KATYA'S CHALLENGE

KATYA'S CHALLENGE

The fight for critical electronics raw materials

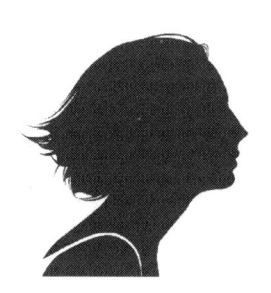

John Breckenridge

KATYA'S CHALLENGE

An adventure story dedicated to Elizabeth,
Andrew and Helen

Copyright © John Breckenridge 2019
All rights reserved

First published in Great Britain in 2019
ISBN: 9781075701450

The right of John Breckenridge to be identified
as the Author of this Work has been asserted
by him in accordance with
The Copyright, Designs and Patents Act 1988

While places are real, all characters in this
publication are fictitious and any resemblance to
real persons, living or dead, is purely
coincidental

"Nature is in earnest when she makes a woman"

Oliver Wendell Holmes Jnr

FOREWORD

In 2010, the Chinese Government implemented a plan to use its commercial dominance of global supplies of rare-earth elements to turn China into the world's centre of all electronic equipment manufacture. Although only used in small quantities, these elements are critical to the manufacture and efficient functioning of most modern electronic devices from wind turbine generators to smartphones.

They planned to eliminate global REE competition through predatory pricing, export controls and offering major electronic companies security of supply, provided they manufacture in China. This is the background to the story; the rest is fiction.

KATYA'S CHALLENGE

Map of Mozambique showing Camp 25 and the Chinese Camp in Zimbabwe

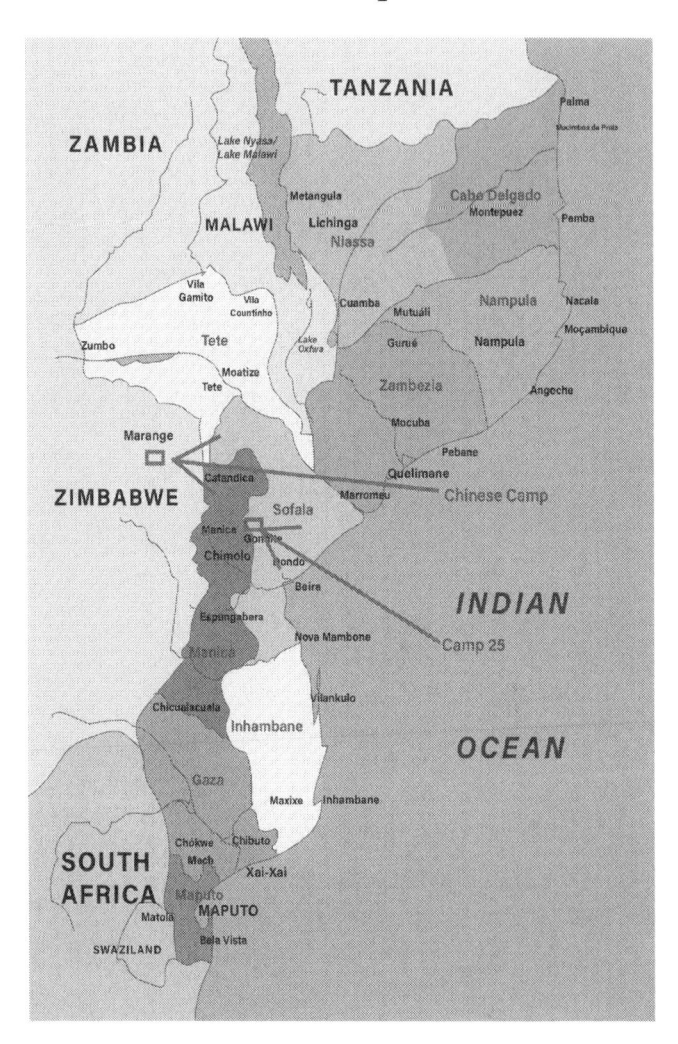

CHAPTER 1

Bloody hell thought Katya to herself, as she tossed and turned in her bed, her mind spinning at Tommy's news. Reckoning further sleep would be impossible she pushed her duvet to one side, got out of bed and padded into her bathroom. Standing under the shower, she turned it up as hot as she could stand it and let the water cascade onto her head and run down her body, trying to wash the anxieties of the night away. She replayed in her head the telephone conversation she'd had with her man Tommy in Beijing late last night. Could this be the end of the line for her trading business?

"It's bad news. All, and I mean all of our orders, have been suspended on direct instructions from the Ministry of Mineral Resources in Beijing."

'Bloody, bloody, bloody Chinese!' How was she going to keep her firm going without supplies? There would be panic in the market, not just in KF Trading, as the news spread.

Dried and dressed, she stood at the window and watched dawn breaking over London, the

KATYA'S CHALLENGE

Thames still sullen under the orange street-lamps, a police car speeding along the empty street below her, a few early pedestrians heading for the underground. She was in trouble, big trouble, but it wasn't the first time. As long as her nerve held, she told herself, something would turn up; she'd find a way through.

Arriving at her office in Bruton Street in Mayfair and swiping her entry card, she ran upstairs to the second floor and the offices of KF Trading Ltd. Inside the office suite, she picked up the overnight faxes from the machine behind Jean's desk in reception and walked through into her own office, trying not to feel the walls closing in and all too aware that now was the time to show her leadership; but also dreading the next couple of hours.

*

She heard Jean come in just before eight o'clock and walked through to the reception area, standing up straight, shoulders back, ready.

"You're in early, boss."

"Yes, we're in real trouble. The bloody Chinese have put the block on our forward REE[1] orders and our last one only just cleared port before the ban kicked in. When the troops arrive, please

---

[1] REE = Rare Earth Elements – a group of 17 metallic elements whose properties make them essential to the manufacture and functioning of most modern electronics.

bring them up to speed and ask them to come to the boardroom at nine o'clock, prepared to discuss our situation in detail: inventory, orders, forward commitments and finance."

"Will do."

Over the next half hour, Marijke van Hattum, David Fewster and Mark MacDonald arrived in the office and were given the same briefing. At five to nine, Jean picked up her notebook and headed for Katya's office. As she walked through the door, she asked, "Do you want me to do anything, boss?"

"Yes, Jean, can we have coffee for five in the boardroom, please, and would you sit in on the meeting and take the minutes for me?"

Half an hour later and surrounded by worried faces, she summarised, "Well, our pre-sold inventory will let us meet our key customers' scheduled requirements for the next four months or so. Add in the material currently en-route from Shenzhen and we might just hit the six-month mark without upsetting anyone important, but we have absolutely no spare material for anyone else, not a single gramme. So, we have three, maybe four months to find other sources in North America, Australia, or Greenland. I don't want us to have to declare force majeure; it takes so long to recover from it. The only consolation is that our competitors are probably in the same boat." She hesitated for a moment and then continued, "Unless the Chinese come directly into the market . . . but I don't think they will . . . yet.

KATYA'S CHALLENGE

I think this is part of a Chinese strategy to develop their own high-tech products and the accompanying manufacturing base. Manufacturing computers and gadgets like iPhones for foreign corporations like Apple doesn't leave much of the added value in China, while developing and manufacturing their own competing devices delivers much more – especially if they have a grip on key raw materials, like rare earth metals."

The boardroom phone rang. When she it picked it up, the telephonist said, "I have a Mr de Bruin for you."

Katya sat up straight in surprise, but after a moment said, "I'm in a meeting, but I'll take it in my office in a moment." Turning to the others she said, "Look, this is a private call which I really should take. Can you give me ten minutes or so, then we can get back to our workaround on these blasted Chinese export restrictions? Thanks."

Picking up the phone in her office she heard a rich and very recognisable South African-accented voice: "Hey Katya, hoe gaat het?"

"Piet de Bruin! Heel goed, en met jou?" She then switched back into English. "Long time, no hear - what are you after, you old bandit? Just a moment while I close the door." A couple of moments later she uncovered the phone and said, "Right Piet, I can talk now. I have a suspicion that this may be confidential."

KATYA'S CHALLENGE

"Correct. I want your advice on something I don't want shared outside your office, and certainly not at the moment. I chair a new business that has an exploration license on a concession that appears to be rich in rare earth metals just inside Mozambique near the South African border. We are called Future Metals."

"You've heard about China's suspension of supply contracts?"

"Yes, which adds impetus to our plans. I'm coming over to London next week with a couple of colleagues and wonder if we could meet up?"

Katya looked quickly at her diary. "I've a fairly quiet week ahead, though I have to go to Brussels on Monday. How about Wednesday? We could meet up at my club for lunch."

"I'm staying at the Mandarin Oriental in Knightsbridge next week and would rather set up lunch in my suite. I'm not particularly keen for us to be seen together just now."

"Very cloak and dagger."

"Not really but the whole project is at a critical stage. The bloody Chinese have been following me around and I don't want people to see us together and join the dots in a way that could work against us."

"So they're breathing down your neck as well? OK, I'll come. By the way, who are the colleagues?"

"Luc Kruger, our mining and mineralogy expert, and Ton Botha, our money man. We are putting a PEA[2] together and need your technical and marketing expertise on the current state of the rare earth metals business."

"Can you e-mail me a brief, so I can get up to speed?"

"Will do, tot volgende week, 'ziens Katya." He broke the connection.

Her mind racing, Katya returned to the boardroom and asked the others, "What are our options?"

As they talked, Katya looked at them: Marijke, smartly dressed in a white blouse and navy skirt, composed, practical, expectant; David, white shirt, gold cuff-links, red tie, fired-up, ready for a fight; Mark, black three-piece suit, white shirt, Pound-symbol cuff-links, plain blue tie and unemotional. She sometimes thought that if you opened his skull, you'd find an endless spreadsheet printout – but a good man to have in a business like this that required strict financial control. He'd lobbied hard for the installation of advanced trading management software, which will come into its own in the coming months.

---

[2] PEA = Preliminary Economic Assessment, the first step in taking a new mining project through to commercial exploitation.

KATYA'S CHALLENGE

I'd better talk to my competitors, she thought, *and see if they're all in as much trouble as I think we are. At least I think I know them well enough to know when they're putting a gloss on a bad situation.*

*

CHAPTER 2

On Wednesday morning Katya decided to 'dress to impress.' After her session at the gym, followed by an invigorating shower back in her apartment, she put on a silk kimono and wandered through to her kitchen. Breakfast was fresh orange juice, fresh raspberries with yoghurt and a croissant with butter and apricot jam. Taking a mug of coffee through to her bedroom, she dried her hair and put on her makeup. Choosing a black Armani trouser suit from her walk-in wardrobe, together with a white, open-neck shirt, set off with a scarlet silk chiffon scarf. She finished the look with a pair of black patent leather Jimmy Choo heels. Phoning for a taxi, she made her way down to the entrance hall to await its arrival.

As she walked into the office, Jean looked at her and said, "Nice! Going somewhere special?"

"You know I'm meeting an old friend and a couple of his colleagues for lunch. I have a feeling that first impressions are going to count for a lot today, hence the outfit."

"It should definitely impress. Do you want some coffee?"

"Please. Is there anything urgent that I have to deal with this morning?" Katya asked, walking through into her own office.

*

Katya walked up the steps into the Mandarin Oriental's lobby, over to the reception desk and asked the receptionist to let Mr de Bruin know Ms Francis had arrived. The receptionist made the call and, turning back to Katya, passed her the handset.

Piet said, "Hey Katya, glad you could make it. Listen, I have a suite on the third floor, so could you take a lift to the second, where I'll meet you?"

"You are really serious about secrecy, aren't you?"

"Secrecy preserves profits. Will you do that?"

She stepped out of the lift a couple of minutes later to see Piet walking towards her with a big smile on his face and his arms outstretched. "Katya," he said embracing her. Stepping back, she looked at him and thought he was ageing well. He must be about the same age as her father, but he was still slim, with a full head of salt-and-pepper coloured hair surmounting a tanned and humorous face with pale blue eyes.

"You are looking good; this trading life must suit you."

"I can't complain, and it keeps me in the style to which I have been accustomed. Actually, it's damn good fun, or at least it was until last week"

"I can see that; anyway, come and meet the rest of the team."

Piet turned around and led the way to the stairs to the third floor and across to the door of his suite. He knocked three times, waited a moment 'till the door was opened by a tall, athletic, tanned and brown-haired man. "Luc Kruger," he said, smiling, "and you must be Katya. Please enter our humble abode - oh and call me Luc."

As she walked into the suite, another tall, thin man with a deeply lined face and a totally bald, tanned head, who had been standing by the windows came toward her with his hand outstretched. "Ton Botha," he said, looking hard at her. "So you are Katya Francis. Delighted to meet you at last. Please call me Ton."

She smiled and shook his proffered hand.

"Right then, let's have a glass of champagne to celebrate! This little gathering is more important than you might imagine," said Piet.

Luc went over to the sideboard, took a bottle of champagne out of an ice bucket, removed the capsule and twisted the cork out of the bottlc. Turning to a row of crystal flutes, he poured everyone a drink.

Handing Katya hers, he was immediately struck by her wide-set grey-green eyes, which seemed to look inside his mind. *Not your usual trader* he thought, *and good-looking with it. I think I might want to really get to know this one.*

Glasses in hand, they turned to Piet who said, "A toast: to Katya Francis – a talent in the rare earths business – Katya!"

As she turned slightly pink, they echoed, "Katya."

"Let's eat," said Piet. "We can get down to business over the coffee."

*

Lunch was oysters, grilled halibut and crème brûlée, the wine an excellent Cape Sauvignon Blanc. The butler served coffee, and as if on cue the light conversation died away and she saw Piet's face change to business mode, but she squeezed her question in all the same. "Who selected the wines?"

Piet answered, "Luc did, and he ought to know. He was brought up on a vineyard in the Western Cape and his old man is a noted wine pundit."

"Well, they were excellent." She smiled at Luc who grinned back in a 'Who, me?' sort of way. As the laughter and chit-chat died away, Katya sat up straight and said, "Piet, I read your briefing notes, but you need to tell me more."

"It all started eighteen months ago when Luc came to see me. He'd been prospecting in

Mozambique and had discovered what seemed to be a large deposit of monazite rare earth element ores just inside the Mozambique border near the Rio Púnguè. Given how the Chinese are steadily edging into global number one position in the supply of rare earth elements and appear to be trying squeeze everyone else out, this looked like a real commercial opportunity.

"I negotiated an exploration license for 24 square kilometres of land with their Ministry of Mineral Resources and put up the cash for Luc to assemble a surveying and drilling crew to scope out the deposit and arrive at a realistic estimate of the recoverable reserves. This is nearly complete, although it has turned out to be a tougher assignment than Luc expected. We are on the last few weeks of the drilling programme and, based on the assay results so far, Ton and I have been encouraged to spend some time putting a PEA together. It looks good, very very good, but we still have to solve two problems, one difficult, one less so - and this is where you come in, Katya."

"Oh, how?"

"You know that good chemists are as necessary to this business as wings are to an aeroplane. Our exploration license needs to be converted into a mining and refining one. Rare earth extraction and refining as presently carried out is the filthiest of processes, contaminating the precincts of the mine and waterways for kilometres in every direction. The guys at the Ministry know this and are very protective of their mighty Rio Púnguè which flows near to our claim. I've been advised that I need to demonstrate a clean process if we are to get the license.

When you were in the final year of your doctorate and I became your academic supervisor, I saw your talents. In your thesis, you proposed a generic smelting and refining process for these ores which was very clean and delivered a high purity rare earth concentrate with only calcined mother ores as waste products – useful as road foundation or as a replacement for sand in concrete – a totally benign waste."

"Yes, but that was then, and it was largely theoretical work."

"Well, I've talked to some experts since and they all say that it would be a really ground-breaking process – if you'll excuse the pun. So much so, that I have funded two groups of post-docs to look at it. One focusing on ore smelting at Witwatersrand University in Jo'burg and one at Delft in Holland focusing on refining."

"Hmm, what do you want me to do?"

"I want you to do two things: supervise the two research groups - weekly Skypes and monthly meetings should be enough and to work with Ton to develop best case/worst case/most likely cash-flows for the project."

"Do I get paid?"

"I can offer you a seat on the board as Technical Director with a monthly bank transfer of $20,000 plus expenses, until the project is either abandoned or the refinery starts operating. At that point, we'll review your remuneration to include a profit share."

"How much of my time will you need?"

"It should work out at less than one week a month to begin with, and then we'll see."

Katya stood up and paced up and down in front of the windows for a few moments, *that'll be fun; I'll have go back to school and go over the work I did for my doctorate, plus what I've learned since, if I'm to have any credibility with Piet's research groups.* Then mentally running through her business commitments, appointments, negotiations, visits, and travel plans, before she turned back to the expectant faces with a smile on her face. "OK I'm in in principle," she said. "But thanks to the bloody Chinese, my business is facing real challenges just now and I need to go over this with my team to be sure that things will be able to carry on OK in my absence. So, regard this as a provisional acceptance. I'll confirm it tomorrow."

There were smiles all round. Luc stood up and returned to the sideboard for another bottle of champagne. Piet stood up and, looking at Katya, said,

"Gentlemen, a toast – to Katya and the completion of Future Metals' team."

*

CHAPTER 3

As the taxi drove her back to Mayfair, Katya's thoughts tumbled over each other. *This could be a show-stopping opportunity. If it really was exciting enough for Piet to have funded the exploration and offer her a salaried director's position now, before a single gramme of product had been extracted, then this had to be an opportunity to grab with both hands.*

Provided they could sort out the immediate supply problems, she could leave KF Trading in her colleagues' hands while she flew out to Africa to evaluate progress on the project. That would be interesting, she thought. Luc was ex-military, South African, definitely a hard man but he'd made her laugh, his twinkling eyes and dry sense of humour hinting at the possibility of an oasis in the desert of her current private life. It could be fun to get to know him better.

Ton, she thought, was a typical "mining and minerals accountant," a bit of an introvert and apparently preoccupied with managing risk. Great, very important, but not much fun. Anyway, her time with him would be limited to board-level project management discussions.

She smiled to herself – great to be part of a project on this scale and with at least two colleagues who were fun to be with.

Assuming she went ahead, her involvement would kick off in three weeks' time, when Piet said he'd send a jet to Heathrow to collect her and take her to the concession in Mozambique. A nice touch, that! Time to get her shots up to date and get her visas for Mozambique, Zimbabwe and Zambia.

*

Back in the office, she called the rest of the team together and told them that she had just been offered the opportunity of a lifetime, one that could guarantee KF Trading's future, not immediately but in the medium to long term.

"I can't tell you much about it at this stage as I am under a strict secrecy obligation but, as I am sure you have guessed, it's a REE project and if successful, will guarantee us uninterrupted future supplies for the business. With any luck, we can turn KF Trading into one of the, if not *the,* largest non-Chinese REE businesses in the world. It will mean a lot of travelling for me over the next few months and a lot of extra work for you."

"Who are you leaving in charge?" asked Marijke.

"No one – I want you to carry on working as the team you are. David, as Sales Director, keep on selling. Mark, as FD, keep our exposures balanced out each evening. I don't want to come back and find that we are about to go bust and Marijke, you and I will continue sourcing. I suggest we have a teleconference every two or three days at 08:00 GMT, as I'll mainly be in countries that are GMT+1 or +2. I'll take the satellite phone, as landlines are few and mobile connections patchy. I'm sure we'll manage fine; anyway, I'm not starting my travels for three weeks and I'll only be out of the UK for 10 to 14 days at any one time.

Do you think you can keep the show on the road while I do this?"

"Yes!" came back the enthusiastic response.

She slept on it overnight and rang Piet in the morning. "I'm definitely in."

"Excellent. I'll courier you all the necessary details and paperwork. I couldn't be happier. Oh! Luc would like a word."

"Hi Katya, I've just overheard you talking to Piet, so you're in. Great, are you doing anything tonight?"

Katya thought for a moment before saying; "No, why?"

"I thought that since you've joined the team, we should get to know each other better and the best way to start doing that would be to have dinner this evening."

"Sounds like a good idea, where?"

"Your call, I don't know London that well."

"Why don't I come to your hotel and we can go on from there? We can start with a drink then decide where we're going to eat."

"Fine, what time do you want to meet?"

"How does seven o'clock sound?"

"Great, see you then."

She was smiling to herself as she put down the phone; yes, Luc was an attractive man and yes, did she want to know him better, yes!

*

Arriving at the hotel, when Katya contacted Luc she was asked to repeat the second-floor subterfuge as at lunch time. Coming out of the lift she saw Luc striding to meet her. He took her hand and kissed her on the cheek before leading her up to the suite they'd occupied at lunch. Luc knocked on the door and they were admitted by Piet with Ton standing over by the window.

More kisses and Piet apologised for gate-crashing their date.

"I just wanted to be sure you had all the info you need."

"Your paperwork arrived about an hour after you phoned, I've looked it over and it seems OK. I'll look at it again in the morning and sign it off if it still makes sense."

"Good! Anyone for a G&T?"

"Yes!" They chorused.

Drinks in hand they toasted their new venture and then Piet said. "Ton and I'll head off and leave you two to it - wait a minute, where are you going for dinner?"

"I thought we might try Wheelers for a fishy dish, unless you want a steak Luc?"

"Fish is good for me."

"OK." She called the restaurant and made a booking.

*

As the waiter cleared the table and brought their coffee and cognacs, Luc leaned back in his chair and asked. "How come someone with a strong academic background like yours ends up running a trading business?"

"Simple; I am a really nosy bitch; I need to know how any technology works before I start. Once I understand it, I can see who will use it to greatest effect and then persuade them to buy from me. Because I can understand what they're doing, I can empathise with buyers and technicians, with production managers and QC. I put a great deal of effort into understanding how my customers operate and work at building strong relationships with them. Seeing orders coming in every month from carefully nurtured contacts is the lifeblood of the business, but these contacts also bring me the industry gossip and it is very seldom that anything appears in the trade press that I haven't already heard about. Coincidentally it means that I am usually first in the door of a new opportunity."

"So that's how it works is it?"

"Yes, but I also do due diligence on my suppliers, customers and competitors. Who's doing well, who's losing money, who's involved in a takeover and so on. Provided you can put the 'market jigsaw' together, you can see the opportunities to make money."

"Are you totally focused on the bottom line?"

"No but it is never far from my thoughts, although I do have other interests."

"Such as?"

"Painting, sculpture, the theatre, ballet and keeping fit."

"So you're a bit of a culture vulture."

"Huh! You need something gentler to balance the hard-edged nature of the trading game, but what about you? How did you make the leap from security to mineral prospector?"

"It's a long story which I won't bore you with, but it is basically all Piet's doing."

"So, he's the moving hand behind both of our career paths."

"Hmm! Looks like it. But more to the point it's brought us together and on the basis of our short acquaintance, I'm extremely glad about that."

"Flatterer!"

"Simply a speaker of the truth."

*

CHAPTER 4

On the top floor of the Ministry of Commerce in Beijing, the minister's senior secretary knocked on Minister Zhang's door and entered. "Comrade General Tang has arrived, sir."

"Send him in."

A somewhat nervous Tang entered the Minister's lavishly appointed office, wondering what exactly the minister would require of him. He was certain that this was no social call and that Zhang would expect him to follow any 'request' as though it were a direct order from the Chairman of the Party.

Zhang's richly furnished office was completed by large portraits of Mao Zedong and Hu Jintao on the wall behind his desk, presiding over the proceedings in front of them. He closed the door behind him, walked over to the desk and stood to attention. "Comrade Minister, you wanted to see me?"

There was a knock on the door and the secretary walked in with a tray of cups and a teapot. Going over to the table, she set them out and poured two cups. Bowing her head, she said, "Comrade Minister, Comrade General" and left.

The two men walked over to the table and sat down. When Zhang heard the click of the door lock, he turned to Tang and began, "You have been fully briefed on Project Golden Lion?"

"Yes, sir."

"And you've heard about the activities of this South African group whose activities threaten to undermine our plan, risking our ability to control the rare earths business?"

"Yes."

"I now have reports that the South Africans are on the move. Their leader arrived in London yesterday, presumably to advance his project. I have a team keeping him under surveillance to see who he meets."

"We can't do anything in London."

"I'm not asking you to, but we need to stop them. Our sources in Mozambique say that their concession seems to be both large and rich in rare earth elements and if successfully developed, will undermine our global strategy. In turn, this could seriously undermine our Project and the whole plan to develop the future competitiveness of our domestic electronics industries. I don't want them to succeed. Ideally, I'd like them to give up and go home so that we can take over the concession for China, Tang."

"Surely this goes well beyond the objectives, strategy and tactics of the Project, sir."

"You may say that, Tang, but I am putting the overall interests of China ahead of the detail of the Project. As a soldier, you must agree that it is easier, quicker and cheaper to destroy an army on the march, rather than waiting for it to establish fortified positions. Creating market dominance through supply constraints and price manipulation will take a long time, much better in my view to simply eliminate competition at source.

I want this concession for China and if I succeed with your help, it will be very good for both of our careers. But we must keep our activities absolutely secret. Do you understand?"

"Yes, sir, I understand, and I'll see what I can arrange. By giving up and going home, may I assume that you would be happy to see them go home in body bags?"

"Yes – so long as no one can see our hand in their travel arrangements."

"Do you want a briefing?"

"Absolutely not, Tang, your activities must be both invisible and unattributable. I only want to know when your activities begin and when the South Africans leave so that we may use our friends in the ministry there to acquire the concession."

"I'll need to see what I can arrange. I'll probably send a unit from the Chengdu Special

Forces Unit. They have some African experience and we have a growing number of assets in East Africa they can liaise with. What is the timeline on this and what is the target area where the South Africans are working?"

"I need you to be operational in no more than ten days. I'll get my secretary to give you the location details."

"Do you want a plan briefing when we're ready to go?"

"No, Tang."

"Understood." He stood up and turned to leave.

*

When Tang returned to his office, he found a thick file on his desk containing maps, aerial photos and a list of embassy contacts in Zimbabwe. He looked through the file then asked his secretary to track down Colonel Chen and have him report to him. Fifteen minutes later, there was a knock on his door and the secretary ushered Chen into the room.

He stood to attention. "Comrade General?"

"Yes, Chen, you have new and urgent orders. I want you to pick a small squad, travel to Mozambique and take out a bunch of South Africans who are reaching the end of a drilling program on a rare earth ore body. We need to take this concession over to maintain our grip on the global supply of these minerals so we can develop our competitive position in electronics.

This will be a covert, unattributable and totally deniable operation. I suggest that you and your team travel as civilians to Zimbabwe, establish a base somewhere near the eastern border with Mozambique, opposite their exploration camp, and launch your raid from there. The equipment necessary for you mission will come through our embassy in Harare."

"How many are there at the site we need to hit?"

"Intelligence suggests that there are around twelve civilians and a security detachment of about thirty men."

"This sounds like I'll need more than a small squad, sir."

"I have arranged for you to be given command of a squad of Zimbabwean soldiers. The idea of getting paid seems to be attractive to them. Speak to the military attaché in our embassy when you get to Harare. He'll arrange their transfer to your command."

"Does he know what we're going to do? Will he keep things confidential?"

"Chen, he's a cousin of mine, he knows how to keep his mouth shut."

"OK sir but why don't we just drop in on them directly in a surprise attack and leave, again as civilians, through the airport in Beira?"

"Diplomatic necessity, Comrade Major. If your base is in Zimbabwe and you don't upset the locals, then there will be no repercussions. If your attack comes from across the border, even if the Mozambican authorities find out about it, there will be no evidence that we did it, no camp for them to find – do you understand?

"Yes, sir, it looks as though our mission will have an excellent start. I'd better get busy with the detailed planning."

"Good. I need you and your men to be ready to leave in no more than 10 days. If your quartermaster has any difficulty in getting what you need, speak to my adjutant."

"Yes, sir."

"And Chen, I want you back here in 48 hours to brief me with your plan."

"Sir!"

*

With the team checked into a cheap tourist hotel near the centre of Harare, Colonel Chen took a taxi to the bright, white Chinese Embassy building on Golden Stairs Road. Inside the cool entrance hall, he was challenged by a smartly dressed young woman wearing a black blazer and skirt over a crisp white shirt. Identifying himself, he asked for the Military Attaché and was asked to wait in the reception area. After a few minutes, a tall, heavily built man wearing a colonel's uniform came through the internal doors and made his way over to Chen.

"Comrade Colonel Chen, I am Senior Colonel Hsiu, the Military Attaché here in Harare. We were expecting you yesterday. Did you have problems?"

"Yes, Comrade, you know we are travelling incognito as civilians? Well, one of my men was identified by an idiot officer at immigration control in Beijing as a 'person of interest' and held for questioning. It took more than two hours to demonstrate to their satisfaction that he was a first-class junior officer in the PLA and although he had the same name as the man they were looking for, they'd got the wrong man. After General Tang spoke to him, I suspect he may well be on his way to a new posting on our north-eastern border near Murmansk. He resolutely refused to take our army documentation into account or listen to me. A man of limited intelligence – and an even more limited future, I think. The upshot was that we missed our original flight and didn't get into Harare until late last night."

"Come, let us take tea while we discuss your requirements. I assume they haven't changed from the list sent through by Tang's quartermaster."

Once through the internal doors, Hsiu led the way to a plainly furnished conference room with the statutory pictures of Chairman Mao Zedong and President Hu Jintao on the wall above the conference table. Producing two folders, he gave one to Chen and gestured for him to sit at the conference table, which had a tray of tea on it. Hsiu poured and they drank noisily before opening the folders.

"So," said Hsiu, "the materiel is not a problem. Your guns, ammunition, RPGs, electronics, camping gear, generators and insignia-free bush uniforms all came through in the diplomatic bag last Wednesday and are here in the Embassy Compound. I spoke to our Zimbabwean Army liaison General Mutasa the same day about troops and transport. He eventually agreed to let us hire – yes, hire - 36 troops and two trucks to transport them, us and our gear through the bush to a suitable campsite he has identified on the edge of the Marange diamond fields on the south-eastern border with Mozambique."

"You say 'troops' - what calibre are they?"

"He says they're hard enough for a fight and happy soldiering in the bush. Personally, I would classify them as sloppy and ill-disciplined. You may have trouble making them do what you want, when you want and the way that you want. Anyway, they will be handed over to your command this afternoon and you will have a day or two to impose your authority on them and get to the campsite."

"What language do we speak?"

"I'm assured they all speak, or at least understand, English. It is apparently an educational requirement for all Zimbabwean army recruits. That's not a problem for your men, is it?"

"Fluent English is a requirement for all ranks in the Chengdu Special Forces command."

"All ranks?"

"Yes, all ranks. It means we can be deployed all over the world without problem. What's the proposed campsite like?"

"If you look at the back of the folder, you'll find detailed maps and a couple of aerial photos. It is in an isolated hollow, well away from any diamond mining activity and with access to clean spring water."

"Not the worst start for a mission, but I don't like relying on local troops for such a sensitive mission."

"Why?"

"Look, this is supposed to be a covert mission, invisible, unattributable and 100% deniable. With my own men, I can be sure of the security. With this lot, I'm not so sure. What happens if any of them get killed during our op?"

"Our Government will pay $1,000 to the family of anyone crippled or killed in action."

"$1,000! $1,000! That's ten years' pay for my men. What do these troops earn, anyway?"

"I'm not sure but I think they are pretty much on a par with our pay scales. Mugabe must pay above local Zimbabwean labour rates to ensure the loyalty of the Army. In fact, our understanding is that the army have been running the country for the last few years anyway and set the agenda for most things. The choice of the Marange diamond fields is no accident. The diamonds are dug out using slave labour and find their way to market via the Army High Command and the upper echelons of ZANU-PF. That's how they sustain their luxurious lifestyles. The rest of the economy has gone down the toilet and barely supports the populace on a diet of the local maize porridge and a shared bicycle.

"Anyway, let's go and have something to eat. We'll pick your men up after lunch and go see your local troops."

*

Back at their hotel, Chen called his men together in the hotel's so-called conference room for a briefing session. "Well, now you've seen them, what do you think?"

"I'm sure we can do the job with them," said Captain Xiao.

"OK, we'll go to their camp first thing in the morning and collect them and our transport, drive to the embassy and pick up our gear."

Pinning a map up on an easel in the corner of the room, Chen continued, "We will establish our camp here, just north of Mutare, about five miles from the Mozambique border. The South African camp is here, about 50 miles north of a town called Chimoio. The distance between the two is about 130 miles. We'll drive to the Mutare camp site tomorrow morning, build a defensible base and then split the Africans up into three squads, two for the attack and one to defend our base, and who will remain there in case of intruders."

Pinning an aerial photo on top of the map, he said, "As you can see, the South African camp is rectangular, about two hundred and fifty by three hundred and fifty metres. Earthen walls with wooden palisades on top and a large wooden gate in the middle of the southern wall. They have built watch towers at the four corners, each with a heavy machine gun and a searchlight.

"One of the squads should attack from the north, the other from the south. Use RPGs to take out the watch towers and breach the gate. The rest of the attack should simply be a question of mopping up.

"Xiao, I want you to lead the attack on the South African camp, so when we get to our base tomorrow, sort the soldiers into the three squads and we'll practice the attack. The attack squads will take the trucks to within three miles of the target on Tuesday afternoon and bivouac. Leave the trucks there and march to the target, ready to start the attack at 02:00 am on Wednesday morning. Rules of engagement are simple: if it breathes, kill it. We won't take any prisoners, but before we destroy the camp and its equipment, collect any computer equipment, files and other sources of data on their operations that you can find."

*

CHAPTER 5

As her Gulfstream touched down at Beira airport, Katya looked out of the cabin window with interest. A modern-looking airport with a handful of commercial planes drawn up in front of the terminal and off to one side, what looked like several private aircraft. Among them was a Chinook helicopter painted drab olive, with only a South African registration number visible on the fuselage.

The Gulfstream taxied over to the private aircraft section and was met by a Jeep with 'Immigration' painted on the side. It stopped at the aircraft steps and two men jumped out: a tall, heavily built black man in a tan uniform with "Mozambique Imigração" flashes on his gold braid decorated tunic, followed by Luc Kruger, looking every bit the big white hunter in khaki shorts and shirt, desert boots and a wide-brimmed hat.

"Hi Katya, good trip?"

"So far," she said and before she could say anything further, she was interrupted by the immigration officer, who demanded, "Passport Madame, por favor."

KATYA'S CHALLENGE

Reaching into her bag, Katya took out her passport and handed it over. He leafed through it carefully before coming to the page carrying her visa, studied both Katya and it thoroughly and then compared her face with the photo. Expressionless, he turned back to the Jeep, reached in and took out a stamp and ink pad, laid her passport down on the bonnet and stamped it. Handing it back he said, "Welcome to Mozambique, Madame." He turned back to the Jeep and was driven away.

Luc said, "Ready for the last lap out to our concession, or do you want to freshen up first?"

"I'm still in travel mode, so we might as well finish the job."

"OK, I'll get your bags." With that he climbed up into the Gulfstream's cabin, went through to the cockpit, told the pilots to be ready for departure the following evening and collected her bags from the flight attendant.

Back on terra firma, he pointed to the Chinook and said, "Our taxi!" and started walking towards it.

"Have we far to go?" she asked.

"About 200 miles as the Chinook flies, just over an hour's flying time."

"Kind of big for a taxi."

"We need it to bring supplies up to the camp. There is a road up to it from Beira, but it is so bad that even an all-terrain truck like a Mercedes Unimog can barely make 30 kph and that's with a restricted load, so it's air-freight all the way. It's all loaded up now and just waiting for us to take off."

"Nice weather," she said.

"Good most of the year, but you should see it around the end of the year when the rainy season kicks in. Torrential downpours and a Turkish bath atmosphere. Anyhow, we're within days of finishing the drilling programme and packing up for now."

*

The Chinook touched down in a cloud of dust and as the rotors slowed to a stop, Katya and Luc disentangled themselves from the bales of supplies, stood up and headed for the door. The sudden silence after the clattering and vibration of the helicopter was bliss. Luc opened the door, kicked out the ladder and helped her down. "Welcome to Camp 25."

Looking around, she saw they had landed inside a large stockade with cabins at one end, what looked like a warehouse in the middle beside the helipad and a drilling rig at the other end. The helipad had high earth ramparts around it with offset access, meaning that the helicopter was shielded on all sides. Watch towers stood at the corners of the stockade and she could see what looked like a searchlight mounted above a machine gun pointing outwards from the platform at the top of each one. A tractor headed for the helicopter, towing a large flat trailer carrying a group of men holding on desperately to avoid being bounced off while some H&K MP5[3]- toting soldiers looked on. Once at the helicopter, they jumped off, opened the main door and started to unload the cargo.

Luc grabbed her luggage and headed for one of the accommodation huts with Katya following on. Throwing open the door of the second hut, he bowed and said, "Your suite, Madame," walked in with her bags and set them down in front of a large wardrobe. The other furnishings were a double bed with a mosquito net, a small fridge and a chest of drawers. An open door at the other end led to a simple bathroom; shower, toilet and a hand basin.

"Water is limited here and we need most of it for the drilling rig, but it is available for personal use in the accommodation huts between 05:00 and 08:00 and again between 16:00 and 18:00. Please drink only the bottled water in the fridge and make sure you use it to clean your teeth – unless you'd rather use whisky." He grinned.

Looking at his watch, he said, "I'll give you fifteen minutes, then I'll give you a guided tour of the camp."

A quarter of an hour later she heard his knock on the door and shouted, "Come in!"

---

[3] MP5 – the MP5 or Heckler & Koch MP5 is a German-manufactured submachine gun with fifteen and thirty round magazine options. Rapid firing and favoured by security and armed police forces around the world

Dressed now in khaki combat trousers, boots and a bush jacket, she went over to him, thinking to herself that he really was quite attractive in an alpha male sort of way, even if he was kind of short on idle chit-chat. She looked up at him and, smiling inwardly, said, "Let's go."

As they walked out into the compound, he pointed out the soldiers' barracks, the canteen and the rest of the accommodation huts.

"This is not what I expected," she said.

"What did you expect?"

"Just a mobile drilling rig and some tents. This looks more like a permanent military camp. The whole operation must have cost a hell of a lot of money. Who's funding it?"

"Piet has been our fairy godmother. He has been very generous, as we've spent around $15 million so far."

"Is it his own cash?"

"I don't know but he has kept paying the bills and funded the construction of this proper base camp. I think that's because of the trouble we had early the project. The first three drilling camps we set up were just as you describe. But, and it's a huge but, we were attacked at the last two and if we hadn't been on the qui vive, we might all have been killed."

"Who attacked you?"

"A bunch of down-and-out locals. Fortunately, we were armed and alert and took them out. We've been like the ancient Roman Army ever since, building a basic fortified encampment at each drilling site, but nothing like this."

Walking past the Chinook, they entered the warehouse, a large canvas structure supported on a steel skeleton, with assorted bales, crates and bits of machinery along one side and a stack of what looked like rifle crates along the other. Down at the far end was what looked like a large WWII concrete air-raid shelter.

"What are those crates, weapons?"

"Nice idea but no, they're core sample boxes. We take the drill cores and pack them sequentially in these boxes, marking the co-ordinates of the bore and depth they came from, they are then sealed and sent to the Alex Stewart Labs in Zambia for assay."

"Presumably you've got loads of data now if this is the last hole you're drilling?"

"Yes, and it's all good. The results from the first ninety-nine bore holes show rare earth ore deposits starting only 10 metres below the surface and as going as deep as 450 metres in places."

"Promising, but why so many bore holes?"

"The ore body itself is fairly soft monazite rock, quick and easy to drill, so we decided to drill lots of holes so we could profile the deposit with some accuracy. Better than that – it's actually a very unusual mixed sedimentary multi-metal ore body, not really a true Monazite ore. Rich in samarium, lanthanum, dysprosium and neodymium and mercifully free of thorium. I think the deposit is the bottom of a huge lake formed around the end of the last ice age, about 100,000 years ago. My best guess is that the minerals were washed down from the Bvumba mountains to the west of here, in Zimbabwe's Eastern Highlands. This would account for the unusual mix of elements and its nearness to the surface. The ore as sampled assays at between 20 and 33% metal oxides."

"That's huge. No wonder Piet is keeping this as tight as possible. How far across the concession does the ore body run?"

"It seems to be an ellipse with an area of around 16 square kilometres. As you would expect, the ore body thins at the edge, but if this last bore meets expectation, it'll come out around 16 million tonnes of recoverable ores in total, somewhere between thirty and fifty-five million tonnes of rare earth oxides."

Doing the mental arithmetic as she stood there, she came up with a number. "Bloody hell! That's between twenty-five and forty year's current world demand, conservatively worth six to ten billion dollars at 2009 market prices. The deposit may be worth considerably more, as there isn't much topsoil to remove and there isn't any thorium. It's worth much more at today's market prices, but I'd rather base our valuations on the prices prevailing before the Chinese got antsy. High prices like now never last; consumers use less wherever possible and there is always a substitution threshold, using more of a cheaper alternative to achieve the same result. Not as elegant, but cheaper. Depending on the results of the smelting and refining laboratory teams, the profits are going to be well into the billions of dollars. Wow! What do you reckon the life of the mine will be?"

"I haven't talked it through with Piet yet, or you for that matter, but my guess is that we don't want to go at it too enthusiastically - spread it out over say, fifty or even a hundred years."

"Agreed – we need to drip-feed the market and keep prices up to maximise the profit."

"Let's go and have a look at the rig."

As they walked over to the drilling tower, she saw that it was mounted on a huge truck chassis fitted with caterpillar tracks, carrying what looked like a large diesel generator, an air compressor and various pumps. She could see the drill pipe turning and feel the vibration from the generator powering it. Water leaked from the drilling table onto the ground, turning the surrounding earth to a glutinous red mud slurry. Duckboards made a path over the mud to the rig. A stack of sample crates stood at one side and drill pipes at the other.

"How the hell did you get that monster up here and why the elaborate camp? I understand the need for security, but this looks like a 21st century Foreign Legion outpost."

"We drove it up here very slowly and with great difficulty. It took us eleven painful days to drive it the 250 miles up from Beira, in convoy with a pipe truck, a mobile engineering workshop and a guard truck.

"By the time we got the results from the first dozen drill sites, it became obvious that we'd hit on something huge and that we should build and equip a proper compound where we thought operations might eventually be centred. Piet and I decided that as this edge of the deposit is closest to Beira, we should make it the centre of operations, hence the semi-permanent exploration camp. We think that the best approach to exploiting the deposit is to do the mining, smelting and refining here on site to minimise logistics costs and environmental impact."

"It'll keep operating costs down too, I imagine. Good thinking."

"Why, thank you, ma'am." He smiled at her, noticing that as soon as he'd started quoting numbers, she'd suddenly gone all business-like.

As they approached she saw a very tall, very thin white man in a hard hat directing the operators. His movements were spider-like, his arms making pecking motions as he directed the men. Seeing them approach, he climbed down from the tower and walked over to them.

Luc and Katya went over to meet him. Luc held out his hand to the man and, turning to Katya, said, "Meet Ken Collins, otherwise known as 'Spider,' our drilling superintendent. Ken, this is Ms Francis."

"Hi Ken, call me Katya. You look busy. Luc tells me you're almost at the end of the drilling programme."

"Yes, we're already at 1,250 metres and the last core samples are a bit of a surprise. Pressure is building in the bore and I'm 99% certain that there's a natural gas reservoir down there."

"So shallow?"

"It's maybe not such a surprise. The last 300 metres have been through solid basalt, which would be an effective cap on the gas, and it looks as though we're breaking through it into sandstone, which must be the gas reservoir."

"You should stop, Spider. We're not equipped to handle a gas blow-out and I don't want to see the whole place go up in a sheet of flame."

"OK, not nor me neither. I was just going to come and see you."

"Can you pull up the drill and put a temporary cap on the hole? I'll talk to Piet and arrange for the additional kit you'll need to complete the bore. I don't know for sure how long it'll take to get it to Beira, but my guess is around a week."

"OK, I'll fix that. We can discuss the details over dinner this evening once you've spoken to Piet and got a steer on how quickly he can get the kit here."

"See you in the canteen around six o'clock then."

*

CHAPTER 6

The canteen was one of the larger huts along from Katya's quarters, with an open veranda at the front, long tables inside and a kitchen at the back. Looking inside, she could see the drill crew and crew leaders sitting on one side, with the soldiers on the other. All of them were piling into plates heaped with what looked like chicken curry. It smelled delicious. Luc led Katya to one of the tables on the veranda and asked what she'd like. "I hope you like piri-piri chicken. It's a dietary staple here; they say that the spices prevent bugs like salmonella from flourishing. I have certainly never had a problem so long as I've stuck to the spiced dishes. We sometimes have a prawn curry instead, provided the terminal handling crew in Beira can get their act together – but not this week."

"Yes, that sounds good – I wouldn't want to go against local advice. I'll have some of that, and I don't suppose you can magic up a nice, cold beer?"

"Sorry, not here. We can do you fresh orange or guava juice, mineral water or Coke. We do our best to keep the camp booze-free, although every now and again the guys brew up some maize beer and can become a bit noisy until we get rid. Spider, Hennie and I have a lounge cum office in the next hut where we can talk and have a drink away from everyone. We'll go there after dinner."

"Who's Hennie?"

"Chief Hendrik Coetzee, guard commander, ex South African Defence Force, tougher than old boots and responsible for our security. He also runs my personal security business back home on a day-to-day basis. You'll meet him later."

"I saw guard towers at the corners of the stockade. Are they really necessary?"

"Ab-so-bloody-lutely. Out here in the bush the people are very poor and every now and again some of the men will form a gang and, with weapons left over from the civil war, attack compounds like this for food and anything that can be looted and sold. It's totally lawless. The local military are supposed to keep things under control, but they disappear like a puff of cigarette smoke at the slightest hint of a gang raid and leave people like us to fend for ourselves. The gangs don't worry about killing people or destroying operations like this, so we have to be on our guard all the time – hence Hennie and his boys. Apart from the fact that the roads are dreadful, that's why we only come and go on the old Chinook."

KATYA'S CHALLENGE

A canteen boy brought their food over. Katya looked at hers before carefully trying a forkful. "Mmmm, that's good. I thought everyone here would be living on maize porridge and vegetables."

"No, this is a holdover from Portuguese colonial days. Between them and the Arabs, Mozambique's food is quite varied, rich and spicy. If we were nearer the coast, as well as chicken, we would be eating lots of seafood and fresh veg."

As they were finishing, Spider joined them and after the pleasantries had been exchanged, Spider asked Luc he'd contacted Piet. "We had quite a discussion. He's excited about the prospect of finding natural gas under the ore body. It would simplify the development of the mining and refining operation; we could do everything on site and only need to ship processing chemicals in and finished product out."

Turning to Katya he asked, "Your process – can you use natural gas as the energy source?"

"Perfect, provided it isn't sour gas, contaminated with sulphur. It means that we wouldn't end up introducing further impurities to the ore as we process it."

"Well there hasn't been a sulphurous smell from the bore so far, just a hydrocarbon whiff," said Spider and asked when the additional kit would arrive.

"It will be at Beira Airport one week from today, so you can stand the crews down tomorrow after you've put the drilling operation on hold. They can fly down to Beira tomorrow for a few days' R&R and spend some of their back pay."

He handed Spider a handwritten list of the equipment that would arrive the following week. "Is there anything there you need to know more about?"

He looked it over carefully before turning back to Luc and saying, "No, it is all stuff I have used before, so I don't see any problems and if you'll excuse me, I'll go and grab some food before it's all gone, and I have to spend the rest of the evening chewing on strips of biltong."

*

Dinner over, Luc and Katya retired to the office and lounge which were in a similar sized hut to Katya's but furnished with cane armchairs, a low coffee table, a large fridge and a desk at one end carrying a computer and satellite phone. "It's the only way to talk to the outside world from here," said Luc, noticing her gaze. "Coffee? Do you still want a cold beer, or would you rather have a brandy?"

"Coffee, brandy and a large glass of mineral water, please." She settled into a chair and watched him prepare her drinks, thinking, *I know virtually nothing about this guy beyond what Piet has told me, yet he makes me feel comfortable and safe – better than that, he's really attractive and gives me that deep-down tingling feeling.* As he set her drinks on the table, she snapped out of her reverie. "Thanks."

Picking up the brandy, she looked straight at him and said, "Gesondheid!"

"You don't speak Afrikaans, do you?"

"No, but there is a fair overlap with Dutch, which I learned from my mother. I'm half-Dutch, half-English. I spoke Dutch at home and English at school, but you can teach me some Afrikaans." She laughed. "But what about you? All I know is that you grew up in a vineyard, did your military service with South African Special Forces at the end of the Angolan border war, and that you were working for Executive Outcomes when Piet met you on another of his projects. How did you switch from grape grower to soldier to mineralogist?"

"It's really down to Nelson Mandela and Piet de Bruin."

"How come? I would have thought that a life in the world of wine would have been more fun."

"No, it is a world that doesn't attract. Most winemakers work bloody hard to scrape a living and for the majority it's just a lifestyle choice. The few that make it big are still at the mercy of the weather, the wine critics and the buyers from the retail chains in Europe and the USA. Anyway, being a fairly physical sort, I thought I'd give the army a go."

"Did you enjoy it?"

"Not at first, but once I got my commission things improved, and when I managed to get into Special Forces I felt I was doing something worthwhile . . . and it was for a while . . . but the last few months of the Angolan Border War sickened me. By then we were fighting boy soldiers pressed into the conflict, hopped up on drugs and given a Kalashnikov to fire at us. Apart from the fact that these kids had had their childhood stolen and been completely brutalized, many of them became ruthless little killers. Even if the kid in your sights is pointing a gun at you and is happy to use it, it still makes you sick to have to take him out."

"I can imagine - not the sort of experience that makes for dreamless sleep."

"No, so when we came back from Angola in 2002, my old C.O. asked if I'd like to leave the army and join Executive Outcomes with him. Similar work, much better pay and no bullshit. Hennie had been my senior NCO in Angola and he came with me. We ended up running security for mining projects in the Congo, which is where I met Piet and got interested in prospecting for minerals. I left Executive Outcomes and used my back pay to fund a combined degree in geosciences and mining engineering at Witwatersrand University and started prospecting. The point being that if you discover a deposit of something the world wants and can secure the rights to it, the only dust you are ever likely to find in your pocket is gold dust. After a couple of years of scraping around, I found this deposit and went to see Piet as being the ideal 'angel' to come up with the funding to take the project to Bankable Feasibility Study status."

"But how come you've got this private army here, along with your friend Hennie?"

"When I was getting towards the end of my degree, Hennie approached me with a proposition that I should set up a smarter security company, handling not only personal security but also internet security. It seemed like a good idea, especially as I wanted to go prospecting and wanted to stay alive. The internet security was the real teaser, but what a good bet that has been. That business has really taken off over the last two or three years.

Well, that's my life story; what's yours? All Piet has told me is that you're a chemist and a trader with specialist knowledge of the rare earths business."

She smiled and said, "Refill my brandy and I might just tell you, but before that, is there a Vrouw Kruger?"

"There nearly was but my lifestyle doesn't seem to hold much long-term attraction for many women."

Once he had replenished her glass and settled back in his chair she leaned forward and began, "As I told you I'm half-Dutch, half-English. My father works for Shell and is now CEO of its Exploration & Production business, based at headquarters in The Hague, which is where he originally met my mother. She was PA to my father's boss back in the day and once I was old enough to travel, we accompanied him on most of his postings, which gave me a grandstand view of an awful lot of places."

"Industrial gypsies."

"Yes. In my teenage years I was sent to boarding school in Scotland and from there I went to Cambridge, where I studied chemistry. From there to Germany as an analyst in Reacorchemie's laboratories in Munich. It didn't take me long to decide that if I wanted to be taken seriously, I needed to become Frau Doktor Francis, so I went back to school and got my doctorate in the chemistry of the rare earth elements, one of Reacorchemie's specialties. I then got an offer to work for Critimetaal in Brussels, which is where I first saw metals trading. I managed to transfer from the laboratories to the trading division and learned the ropes from a Dutchman called Jan van Vliet. After about six months, I had my own trading book, small to begin with, but it grew rapidly until I was turning over north of $20 million, mainly in rare earth metals sourcing and recycling. Then I had my 'light bulb' moment. Here was I turning over all this business on a salary which, while generous, was only a small percent of the money I was making for the company. Why not do it for myself? After all, it is relatively easy money provided you know your market and keep your emotions out of the dealing room."

"Why doesn't everyone do it then?"

She laughed. "Because they don't have the contacts, the understanding of the market, the enjoyment of and freedom to travel and get a certain buzz from taking calculated risks."

"But don't you have a family - a regular life outside the office?"

"Life outside the office? I'm hardly ever in it - I usually clock up at least 250,000 air miles in a year. There really isn't time for much else."

"How did you meet Piet?"

"When my father's work took us to Nigeria, he met Piet, who had some deal or other going on with Shell, and he was a regular visitor to our house. Over two successive long vacations from Cambridge, we got to know each other well. He used to test me, not on my knowledge, but on my understanding of what that meant. When we moved back to The Hague and I went back to Cambridge to do my doctorate, he had been appointed as a visiting professor at Delft and persuaded me to complete my thesis there, and we have been in regular, if intermittent, touch ever since. He also helped me get the backing to start my own business. That's why I wasn't totally surprised to be asked to come and meet you three weeks ago."

Looking at her watch, she yawned and said, "It's been a long day and I have to go to bed."

They both got up and Luc put his hand on her arm as he walked her back to her hut. "Have a good sleep but if you hear a klaxon going, get your kit on and head for the Control Room at the bottom of the north tower as fast as you can."

"Are you expecting trouble?"

"No, but if trouble does kick off, we're ready. The control room has reinforced concrete walls. As a fall-back, head for the shelter in the warehouse. It's an armoured refuge to keep the civilian workers safe in the event of an attack on the camp."

As she entered the hut, he leaned over and kissed her lightly on the cheek. She looked up, surprised, hesitated a moment, then stood on tip-toe to kiss him back.

"Sleep well," she said and shut the door.

*

CHAPTER 7

Hennie woke to the sound of the emergency buzzer beside his bed. Looking at the clock, he saw it was two thirty. He reached for his radio, pressed 'transmit' and growled, "Sitrep Jan – over!"

"Intruders advancing from both north and south – over!"

"How many? Over!"

"About a dozen each from the north and the south - Over!"

"Do you think they know we're watching 'em? Over?"

"No – we're just tracking them with night-vision binocs at the minute – Over!"

"Sound the 'attack' buzzers and have the lads take up station as silently as possible. I'll be up in the command post in a couple of minutes – over and out!"

One hundred twenty seconds later Hennie walked into the command post in the base of the north tower and looked at the sensor display screen. They had planted three concentric arrays of remote ground sensors around the outside of the stockade and had cleared the surrounding bush to a radius of 500 metres to prevent intruders creeping up on the compound's walls unseen. The north and south segments of the outermost zone were flashing red, denoting multiple intruders. The middle array of the northern zone started flashing as he looked at the screen.

As Luc and Katya walked in behind him, his radio buzzed again. "We can see the northern intruders clearly now. They look like a well-organized squad and they're comfortably in range of the Brownings – over!"

"Sound the klaxon and give them a 'Happy Hennie' welcome – now! Over!"

With that, all four watch-towers switched on their searchlights, turning the night into broad daylight around the camp. Their klaxons sounded, flooding the night with noise, then came the staccato *Taka! Taka! Taka!* of heavy machine gun fire. The surviving intruders scattered back the way they had come, leaving more than a dozen bodies lying on the ground.

KATYA'S CHALLENGE

"Jan! Status! Over!"

"No worries, Hennie, we got most of the bastards and the rest ran for it. None of our guys hurt."

With that there was a sudden whoosh, followed by an explosion immediately under the gun platform of the south tower, the blast sending searchlight, gun and soldiers flying.

"Jan! What the fuck was that?"

"One of the bastards popped off an RPG."

"Can you see them - see who did it?"

"Yes."

"Then take them out – everyone fire at will!" The searchlights and machine guns on east and west towers swung around to cover the approach to the remains of the south tower.

Taka! Taka! Taka! went the Browning M2s[4] again as the gunners hosed down the southern approaches to the camp. The noise of the Brownings was punctuated by the ripping sound of MP5s being discharged, magazine after magazine.

---

[4] The Browning M2 0.5" calibre machine gun was originally developed towards the end of WWI. In its current iteration, it is the chosen heavy machine gun for NATO infantry forces and for more than 80 other armies around the world. Simple, robust, reliable and effective.

KATYA'S CHALLENGE

When the last intruder lay motionless on the ground, Jan ordered, "Cease firing, cease fire!" and the night fell silent, but for the throbbing of the diesel generator powering the camp.

Back in the control room, Luc turned to Katya. "It looks like the fighting is over, for the moment anyway. Hennie and I are going to meet up with Jan and see what's what." Handing her a Glock 9mm automatic, he asked if she knew how to use it.

"Yes," she said, releasing the safety and removing the magazine. Working the slide, she ejected the round from the chamber, pressed it into the top of the magazine, reassembled the weapon, chambered a round and put the safety catch back on.

"Great, please stay here 'til I get back and use it if you have to."

Picking up the walkie-talkie, he spoke. "Hennie, Jan, meet me at the gate and we'll see what we can see. Get some of the guys to walk round, make sure the dead really are dead and collect their weapons and anything else that might be of use."

When they met up, Jan was grim-faced. "We lost Marius de Jong and Gert van Zyl when the RPG hit the south tower. They were on the gun platform, right on top of the blast."

"Anyone else injured?"

"No – let's go and see what we've been fighting."

They walked through the gate, MP5s at the ready, and walked over to the bodies scattered on the ground on the south side. "All Africans - all wearing camos. These aren't random villagers looking for an easy target; these are soldiers. I wonder who controls them."

Hennie looked thoughtfully at the body of the man who was lying on top of an RPG launcher which he had presumably fired. "Well, they're not Mozambican regulars. They're not wearing any insignia or name flashes, so it could be anyone, but my bet is that they are controlled, financed, trained and equipped by our Chinese friends. At least none of these buggers will be able to pull this stunt again. Let's go around to the north side and see what we've got there."

As they walked round the outside of the stockade, they heard a couple of pistol shots. "Some of the bastards were still alive, it seems," said Hennie.

As they rounded the edge of the stockade another of Hennie's section leaders came up to them and said, "Come and look at this, boss! We've bagged ourselves a couple of Chinamen."

The three of them trotted over to where a soldier was kneeling beside two bodies. Also dressed in camos, they appeared to have died from M2 rounds which had destroyed their chests and knocked them onto their backs. They were looking sightlessly up at them. Jan knelt and closed their eyes, then started going through their pockets.

"Anything?" asked Hennie.

"Four spare Kalashnikov magazines and the remains of a couple of satellite phones."

"Damn - any clues?"

"Possibly. They're Chinese and I think the SIM cards may still be OK. We might get some useful info from them when we get back to camp."

"So, the Chinese are definitely muscling in on our operations. This gives us a real problem."

"Look! What's that over there, Jan?" said Hennie, pointing to a small black box lying on the ground about two metres from the furthest body and walking over to pick it up. "Bloody hell! It's a hand-held GPS, and undamaged to boot. By all that's wonderful, we should be able to use it to see where they've come from."

"So, it was worth getting all that hardware installed then, Hennie?"

"Dead right Luc – and I mean dead! The sensors gave us a clear ten minutes' warning of their arrival, so we were ready to accelerate their progression to the afterlife. How many bodies are there?"

Jan walked over, stiffening to attention when he saw Luc. "Twelve on the north side, including two Chinamen; ten in the south, sir."

"Twenty-two in all. Any idea how many got away?" asked Luc.

"Not many. My guess is no more than three or four who panicked and ran off. There's blood on the ground to the north where they went, so at least some of them are seriously wounded and may not be a further threat."

"You can't make that assumption."

Hennie chipped in, "I'll send out a scouting party and track the bleeders down – pun intended. They're still unfinished business."

"You're right," said Luc. "If you can get them all, the Chinese will have no idea of what has happened. They may even think that their 'soldiers' killed their leader and ran off into the bush. If you take a good look at them, most are sloppily dressed, and I would guess that their attitude to soldiering matches. Send Mobutu with them - he could track a beetle through a thunderstorm – and do it silently.

"And now, we'd better collect their weaponry and dispose of the bodies. We don't want anyone coming across an unexplained mass grave, and apart from anything else, they make the place untidy and the smell will be seriously unpleasant by tomorrow. I suggest we strip the bodies, load them onto the Chinook and dump them in the river. The crocs or whatever will soon reduce them to unrecognizable bits and pieces."

"What about our guys?" asked Hennie.

"Let's cremate them here and we can take the ashes back for their next of kin."

*

Luc, Hennie and Katya sat round the table, each with a plate of fried chicken and a mug of coffee.

"Hennie, what's the final score?" asked Luc.

"Two of our boys are dead and the top of the south tower destroyed. The searchlight is damaged beyond repair, but the Browning will be OK with a new barrel and sights. The breech and belt feed mechanisms are undamaged. A good choice of weapon. Apart from the loss of our boys and the damage caused by the RPG, we seem to have got off lightly. There's no damage inside the compound, so our early warning system really worked. I know we trained extensively with it, but nothing tests your training like a real-life attack."

"Well done, Hennie, I knew you and your guys were the best."

Turning to Katya, he said, "You've been very quiet, are you OK?"

"Ja, just a little shocked."

"How come you're so at ease with guns?"

"I've been in a real 'them or us' firefight once before. When my father was working in the Niger Delta, I went out there one summer holiday. We were travelling to an oil pumping station when our truck was rammed, probably the precursor to a kidnap attempt. Happily, our bodyguards were on the qui vive and there was a short, sharp firefight which left the would-be kidnappers lying dead. I was scared witless but soon recovered.

That's when my father asked the bodyguards to train me in assorted weaponry, like your Glock, for instance. He asked them to train me in using pistols and machine pistols in case anyone tried to kidnap us. I was signed off as fully proficient with Glocks, Uzis, MP5s and AK47s, although there's not much call for that kind of expertise in Mayfair. The black hats there tend to fight with lawyers, lobbyists, connections and money instead." She laughed, then paused for a moment. "Yes, I found tonight's attack frightening, but I'm OK, especially as they lost, and we won. By the way, do you want your pistol back?" she asked, pulling it out from her trouser belt and checking the safety before setting it down on the desk.

"No, I want you to hang on to it until we can be certain you won't have to use it, but are you really OK?"

"Yes, really, I'm fine. But if I'm holding on to it, do you have a holster? It's bloody uncomfortable stuck down my backside."

Opening a desk drawer, he pulled out a holster on a belt and laid it down beside the pistol. Turning to Hennie he asked, "Any word from the search party?"

"Not yet, but we've got all of the bodies on the Chinook ready for whatever Jan brings back from the bush. I thought we should fly them up the coast and dump them in the sea off the mouth of the Zambezi. There aren't many people around to see what we're doing and there's lots of sharks there. As soon as they smell the blood in the water, they'll find the corpses and demolish them."

Katya sat quietly listening to them, thinking that this was just about as far from her Mayfair office as she ever wanted to get. Luc and Hennie seemed totally unmoved by the deaths of some twenty-four African soldiers. What experiences in the Angolan War had conditioned them this way? Last night she had gone to bed with a tingle in her tummy when she thought of Luc; this morning she saw another darker side, the soldier, and wasn't sure what she felt any more.

Hennie interrupted her reverie by asking if anyone had looked at the Chinese GPS set.

"Give it to me," she said, "and I'll have a look. By the way, do you have any good large-scale maps of the area? Because if I can find their starting coordinates, I'll need a decent map to identify the actual location of their camp."

"No problem, I've got 1: 50,000 scale maps covering all of Mozambique and about 200 miles of the surrounding countries' border areas into South Africa, Zimbabwe and Malawi. It's all part of my prospecting kit," smiled Luc.

As she went to work, Hennie's radio buzzed. "Jan, what news?"

"We found the bastards, Hennie. Three Africans and another Chinaman. They'd bivouacked about three miles north of the compound. Two were already dead from their wounds, one was badly injured and the other one was completely shattered, curled up like a baby."

"What have you done with them?"

"There are three bodies out there now and we have one prisoner with us. We should be back at the camp in about an hour."

"Well done! We'll see what your prisoner can tell us – over and out." Turning to Luc, he said he'd send a larger party out to recover the bodies.

"Yes, I want to remove all evidence of the attack."

With that, Katya exclaimed, "Gotcha!" and went over to the coffee table with the maps under her arm. Sitting down, she searched through them until she found one of the Zimbabwean border area by the Marange diamond fields. A couple of minutes later, she called Luc and Hennie over and, pointing at an area she had ringed on the map, said, "That's where they started out from."

CHAPTER 8

When Piet de Bruin returned to his office after lunch, he'd just sat down behind his desk when the phone rang. When he picked it up, his PA Mary said, "Luc Kruger on the phone, boss, do you want to talk to him?"

"Put him through." After a few clicks and buzzes on the line, Luc's voice came through. "What gives, Luc?"

"Our friends came around last night for a game of flood-lit field hockey."

"What was the score?" asked Piet, immediately picking up on the coded references.

"We got twenty-six goals to their two before they gave up and set off for home."

"Sounds like an unequal game. Any broken goal posts?"

"Only one badly broken set of goalposts and a floodlight. They were a rough team, but we were rougher. We've cleaned up the pitch and, in an hour or two you'll hardly know that we had even kicked off."

"Any idea where their clubhouse is?"

"Yes, and I've sent some people over to see whether a return match is a realistic possibility."

"And?"

"It seems we've got a good chance of a show-stopping return match tomorrow."

"No problems with the team?"

"No, but I'm really surprised at how well our latest recruit has fitted in. Much tougher than I expected and seems to be pretty unflappable with it!"

"You know I choose my team very carefully, Luc; that's why we usually win."

"OK Piet, I'll keep you posted – 'ziens."

Piet hung up the phone and leaned back in his chair. *So, the bloody Chinese were really serious. Beaten in this encounter, they wouldn't give up. If Luc had found their base and if they could destroy it, then the boys in Beijing would be even more intent on destroying him and his project. Glad that Katya had acquitted herself well, good choice!*

*

Katya walked into the hut, made herself a coffee and sat down at the coffee table.

Luc looked up and asked, "Are you OK?"

"Yes, fine thanks, although that was a pretty disturbed night. That was a real attack and when they blew up the south tower, I thought everything was going to hell in a handcart and I might actually have to use this in earnest," she said, pointing to her holster.

"When Piet said he was going to bring you on to the team, to be honest, I had my doubts, reinforced when he introduced this poised, good-looking woman at the hotel. I wondered to myself how you would stand up to the reality of our operations on the ground."

"And now, flatterer?"

"Happy, no doubts. You're much tougher than you look and you're most welcome on the team."

'Thank God for that,' she thought. For all the chit-chat yesterday evening, and the evident attraction between them, she had no illusions that an ex-special forces South African soldier would see her as anything other than a liability outside of a civilian environment. Well, it seemed that she'd changed that. Good!

"Thanks, but now I'll have to get on with my grand tour; first to Witwatersrand University and then to Delft to see whether my lab-scale work on smelting and refining translates to pilot scale and through to production."

"Surely that's not important - the game plan all along has been to take the project through to a PEA, maybe to a Bankable Feasibility Study and then sell it on to someone else to commercialise."

"Yes – but."

"Yes - but what?"

"You know that permitting a mining development can be a really difficult exercise nowadays. Governments have woken up to the fact that mining and refining operations can be absolutely filthy and a project that comes with a novel and relatively clean refining process will have a much easier passage to approval and consequently be worth a great deal more."

"Makes sense. But I'm afraid you're stuck here for another day. Hennie's gone on to reconnoitre the Chinese camp and won't be back until early afternoon. My guess is that we will spend the rest of the day planning an attack and, knowing Hennie, he'll want to hit them just before dawn tomorrow. Maximum surprise, maximum impact.

Assuming all goes well, they'll have done the job and be back here in time for a late breakfast, but we may need to use the Chinook later for a bit of what you might call 'housekeeping'. We need to be bloody sure that we eradicate all evidence of the Chinese attack here, and all evidence of our involvement in the destruction of the Chinese base in Zimbabwe.

Fortunately, I don't think the Chinese will be any keener on publicity than we are."

"In that case, I need to make some calls." Standing up, she left for her hut and satellite phone. Moments later she was on the phone to her office in London. "Can you put me through to Marijke, please?" After a short delay Marijke came on the line, asking how things were.

"Interesting in a Chinese way."

"What?"

"Don't you remember the old Chinese curse: 'May you live in interesting times'?

"Ah, yes, so it isn't going smoothly, is it?"

"No, but Luc and his boys are a formidable bunch. Anyway, that's not why I'm calling; how's the business doing?"

*

CHAPTER 9

Slurping yet another cup of tea, Tang looked at his in-tray; nothing from Zimbabwe. He buzzed his secretary. "Any word from Colonel Chen?"

"Not yet, sir."

"Wasn't he supposed to let us know when he was about to attack the camp?"

"Yes, he did that, but the squad would take several hours to reach the target and we've not had any further signal from him."

"Let me know the minute you hear anything."

"Yes, Sir."

Tang sat back in his chair, wondering what might be going on in Zimbabwe. Chen's team had cleared the embassy in Harare a week ago to set up their base camp. He knew they were on their way now, but it was all taking a long, long time, much longer than it should have. He knew he'd insisted on only two bulletins for the duration of the operation, "Going In" and "Results", but he couldn't help worrying that it wasn't all going to plan. However, he would just have to be patient and hope that Director Zhang wouldn't make his life a misery in the meantime.

*

Hennie dropped to his knees behind a large bush about half a mile from the Chinese camp and pulled out his binoculars. He, Jan van den Heuvel and Oké Mobutu had been dropped off from the Chinook about five miles from the Chinese camp and trekked up to the spot indicated by the Chinese GPS handset. The camp lay in the centre of a depression in the hillside in front of them, three long huts surrounded by a wooden stockade about two metres high. An observation platform stood at one end, allowing a sentry a view all around the perimeter.

"Not much going on, Jan. There's an observation tower but it's not manned. There are, let me see, a couple of African troops sitting on a bench and watching a game of five-a-side football, say twelve in all. There are also three Chinese sitting round a table at the base of the observation platform. They don't look as though they are expecting visitors."

"Well, at least that agrees with the information we got from the prisoner."

"Here, look for yourself."

Jan took the binoculars and studied the camp. "They may not be on guard but taking them by surprise in daylight won't be easy. I'd favour a dawn raid, using a couple of our M2s mounted amidships on the Chinook, gunship style, to take out the observation platform, strafe the cabins and knock a hole in the stockade. We could then drop in and mop them all up. From first bullet to 'cease fire!' it should be possible to take out the entire camp in five to ten minutes at most."

"Agreed, but that leaves us with the problem of tidying up afterwards. We'll need to think this through back at Camp 25. Make sure you have photographed everything. We need to have as much data as possible for planning our raid."

Handing the binoculars back to Hennie, he said, "Look at the north side of the tower - that looks like a satellite dish. That must be how they communicate with China. I wonder if it points at a geostationary Chinese satellite or if they use an orbiting satellite, giving them a comms window of just a few minutes every couple of hours or so."

"My guess would be that they're not linked up to a geostationary satellite, but Luc should be able to find out about the Chinese satellites through his contacts."

"Not necessary, Hennie, we can take their comms out with a couple of RPGs on our first pass. They won't have time to do anything."

"True. Right, Jan, have we got all the photos and data we need?"

"I think so. We can put a pretty accurate site layout together and plan our attack."

"OK guys let's head back to the rendezvous and our lift home for a late breakfast."

As they set off for the helicopter rendezvous, Jan radioed ahead to the pilot and told him to be ready to pick them up in ninety minutes. As they neared the rendezvous point, Hennie suddenly stopped and said, "We didn't see any transport in the Chinese camp, and I don't believe that the bastards who attacked us last night walked from here to Camp 25."

Oké turned to Jan. "Baas, we crossed two sets of vehicle tracks on the way to their camp."

Hennie heard and asked, "What kind of tracks?"

"Trucks – maybe 10 tonners - troop carriers, Baas."

Hennie thought for a moment before turning back to Oké. "You didn't see any trucks when you tracked down the survivors, did you?"

"No, and no tracks out of the clearing where we found them."

"I think we'd better search the bush around Camp 25 when we get back."

As they neared the rendezvous, Jan sent Oké ahead to scout the landing zone. He returned after ten minutes, looking relaxed. "No sign of trouble, Baas."

Jan radioed the Chinook pilot, giving him the all-clear to come in and pick them up. With that they heard the faint clattering whine of the Chinook's approach, steadily getting louder until they could see it, then settling down into the clearing in a cloud of dust as the main fuselage door was thrown open. They ran forward, shielding their eyes, and climbed aboard, Oké pulling the door shut behind them as they took off again. Hennie, pulling on a headset, asked the pilot to make a low-level approach to the Chinese camp and fly over it at no more than 250 feet. Jan, also wearing a headset, heard this and looked enquiringly at him.

"I want you to get up to the door with your Box Brownie and complete your photo album as we fly over. I'll cover you in case someone takes a pot shot at us, but we should appear out of nowhere, transit their camp and be gone in just a few seconds. OK?"

"OK."

"Camp coming up in ten seconds," came the pilot's voice over the intercom as Jan scrambled to get into position, turning on his camera.

The Chinook rose up over the lip of the depression holding the camp and flew over it fast and low, disappearing over the opposite lip in seconds, giving no-one on the ground time to do anything other than register the fact that a large helicopter has just flown over them.

"Get your pics?"

"In the bag."

"Great."

"Do you think this will have warned them that someone's on to them?"

"Not really, helicopters are the main transport in this area for the military and the richer miners, so no, I don't think they'll be too worried."

The pilot's voice cut in again. "Ready to head back to base, Hennie?"

"Yes, but when we get there, I want you to make a slow recce sweep right round Camp 25 on a radius of around five miles. We think our visitors must have driven to within a few miles of the camp the night before last and yomped the rest of the way. If you concentrate on the north-western approach to our camp and fly slowly, we should be able to spot their trucks."

*

CHAPTER 10

Colonel Chen paced restlessly round the base of the observation tower, stopping on every circuit to look at the door into the middle hut where the radio was housed. Captain Xiao should have reported in first thing this morning on the success of his mission to destroy the South Africans' camp, but nothing. Had his squad mutinied? Run away? He wouldn't be too surprised; he had been disappointed by the quality of the squad the Zimbabweans had given them. Big, hard men individually, he'd thought, but not soldiers - sloppy and poorly disciplined.

However, he had to work with what he'd been given, and he knew General Tang was not good on excuses. You were given an assignment, you requisitioned what you needed, and you got on with the job. Any outcome except success was a very bad career move. It didn't matter who you were related to in the Politburo, failure on a task like this was totally unacceptable and likely to lead to a posting in charge of a border guard detachment in Mongolia or even imprisonment in a labour camp. He shuddered inwardly.

*

After the Chinook landed back in the camp, Hennie, Luc, Katya and Jan met in the office to discuss the next step. Jan projected the photos he'd taken during their reconnaissance of the Chinese base.

Luc asked Hennie to summarize what they had discovered. "The Chinese have a neat little camp built in a hollow at the location Katya identified. A simple wooden stockade encloses three wooden huts. The outer two are probably dormitories, the central one being their mess and officer's quarters. There is a small observation tower at the end of the middle hut which carries a satellite dish, presumably a link back to Beijing. Their only visible transport was a Jeep, suggesting that the trucks we discovered were their only other means of transport. We saw about a dozen presumably Zimbabwean soldiers and three Chinese, who will be the officers leading them. Altogether, about fifteen people who will need to be taken out."

"Do we really need to do that?" asked Katya.

"'Fraid so," said Luc. "They came for us with the intention of destroying our camp and us as well. This has all the hallmarks of a Chinese black op and the only possible response on our part is to make it so black that the Chinese can't see anything at all. If our Chinese friends simply disappear from the face of the earth, no-one back in China will know what happened until a reconnaissance satellite over-flies our camp and theirs, and even then, they will only see our camp standing and theirs destroyed.

"What do you suggest, Hennie?"

"Well, I would follow on Jan's suggestion and configure the Chinook as a gunship and take a dozen of our guys with us in it. I would fit a couple of our Brownings in the doorways as he suggests, fed with a mix of ball and explosive ammo. I would take some RPGs with us and mount a two-stage attack.

"Approaching their camp at low level from the south just before dawn tomorrow, I would take out their observation tower with an RPG, while raking the huts with machine-gun fire. I would land on the track leading to the gate in the stockade, take it out with an RPG or two and send in the lads to mop up. Once the site is sterilised, I'd go in and pick up anything interesting in their officers' quarters before burning the place to the ground – and be back here for breakfast."

"Sounds good. I think I'll come with you. You will need to split into two squads once you land. I'll lead one while you lead the other. I'm particularly interested in seeing for myself just what sort of a setup the Chinese have. I don't have a clear idea of what we are up against, either a rogue Chinese black op or a government-sponsored campaign. If the latter, then we really do have a fight on our hands to protect our claim. By the way, do we have any machine-gun mounts for the Chinook?"

"No, but I know what we need, and Spider's guys should be able to fabricate them easily enough this afternoon while we develop the plan of attack with the lads."

With that, they headed over to the canteen for brunch. Spider was there, and Hennie outlined his requirements. Spider thought he could manage to fabricate and fit the gun mountings easily enough before dinner time.

*

While Hennie and Luc planned the following morning's dawn raid, Katya rang London for an update on the market, concluding her call to Marijke with, "Good work, I think I'm beginning to see a way through all of this" as she was updated on the unfolding alternative supply position.

Time for a bit of a workout, she thought. Given the time, she could fit in a good session, have a shower and be ready for dinner. Realising she couldn't change into her athletic gear and run around the camp in front of a bunch of soldiers, she decided on her gym routine, but without any equipment. As she worked through her routines she was thinking about her personal trainer, Harry Jones. He'd been a real find via the Hurlingham's Fitness Centre. She'd mentioned that she was into kickboxing and asked if anyone could recommend a trainer; an introduction to Harry had been the result.

They'd hit it off from day one and he'd pushed her skill level up to black belt status within two years and was now pushing her to take her 1st Dan tests. When she asked where he'd learned his skills, it turned out he'd been an SAS unarmed combat instructor in his army days. He'd taught her a few moves in that area too, such as how to defeat someone coming at you with a gun or knife. Reflecting on the events of the last twenty-four hours, she was glad that she hadn't had to prove herself for real. It had been quite a night.

After a final fifty press-ups, she'd had a welcome shower, dried her hair, dressed and headed over to the canteen for dinner.

Piri-piri chicken again, like last night, but never mind; it was delicious. Luc and she were at a table together with Hennie and Jan, going over last night's events, this morning's reconnaissance and the attack plan for the morrow when Spider came over to join them,

"Gun mounts fabricated, bolted into the Chinook and ready for you to fit the Brownings. I estimate that they've got a firing arc of around 120 degrees, which should be enough. We've also fitted brackets for the ammunition boxes, so they won't slide around inside the fuselage."

"Well done," said Hennie. "I was wondering about that. It's bloody important to have the ammo boxes fixed in place, otherwise you can end up with plenty of ammo and a jammed belt feed at the worst possible moment.

Well, sunrise is just after five am so Luc, Jan and I will be away from here at four, ready to give the bastards a right kicking as dawn breaks so I'm off to bed."

Luc escorted Katya over to the lounge hut and made sure she had coffee and a brandy to hand before kissing her goodnight and heading off to bed.

As he lay in bed, he found himself thinking about Katya. What a find - calm in a crisis, technically able and gorgeous to boot - very nice indeed. He drifted off to sleep dreaming of her.

*

CHAPTER 11

The Chinook flew over the Zimbabwean border just above the treetops and was gone before anyone on the ground had time to react, as it continued on course for the Chinese camp.

A voice over the intercom said, "Target in 15."

Luc, Hennie and the troops got ready, opening the side doors on the Chinook and swinging the Brownings outboard. Two of the troops picked up RPGs and steadied them ready to aim and fire. Moments later the helicopter breasted the hollow and bore down on the Chinese camp, heading for the observation tower. Half a dozen figures could be seen scrambling from the left-hand hut, guns in hand, looking for the source of the noise.

"Fire at will!" came Hennie's order and with that, two RPGs were fired at the tower, causing it to topple over in a ball of fire. As they crossed over the stockade the machine guns opened up, raking the huts from end to end. With the Chinook hovering over the centre of the camp, they continued hosing the site with 0.5" calibre machine gun rounds until the two outside huts collapsed in heaps of broken panels and nothing appeared to be moving.

"Cease fire, stop firing!" came Hennie's order.

With that the Chinook moved to the track leading up to the gate and set down gently, rotors turning slowly. Luc and Hennie led their men from the helicopter and advanced toward the gate. "Open the gate." ordered Luc. Two whooshes, two flashes, two bangs and the remains of the gate were left hanging from the hinges on the posts at either side of the entrance. Walking slowly, two abreast, the troops entered the camp, ranging their MP5s left and right, ready to neutralize any opposition.

There was no noise from within the camp, so Luc figured that any survivors of their attack were either hiding in the wreckage or were too traumatized to respond. "Hennie take your section and check the left-hand hut, then join me at the centre one. I'll check out the remains of the right hand one and join you. But be careful on entering the centre hut; there may still be some opposition there."

With his MP5 on single shot setting, he walked cautiously to the wreckage of the right-hand hut. It had been trashed and collapsed in on itself. There wasn't a single undamaged roof or wall panel, and in two or three places he could see blood seeping out into the earth. Hearing movement behind him, he turned swiftly to see the barrel of an AK47 being pushed up between the remains of two wall panels.

Aiming for where he thought the soldier would be, he fired a couple of shots and saw the AK47 slide sideways before disappearing from sight. Beckoning to his men, he said, "Let's check this out properly. Work in threes, two to drag the wall and roof panels aside while the third deals with anyone underneath."

Punctuated with the occasional shot, the two squads worked their way along the outside huts, meeting up at the entrance to the central one which, although badly shot up, was still standing. Wishing he had a couple of stun grenades and gesturing to the others to stand aside, Luc kicked the door open and threw himself flat on the ground as a stream of bullets shredded the space he had occupied an instant before. He almost got away with it, but a ricochet off the breech of his gun hit him in his left arm about six inches below his shoulder. He felt the shock of the impact but no pain – yet. Looking at his arm, he saw his combat jacket was torn and blood was spurting down his arm. It must have hit an artery and needed attention - fast. He tore the sling off his MP5 with his right hand and used it to make a tourniquet round his left arm above the wound. Shouting to Hennie, he said, "Hennie, I've been hit, take command!"

Hennie looked across at Luc from where he lay and saw him with blood pouring down his jacket. "Need help?"

"Soon – but get the bastard who shot me first."

Signing to his men, Hennie gathered five of them around him and, using his bayonet, wordlessly sketched out his attack plan. Two would crawl down each side of the hut until they were slightly ahead of the spot where the shooting appeared to have come from. Hennie would give them five minutes to get in position then shout GO! On the command, they would fire down through the walls of the hut, while Hennie and the other soldier would blast their way in the door that Luc had opened. Enfiladed by the fire from six guns coming from three directions, the occupants of the hut didn't stand a chance.

Hennie counted down five minutes and then shouted "Go!" Seconds after the firing started, he ran through the open door, firing off a 30-round magazine in less than two seconds, reloading and repeating the action until he had almost reached the point where the bullets from the others had torn open the walls of the hut.

"Cease-fire, stop firing," he shouted as he walked forward, on high alert, swinging his MP5 from side to side. Looking ahead, he saw bodies piled up as if they had been trying to take shelter from the torrent of bullets. When he reached them, he checked for signs of life, found none and went back to Luc.

Kneeling beside him and saying, "Let's have a look," he cut along Luc's sleeve to get at the wound. "It's deep and it's messy but it doesn't look as though the bone is broken. I'll put a field dressing on it, give you a shot of morphine and get you back to the chopper."

"Check out the office end of the hut before we leave and bring anything you find that might be interesting – then torch the place. I want to minimise the evidence we leave behind. My guess is that we'll have a squad from the Zimbabwean army here well before nightfall and the less they can find, the better."

Hennie took a couple of soldiers into the hut with him, grabbed materials to use as a makeshift stretcher, and sent them back to carry Luc to the helicopter. He wandered down to what had been the Chinese soldiers' radio room cum office. Looking round, the absence of paper was striking. Other than bullet holes, splintered wood and broken glass, the room was tidy, although it was obvious the radio would never work again. He saw a steel box on the floor under the radio and pulled it out. Although dented by some of their bullets, it was still closed and held shut with a security-grade padlock, so rather than waste time, Hennie called another two soldiers over to carry it back to the Chinook.

Stepping back outside, he called the rest of the squad to him and told them to pile all the loose debris, along with any bodies, onto the remains of the huts and torch the lot. "That looks like a generator house and possibly a fuel store just inside where the gate used to be. If there is any petrol or diesel, pour it over the huts first. Make sure everything is burning well and then back to helicopter at the double for our flight home."

Ten minutes later, with a thick column of black smoke rising behind them, they were airborne and heading back to Camp 25 at the Chinook's maximum speed of 170 knots. Dropping again to 50 feet, they shot across the border without incident and landed back at the camp half an hour later. Hennie had radioed ahead to warn Spider that Luc had been injured and to have the camp's medic standing by for their arrival.

As the rotors spooled down, the doors were thrown open and Wim, the group's medic, boarded, going straight to Luc, who was now lying unconscious on the improvised stretcher. He checked his pulse and told Hennie that he was in shock but should be OK. He fitted up a drip and got two soldiers to carry him over to the medical room and onto a bed.

As Hennie and the soldiers de-planed, Katya came running over as she saw Luc being carried off on the makeshift stretcher. "What's happened? Has Luc been shot? Is he going to be OK?"

"He was hit in the upper arm by a ricochet. It didn't break the bone, but I think it hit an artery. He was bleeding badly but had the presence of mind to use the sling from his gun as a tourniquet. I put a field dressing on it, gave him a shot of morphine and got him back here in double-quick time."

"But he's unconscious."

"He's just passed out temporarily from the combined effects of shock, loss of blood and morphine. He'll wake up shortly. He's lost a fair bit of blood, but provided the wound doesn't go bad, he should be sitting up and taking nourishment by this evening."

"Are you sure?"

"Yes."

"I'll go over and see if there's anything I can do."

"OK but come back to the office as soon as you can. There's something I want to show you and we need to bring Piet up to speed with what's happened." Getting the box out of the Chinook, he followed it over to the office, telling the soldiers to drop it just outside the hut. Taking out his Glock, he stood back and fired a couple of shots at the padlock, which gave up its grip and shot across the path. He lifted the lid carefully and looked inside.

*

CHAPTER 12

Katya's thoughts were in a whirl as she rushed across to the medical room. *This was absolutely not what I had imagined. I thought I'd spend a couple of days in a pleasant part of Africa, looking over an exploration concession, meeting the people working to define the scope of the ore body and then going on to Johannesburg to see the first steps of my smelting and refining process being turned into an engineering reality. Not this, not standing on the sidelines of a small-scale all-out war where the only possible outcomes were kill or be killed. And now Luc was wounded, putting the whole project in jeopardy. Was he seriously wounded or not?*

Once in the medical room, she went straight over to Luc, who was lying on the bed, stripped to the waist, with a drip set up near his head. Wim was working on his arm, cleaning up the wound and exposing the damaged artery.

"He's in luck! I've removed the bullet; that's it in the tray there. The artery is split, not cut or crushed, and relatively easy to suture but I'll need a bit of help. Have you done any nursing training?"

"No – just first aid, and this looks to be a lot more demanding."

"Not really. What I am going to do is stitch the split in the artery and if you can help me by holding the edges of wound open and swabbing the blood, I'll have a much better chance of doing a decent job."

"OK, but you'll have to tell me what to do."

"Fine. The first thing I'm going to do is replace the emergency tourniquet with clamps above and below the split. Meanwhile, will you please scrub your hands thoroughly with the sterile wash, put on some nitrile gloves and one of these sterile plastic aprons." Working as he spoke he opened a sterile wound treatment pack and located a couple of haemostats. "Fortunately, Luc is out for the count at the moment, so he won't feel a thing."

Aproned and gloved up, Katya came back over to the bed. "What now?"

"Do you see the swabs in the kit, at the far end?"

"Yes."

"Use them to mop up the blood in the wound. One won't be enough so be ready to take more as you need them. Just mop up the blood as we go along and take them out when I say 'ready,' so I can clamp the artery." Katya got to work and soon the wound was open and fairly dry.

"Ready!" With that, he clamped the artery on either side of the split, stood back for a moment to make sure the haemostats were fitted correctly, then undid the tourniquet, throwing it onto the floor. "It's a good job he didn't lose consciousness before he had time to do this. Please keep swabbing and try to avoid the clamps while I suture the artery, dust the wound with antibiotic powder, then pack and dress it."

Fifteen minutes later he stood up straight and said, "That's the difficult bit done and between us, we've got all the detritus out of the wound. He won't be doing any left-handed one-armed press-ups for a while, but he has a good chance of making a 100% recovery - that is, if you discount the scar he'll be left with."

As she watched him working on closing Luc's wound, she realized that, although she wasn't normally attracted to tough guys, she had found Luc to be interesting as well as exciting, smart as well as tough. He engaged not just her hormones, but also her neurons and she realized that she cared a great deal about what had happened to him. Looking at him lying on the bed, she turned to Wim and asked, "When do you reckon he'll wake up?"

"He shouldn't have been unconscious for as long as this. Hennie said he had given him a full Syrette of morphine but that only really stops the pain. I guess he was only shot about an hour and a half ago. I wonder if he gave his head thump and concussed himself when he was hit. I'd better check his blood pressure again."

Wim wrapped the cuff around Luc's right arm and started pumping it up. With that, Luc opened his eyes and groaned. "Wim . . . Katya," he mumbled. "Where's Hennie? Did everyone get back OK?"

"Yes, you're the only casualty," said Katya. "Now lie back and rest. You were shot in the arm, no bones broken but you've a nasty flesh wound."

"Where's Hennie?"

"He found a locked steel box in the Chinese camp office and has gone over to the office with it, presumably to open it up and see what it contains. It would be useful if it contained any pointers as to who exactly is behind these attacks. I mean, we know it's Chinese, but there's Chinese and Chinese, if you know what I mean."

"Yeah, we need to know exactly what or who we're up against. Look, I'm feeling better by the minute; let's meet up in the office after lunch - you, me, Hennie and Spider - and have a council of war."

Wim said that he'd only let Luc go if he seemed to be up to it, but Luc said that he was and that he would be there in a tone of voice that Wim accepted, albeit reluctantly and with a valedictory 'on your own head be it'.

*

When they assembled after lunch, Hennie pulled the steel box he'd taken from the Chinese camp over to him and lifted the lid. Reaching in, he pulled out a couple of silenced handguns, four boxes of 9mm bullets, a wad of $100 bills, maps, a Chinese/English phrase book and what looked like a radio operating manual, together with a book of what looked like call signs, identifiers and a call schedule.

"I'm not sure what this will tell us as my understanding of either Mandarin or Cantonese is limited to say the least, but there are enough dollars there to pay for the fuel the Chinook used on the raid – and some of the bullets as well. Katya, you're going to see Piet in the next day or so, aren't you?"

"Yes."

"Can you take the papers with you? We've got an 'in-house' Chinaman who can tell us what they say."

"An in-house Chinaman? I thought that we didn't like the Chinese, in-house, out of house or anywhere else on the planet."

"Benny Kim isn't your average in-house Chinaman. He was married to and deeply in love with a very pretty Chinese girl. They both worked at Beijing's University of Chemical Technology. They had a little girl and then she got pregnant again. With China's one-child law, she was compelled to have it aborted. Something went wrong and both she and the foetus died. He was heartbroken and became a sworn enemy of what he saw as the cruel and heartless Chinese state.

"He transferred to Hong Kong's University of Science & Technology, met Piet at some conference and the rest, as they say, is history. Benny is settled in Cape Town now with his little Lotus Blossom and is well on the way to becoming a South African citizen. Being both technically able and fluent in both Mandarin and Cantonese, he's been a great help to us in keeping us abreast of Chinese moves in Africa. He's a valued member of the team and he'll extract whatever is there to be extracted from these papers."

As he talked, Katya saw him getting paler and paler, with a sheen of sweat forming on his forehead. He started shivering and suddenly flopped sideways and fell off his chair onto the floor, unconscious. Hennie and Katya knelt beside him as she took his pulse. "140 and weak," she said. "Call Wim. I think this is more than simply delayed shock - we need to get him to a hospital urgently."

Minutes later, Wim, with Luc on a stretcher, and Katya, with the Chinese documents and her luggage, were on board the Chinook headed for Beira, while Hennie was on the phone to Piet to make the arrangements to get Luc into hospital as soon as they landed.

*

When they landed, an ambulance drew up alongside and Wim spoke to the nursing orderlies, who said they had orders to take him to the Clinica Avicena in town, all arranged by a Dr. de Bruin from Cape Town. Hearing Piet's name mentioned, Katya relaxed and walked beside Luc's gurney as he was transported to the ambulance. He'd recovered consciousness on the flight and she told him where he was going and that it was a private clinic arranged by Piet. He too relaxed and she bent over to kiss him as he was loaded into the ambulance and driven away.

"See you soon, Luc - get well quickly."

She picked up her bag and walked over to flight departures, found that there were no more scheduled flights that day and so rang her charter company to book a flight to Cape Town, checked in for it and sat down in the business lounge with a coffee and a cognac to wait.

After a few minutes, she decided to bring Piet up to speed.

*

CHAPTER 13

Katya stepped out of the elevator, walked across the foyer and through a door marked 'De Bruin Investments (Pty) Ltd.' into a modern reception foyer. A smartly dressed, middle-aged receptionist looked up as she came in and said, "Katya! You're here at last. The boss said you were coming in, but I thought your schedule was fly on from Camp 25 to Jo'burg, prior to flying up to the land of clogs, cheese and tulips."

"Morning Mary, good to see you too. Yes, I'm off to Jo'burg tonight but I need some face time with the boss first. I've had what's called an interesting time over the last week and want to debrief before I go on. Can you tell him I'm here?"

Mary pressed a button on her intercom. "Miss Katya's here, Piet."

"Send her in, please."

As Katya reached the door, it was opened from the inside and Piet reached out and embraced her in a bear hug. "Great to see you again, Katya. I gather you've seen a bit of excitement over the last few days."

"Yes – rather more than I was expecting. You didn't tell me that the Chinese were doing anything more threatening than spying on you, maybe playing political games, but that was all. I sure as hell didn't expect to be involved a firefight with dozens of men killed and then see Luc seriously wounded and carted off to a clinic in Beira."

"I didn't expect it either or I wouldn't have suggested that you went up to Camp 25. However, I've spoken to Luc this morning and he sounded quite good."

"Is he up and about?"

"Yes, his voice was firm, and he was chafing at being kept in the clinic."

"Thank God for that; when we flew down to Beira he looked awful and I seriously wondered if he was going to be OK."

"You needn't worry. The doctors and nurses are the ones I feel sorry for, although it will be a while before his arm regains its full strength. The bullet destroyed quite a bit of muscle tissue and chipped the bone. Fortunately, he's right-handed and knowing him as I do, he'll work like a demon at getting back up to full fitness."

"Have you heard from Camp 25?"

"Yes, I spoke to Hennie this morning and they had a quiet night. The kit they need to cap off the last borehole gets into Beira some time on Monday, so the site can be secured by the middle of next week. Hennie will leave a security detail behind when Spider has finished so that the site will be protected."

"So – everything's under control? Hennie is something else - tough and smart. I wouldn't like to be on the opposite side of a confrontation with him."

"He's a hard man, but a thinking one as well and absolutely reliable. He and Luc have a very close bond going back to their army days. He said you had some Chinese paperwork collected from their camp."

She reached into her briefcase and handed him the Chinese papers. He looked at them briefly, went over to his intercom and asked Mary to get hold of Benny and to bring them some coffee.

They sat down by the table and as she listened to Piet chatting on inconsequentially, she found herself reliving the night of the attack on the camp and the following days – *what a week! It was less than a week, wasn't it? It had a nightmarish quality. She had been woken up by the buzzer in her hut and had heard people rushing around in the neighbouring huts, then silence. She'd shot out of bed, thrown on some clothes and headed for the command post in the north tower as per Luc's instructions. As she entered, it all kicked off and she had a grandstand view of a lethal skirmish around the stockade. Once the fighting was over, she'd felt herself shivering and had wanted to curl up in a little ball. She had signed up as a 'technical director,' not as a bush fighter, and while she felt she'd held it together in front of Luc, Hennie and Jan, it didn't feel good.* Her reverie was interrupted by the words 'bankable feasibility study.' Giving Piet her full attention again, she asked, "Have you got enough analytical data to put a bankable feasibility study together now? I thought we were just going to stop at the PEA."

"We've got the results back from the Alex Stewart Labs in Zambia on the first ninety six bores and should get the last results from Camp 25 in about another ten days. They look good; in fact, at today's market prices, we are looking at more than ten billion dollars' worth of reserves. The ore bodies seem to be relatively shallow and well defined, so much so that the ore can be taken out very cheaply by open-cast mining. A first-cut projection using current refining and purification methods suggests an average extraction and refining cost of around 500 dollars per tonne of metal, or a gross profit margin of 50 to 90%, depending on the metal and its market price at the time. The key to 'copper-bottoming' our projections are your actual extraction and refining process costs."

"Well, Adam and his team seem to have the extraction process pretty well defined and if we can confirm the natural gas reservoir Spider thinks he's found, then primary extraction is going to cost less than five Dollars per tonne of ore, and with no hazardous effluent streams to deal with. I haven't been to the Wit or Delft yet and am not sure how effective or cost-effective the selective metal separation is. But hey! I'll be up at the Wit for Monday and Delft on Thursday and be able to put some detailed costs together."

The intercom buzzed: Mary said Benny had arrived, so Piet said, "Send him in and don't forget the coffee."

With the introductions completed, Piet explained where Katya's papers had come from and asked Benny to tell them what they were. He picked them up and scanned them quickly. "I'll need to spend more time on these before giving you a full translation, but at first glance, these are service pay-books and I/D cards, and this is . . ." He looked up, surprised, with a gleam in his eyes. ". . . and these are their radio and satellite contact protocols, together with email addresses for the raiding party, the Chinese Embassy in Harare and their army controller back in Beijing. Wonderful! I think we can cook up some murky electronic smoke, mirrors and disinformation with this lot. How long is it since their camp was destroyed?"

Katya thought quickly, counting back in time and then looked at her watch before saying, "Just over twenty-four hours. If we're going to mess with them, we'd better get going before they write their raiding party off and start all over again from another direction."

Piet chipped in with, "What exactly do you have in mind?"

"As far as I'm concerned, the obvious thing is to piss off the Zimbabwean military and sow dissent between them and the Chinese. Nothing like a spot of careful disinformation to give you an edge.

Let's impersonate the guy who seems to have been Chinese expedition commander, Captain Xiao, and have him bleating that the Zimbabwean soldiers were useless, ill-disciplined thugs who had panicked at the first sound of gunfire and rushed around like headless chickens. The two halves of the raiding party had got lost in the dark and ended up attacking each other instead of their target and killing three of Xiao's men as well as injuring him. The survivors of the firefight had then run away, leaving an injured Xiao to salvage what he could. Meanwhile the South African's camp was untouched, and we can explain the time Xiao was out of contact as being because of his injuries."

"I like the sound of that," said Piet. "We'll play the good old-fashioned game of 'why don't you and he fight?' Not only will we cover our own attacking activities, but we'll piss the Chinese off opposite their Zimbabwean friends. The loss of his men, apparently at the hands of an ill-disciplined bunch of Zimbabwean soldiers, won't help Xiao's career, while the Chinese military attaché's judgement will be trashed and relationships between China and Zimbabwe will be set back a year or two.

Meanwhile, the Zimbabwean military will blame Chinese idiots for the loss of their men and need really substantial bribes before they consider offering any help to them again. I guess, too, that the general pulling the strings back in Beijing will lose lots of face, whoever gave him his orders will be hopping mad. It spreads the shit around the landscape and makes us look like innocent bystanders. Xiao will then have to 'die of his injuries' before anyone from Beijing tries to get him back. All the Chinese were killed when their camp at Marange was destroyed, weren't they?"

"Yes." said Hennie; "I'm convinced that there were no survivors left before we came back to Camp 25."

'She's not just clever, but Machiavellian with it,' thought Piet. *'I suppose all successful traders thrive in a world of subtly disseminated disinformation and uncertainty, underpinned by the certainty of the hard knowledge of what is really going on in their own particular markets.'*

Katya smiled and looked directly at him. "Welcome to my world, Piet," she grinned. "Your cash and connections got me started, but by playing mind games and messing with the heads of my competitors, I have been able to build up a bloody successful trading business. This is where my skills come into play so let me script this one for Benny and we'll get our campaign under way."

KATYA'S CHALLENGE

*

With a series of spurious reports winging their way to Harare and Beijing, Katya and Piet had a wrap-up session before she left for the airport

"Well, let's see how these grenades explode. Have you got a decent contact in the South African Embassy in Harare who will be able to let us know what happens?"

"No problem, both the Commercial and Military Attachés are old friends of mine and were extremely helpful when I was working in the DRC. Actually, it was the military chap, Derek Doornbos, who introduced me to Luc in the first place. These army types keep in touch with each other and seem to have connections everywhere. I'm not sure how many of them are purely military. I suspect that most of them also have links to the NIA."

"The NIA?"

"The National Intelligence Agency – our spooks."

"Oh – but effective?"

"Yes, very, I'm glad to say, and if you are in a business like ours, good relationships with the NIA are not just helpful, they can make the difference between a risk worth taking and a guaranteed failure, possibly even ending up in one of the delightful prisons for which our continent is so famous."

"How about Beijing?"

"Not sure - I'll have to make a few phone calls. How about your man Chung? Would he be able to find anything out?"

"To be honest, I have no idea. I'll certainly ask him but while he is hugely well connected commercially, I don't know about his links with the PLA."

"Given that the PLA is heavily involved in overseas mineral exploration and exploitation, he will be. Anyway, you pursue that angle and I'll ask my NIA contacts.

"Well, that's that then. How about a spot of dinner?"

"There's no actual need for me to be in Johannesburg before Sunday night for my Monday morning meet with the team at Witwatersrand University. I can fly up on Sunday afternoon so if Mary can book me a hotel for tonight and tomorrow, I'll rearrange my flights.

"I also need to get back to my office ASAP. There's a lot of rustling in the undergrowth, so to speak, and there are some guys' heads I need to mess with, but I can't begin to tackle that before Monday, so yes, I'd love to have dinner.

"Meanwhile, I need to spend some time on the phone to London. Is there a spare office here that I can use?"

CHAPTER 14

A visibly upset ADC, Colonel Wu, was shown into General Tang's office.

"What is it?" demanded the General.

"This, sir." He put two email printouts on the general's desk and stood to one side. "These emails were received overnight from Colonel Chen in Zimbabwe. It seems his operation has been a complete failure. The Zimbabwean soldiers he was given seem to have lost their way on the approaches to the South African's camp and ended up fighting each other. He says that Captain Xiao and his two sergeants were shot in the confusion and that he himself has been badly wounded."

"Was the camp destroyed?"

"No, Comrade General."

"Get me Chen on the satellite phone when we are next in line."

"But sir, we can't get in touch with him. We were scheduled to talk early this morning, but the comms link wasn't activated at his end."

"Don't we have an emergency frequency to call him on?"

"Yes sir, but we get no response. I think his wounds must have been worse than he said. He may be unconscious or even dead."

At this point, General Tang's face went bright red, a sure sign of an impending explosion. "Surely someone must have taken command of what's left of the operation?"

Taking his courage in both hands, Wu said, "You would think so, sir. May I make a suggestion, sir?"

"What do you have in mind?"

"Hsiu, our military attaché at the embassy in Harare, set up the deal with the Zimbabwean army which seems to have gone wrong. As the man responsible and if he is to save his position, sir, it would seem to be a good idea for him to find out what the hell went wrong and do what he can to save the situation."

"OK, tell him from me to get his fat arse into a helicopter, assuming he can persuade the Zimbabwean Army to lend him one with a pilot, and get over to Chen's camp, see what the hell's going on and give me a sitrep with maximum urgency."

"Yessir," said Wu, leaving the General's office at speed.

*

Senior Colonel Hsiu sat behind his desk, perspiration dripping from his forehead despite the air conditioning. He stretched his hands out in front of him - yes, they were shaking. Yes, he was in deep shit and unless he could salvage something from this operation, his comfortable posting here would be over and he would be recalled to Army Headquarters back in Beijing and court-martialled for incompetence and failure to equip the special forces operatives with the support necessary for their mission, leading to the loss of highly trained officers and men. The verdict would be guilty, whatever the evidence. He might get away with being stripped down to private and posted to Nepal, but a firing squad seemed the most likely outcome.

Wu might technically be his junior but there was absolutely no doubt that he spoke Tang's words. He reached for the phone and dialled General Mutasa, his Zimbabwean army liaison contact. As the phone started to ring, he cancelled the call. What the hell was he going to say to Mutasa? The whole mission had collapsed; the Zimbabwean soldiers, bloody apes, had apparently behaved like drunken football supporters, an undisciplined rabble – just a minute – were they drunk or high on drugs? Had they gone into action drunk on maize beer, or high on hashish? That might be the approach to take; if he could get Mutasa on the back foot, he might be able to sort things out.

Picking up the phone again, he called Mutasa, identifying himself when the general answered the phone.

"Colonel Hsiu here. What the hell did your troops do? Were they drunk or high? I don't know what their orders were, but I do know that some of our officers have been killed by your guys and this was before their mission had even made contact with the target. We are supposed to be allies, especially given the millions of dollars we've pumped into your country, and what do we get in return? A bunch of drunken incompetents who get themselves and our men killed, without engaging our target or doing . . ."

Mutasa broke into Hsiu's tirade. "Colonel, your highly trained Special Forces officers have succeeded in getting my men and themselves killed. Highly trained Special Forces officers, indeed! These were well-trained men; my Special Forces combat troops. The fact that your men got them killed will not be forgiven easily. In fact, I will have to reconsider our relationship." And he broke the connection.

Hsiu sat back in his chair quivering with a mixture of rage and fear, his shirt soaked in perspiration. *What in the name of the gods do I do now?* he wondered.

*

Fifteen minutes later, with his heartbeat settling back to somewhere near normal, his military training reasserted itself and he got up from his chair and headed back to his quarters to shower and change his clothes.

KATYA'S CHALLENGE

As he put on clean clothes, his mind was working through the options before deciding to get the embassy's travel department to arrange the hire of a helicopter and pilot to fly him out to Marange and the Chinese camp.

Less than an hour later the helicopter lifted off from Harare International Airport and headed south-east towards Marange. As they approached the camp's coordinates, the pilot asked Hsiu for further instructions.

"Circle the site and look for a place to land."

As they circled the camp Hsiu looked down and could only see the remains of burned-out huts. He saw no sign of life and asked the pilot to land. Once on the ground, he opened the helicopter's door, drew his pistol and stepped down into the dust. Stepping away from the helicopter, he gestured to the pilot to cut the engine and waited until the rotor blades stopped. The first thing he was aware of was the smell - the smell of charred wood and plastic mingled with the smell of rotting meat. He listened intently for a few moments before calling out.

"Colonel Chen! Captain Xiao!" There was no reply, so he called again, louder. "Colonel Chen! Captain Xiao!"

The only sound he could hear was the flapping wings and hissing of the vultures that had been disturbed by the helicopter, as they returned to their interrupted meal. Returning to the helicopter, he collected his camera and a metal rod. He systematically searched the burned-out remains of the camp, concentrating on what had been the centre hut where the command centre had been located.

Poking around the wreckage, he found the remains of the radio transmitter riddled with bullet holes. He came across the incinerated remains of several men, all Africans as far as he could see, but nothing to identify the attackers. He continued his inspection, taking photographs of the destruction for transmission back to Beijing. He returned to the helicopter and told the pilot to get them back to Harare.

*

Back in his office, he called Colonel Wu and told him what he had found, saying that he would email the photos he'd taken of the camp. Asked if he knew who had destroyed the camp, he said he'd not found any evidence of who the attackers were, but maybe the South Africans had managed to find out where they were and mounted a cross-border attack.

"What are the locals saying about this?" asked Wu.

"They're holding us responsible for the death of their men, whom they claimed were crack troops – what a joke - and relations between us have been broken off, for the moment at least."

"You've really fouled up, haven't you? This is a huge loss of face for our diplomatic mission in

Zimbabwe, just when it seemed that they were starting to cooperate with us, rather than just pocketing our investment dollars for their own personal enrichment. You'd better get back here and explain your actions to the general. Catch the first flight you can, and be ready to justify yourself when you get back here. Let me know your flight number and I'll send a car to collect you in Beijing."

Hsiu called his secretary in and asked her to book him a seat on the first available flight back to Beijing and to send his flight details to Colonel Wu. She came back to say that she'd booked him on a flight leaving in three hours for Johannesburg, where he'd change for a Beijing flight with a stopover in Hong Kong, getting him in to Beijing around this time tomorrow.

Clearing his desk and locking it, he picked up his briefcase and laptop and headed for his quarters. As he passed through his secretary's office, he asked her to arrange for a car to take him to the airport in half an hour.

"If I don't come back, please get my belongings packed up and shipped back to Beijing via the diplomatic bag."

"Yes sir," she said, looking at him with some concern and wondering if she would see him again. He wasn't a bad boss after all, and much better than some of the officers she had worked for in the past.

*

Twenty-seven hours later, a tired and dog-eared Hsiu walked out of the customs hall to see a sergeant holding up a card with his name on it.

"Colonel Hsiu, sir?" asked the sergeant.

"Yes – what are your orders?"

"To take you to your quarters, sir, and to bring you to General Tang's office at seven am on Monday morning, sir."

"Let's go, Sergeant."

Following the sergeant to the priority car park, Hsiu climbed into the back of the waiting Liebao CS6, shut the door, fastened his seat-belt and said, "Drive!"

*

Senior Colonel Hsiu stood up from his crumpled bed on Monday morning just after 5:00am. He had hardly slept a wink all night as he worried what General Tang might do to him. The possibilities were few: back to Harare – unlikely; maintain his rank and seniority in Mongolia – more likely; reduced to the rank of Second Lieutenant and posted to Tibet – more likely still; court-martialled and shot – a distinct possibility.

He had written and re-written his report for General Tang more than seven times, trying to demonstrate that he had done his job and that the failure was entirely down to the Zimbabwean military, specifically General Mutasa, whose idea it had been to offer a bunch of ill-trained gorillas to support a Chinese-led precision attack on the South African camp. Worse than that, they'd left enough information behind for the South Africans to locate and destroy their base camp in the Marange diamond fields - at least he was damn sure that it had been done by the South Africans, probably a security squad from their exploration camp. Back in the days of the Angolan war, he'd observed the South Africans in action, and they usually left nothing standing and took no prisoners - very professional and very effective. He suspected that they'd simply spotted the Zimbabwean troops approaching their camp and blown them away.

However, all he could do was lay the blame for the disaster - after all, it had been a complete disaster - at Mutasa's door and hope for the best. It was maybe best to portray himself as the obvious choice to return to Harare and rectify the situation, but for that he'd need to be able to offer some sort of inducement to the Zimbabweans and find another liaison officer to work with.

He heard a knock at the door, his driver . . .

*

Despite the command to be at his office at seven am, General Tang kept Hsiu waiting in an anteroom until just after ten before calling him in. "Sit down and give me your report."

"Comrade General," began Hsiu.

"Get on with it, Hsiu!"

Hsiu swallowed hard, feeling deeply uneasy, and began his many times re-written report. Tang listened without comment until Hsiu was finished before saying that he actually agreed that the fault lay with Mutasa's botched troop selection and that while Hsiu had not covered himself in glory, if he wanted to retain his rank, he would go straight back to Harare and sort things out before the failure of this operation had to be relayed to the Minister.

"You have precisely two weeks to restore relationships with Mutasa. You might remind him that delivery of the next tranche of weaponry and armoured vehicles we have offered them depends on it. Pick another operational squad at the same time and get them over to Zimbabwe, secretly, the same as last time, but maybe a slightly larger and more heavily armed squad might be better. Fewer men and bigger weapons - maybe we should work on a plan that eliminates the need for Zimbabwean cooperation."

Hsiu looked incredulously at Tang. He wasn't off the hook, but he had a chance to redeem himself. "I'll go and start planning immediately."

"Yes, and I want to see the first draft before four pm today. Go! Go! Get on with it."

"Sir!"

Hsiu left Tang's office at the double and headed off to the Special Forces barracks. How was it that he'd been given a chance to redeem himself?

Maybe it wasn't just Hsiu's neck on the block, but Tang's as well. Best not to ask any questions.

CHAPTER 15

As Katya came out of the customs hall at O R Tambo International Airport, she saw a tall black man in a chauffeur's uniform standing by the barrier and holding up a placard with her name on it: 'Dr K Francis.' She caught his eye and walked over to him. He looked surprised.

"Good afternoon were you expecting a man?"

"Noooo, Dr. Francis, Dr. Smith didn't say."

He looked confused for a moment then brightened up as he remembered his instructions. "Do you want to go directly to your hotel?"

"Yes please, I've just been up-country in Mozambique for a few days and would like to freshen up before I meet Dr. Smith."

"OK Dr. Francis, now please give me your bags."

She followed him to the car park where he went over to a new-looking shiny black 7-series BMW saloon. He opened the boot, put her bags inside and opened one of the rear doors for her. Once settled, he drove off, out of the airport and on to the main road. Twenty minutes later he drew up outside the Fairway Hotel and escorted her into reception.

"Please ask Dr. Smith if he would be so kind as to join me here for dinner at seven this evening. Can you pick me up in the morning at eight-o-clock to take me to the university?"

"Sure thing, Dr. Francis."

With that, he turned and left. Five minutes later she was in her room, looking out over the hotel's small garden. Kicking off her shoes, she unpacked her toiletries and started the bath running.

*

Relaxing in the warm bath, her mind replayed the events of the last few days. *Anecdotally, she had had some idea of the difficulties faced by mining and exploration companies, but the reality had been a shock. Somehow explosions and gunfire at close range were so very different from the same events portrayed on TV or in the cinema, especially when real blood and dead bodies lay on the ground, not corpses mocked up by the special effects department. She remembered the time in Nigeria when she was travelling out to an oil pumping station with her father and some bandits attempted to take them hostage. That had been a shock to the system too, as their bodyguards retaliated by shooting their attackers dead. That was probably why she hadn't panicked or gone all 'girly,' and she was sure now that Luc accepted her as a fully paid-up member of the team.*

She wondered how he was. She'd sat beside him as they flew down to Beira where an ambulance, arranged by Piet, had taken him off to a private clinic for treatment. His wound would be explained away as a hunting accident. It must have been hurting like hell and the morphine was making him woozy, but he hid it well. Wim had said that, depending on whether any infection took hold, he would need to stay in the clinic for at least four days before he could be up and about without risking his recovery.

Piet had been very concerned but told her to get on with her trip, as Hennie and his men could be relied on to guarantee the integrity of the camp, while Spider would be able to cap the last borehole, leaving the site ready for eventual development. She'd agreed but had told him she would come to Cape Town to see him first.

Getting out the bath, she towelled herself down and took a critical look at herself in the mirror. *Not bad,* she thought, although her daily exercise routine around the camp had been complicated. It wasn't a great idea for the only woman on site to parade round in skin-tight Lycra in front of a rough and lusty bunch of soldiers and drill operators. So she had exercised in baggy combat trousers and jacket, which took much of the sheer joy away from the physicality of a good workout, plus the inconvenience of having to avoid their barracks and what passed for a parade ground.

As she finished dressing and applied her makeup, she started to organise her thoughts for her first meeting with Dr Adam Smith. She was mildly apprehensive, as it was years since she'd even been in a laboratory, let alone to discuss advanced metallurgical technology. Hopefully he'd make the mistake so many men did of underestimating her intelligence while focusing on her femininity.

Her room phone rang as she finished dressing, with the receptionist saying that Dr Smith was waiting in reception for her. Slipping on her heels and giving her makeup a last glance, she gave herself a couple of squirts of Chanel No.19 and headed for the lift.

*

Dr Smith was tall and slim with greying temples and a bookish manner. He made eye contact with her as she stepped out of the lift. "Dr Francis?"

Katya smiled in return and asked, "Dr Smith?"

"Yes, but please call me Adam. My parents were both economists and I believe they thought they had a sense of humour."

Katya smiled and said, "I'm Katya and I'm dying for a G&T."

Over dinner they both relaxed and he explained how far they had come with replicating the smelting process Katya had outlined in her doctoral thesis.

"It works; the only question I have is how you managed to get the funding for a study of that nature in Holland. The kit was expensive, and the chemistry would have required special permission from the Dean, to say nothing of the health and safety protocols."

"I think you'll find that if Piet de Bruin is your doctoral supervisor and thinks that an idea has promise, obstacles tend to crumble and fade away. He's a remarkable man."

"Agreed - when he wanted me to set up a private lab for Future Metals here within the faculty, the Dean was very supportive until he saw Piet's security requirements and staff contracts. It meant that the university would only get rental income and that both the staff and I would be seconded to and paid for by Future Metals. Also, our research results would be proprietary to Future Metals and would not be published. The arguments over ownership of the intellectual property were fierce but Piet stood his ground and told them, politely of course, that if they didn't agree he would find another research group to work with. They eventually caved in when he said he would carry gold-plated insurance on the facility, leaving them as landlords with effectively no liabilities."

"How about security? The last few days have demonstrated that the Chinese are a real and present danger. They launched an armed attack on us in Camp 25 in the early hours of last Friday morning, killing two of our security squad. We believe they basically want to shut us down by whatever means - politics, bribery, even murder - and take over our claim."

"Oh! I didn't realise it was as serious as that. When you come in to the lab in the morning, we'll go over our security precautions once you've seen our results."

Adam made his excuses shortly afterwards, said that the driver would pick her up at eight in the morning and bring her to the university and wished her goodnight.

*

Katya was up at six and headed straight for the hotel's fitness centre for her morning workout. Glowing, she returned to her room, showered and was dressed in a smartly tailored trouser suit by half seven, having texted Marijke, asking her to call her on her satellite phone at eleven London time (one pm Jo'burg) for a business update. Into the dining room for her usual breakfast of orange juice, fresh fruit, a croissant and coffee, she was ready with her briefcase in hand at the front door of the hotel as the black BMW pulled up outside. The driver jumped out, wished her good morning and opened the rear door for her.

KATYA'S CHALLENGE

Half an hour later they pulled up at the entrance to the Geosciences Building on the East Campus. The driver must have called ahead because Adam was standing at the door waiting for her. "Morning Katya, did you have a good night?"

"Slept like a well-fed grizzly bear. Lovely, comfortable bed and no middle-of-the-night alarms or gunfire. How about you?"

"Fine thanks, although our dinner conversation has been bothering me. Anyway, let's go up to the lab."

The Future Metals lab was on the third floor behind a locked double security door which Adam opened with a magnetic card. Inside was a short corridor with a room off to each side and a large door with a window in it at the end, obviously opening into the laboratory. Adam showed her into the right-hand room, his office, furnished with a desk, a cupboard, a small conference table, two whiteboards and a huge monitor screen.

"Please grab a seat. Coffee?"

"Please, black, no sugar."

Adam made the coffee from the small espresso machine that sat on the cupboard and brought it over to Katya sitting at the table. Pulling out a chair opposite her, he

sat down. "You've given me a lot of food for thought and I've been racking my brains as to just how secure our operation is here. I think it's pretty tight, but I want an outside eye to audit our systems. I gather you have interests in rare earth element trading – presumably security around that has to be tight as the duck's proverbial?"

"Tighter, if anything." She smiled. "In the trading world, knowledge isn't just power; it's also the difference between making a guaranteed loss or possibly making a profit. I find the latter quite appealing. However, before we go into that, I'd like to meet the team, see the lab and discuss the results."

"OK, our team numbers four: Dr Jasmin Kaur is our mineralogist and defines the ore samples and likely extractable metals, Dr Jim Black is our expert on thermal processing and is developing your smelting process, Ravi Singh is our analytical chemist and Leonie Malan is lab manager and our statistician. I'll call them in to meet you."

Five minutes later they filed into the office and the introductions were made. Katya began by saying how exciting it was to see the research she had carried out for her doctoral thesis being developed into a fully-fledged industrial process. She then asked for a tour of the actual laboratory itself before she would sit down with them for a detailed discussion of their results to date and the problems they had encountered.

Walking into the laboratory itself, Katya felt as though she had been transported back in time to her days as a doctoral student. Mostly familiar kit: fume cupboards, balances, an ultra-pure water dispenser, chromatography kit, a mass spectrometer and the usual laboratory glassware, etc. The end of the lab was partitioned off with a notice on the door saying, 'Furnace Room'. The rest of door itself was papered with health and safety notices in respect of hard hats, goggles, protective gloves, gas hazard, etc., etc.

Suitably attired, Jim led the way into the furnace room, where he demonstrated his pride and joy and the heart of the research programme, a highly instrumented pilot-scale fluid bed calciner.[5] A ball mill in a sound enclosure stood off to one side and there was a gas cylinder cage holding around a dozen differently labelled gas cylinders and a liquid nitrogen tank. Stacked next to the mill were the familiar wooden core sample boxes.

Jim said, "It's all in here - the action, I mean. We mill the core samples to powder and then run them through the calciner. So far, we've managed to get yields of more than 73%, but I think I can improve the process to take us into the mid-nineties, which would put us on a par with conventional technology, but without the effluent."

She'd taken an instant liking to the man. Enthusiastic, radiating competence and with a bit of a twinkle in his eye, he matched up to the profile

---

[5] A calciner is a high-temperature fluidized-bed oven. Easy to control, with a potential for high throughput and the way in which it allows the introduction of other gaseous reagents during processing.

provided by Piet, a good solid researcher with the bonus of an outgoing personality.

"Impressive. What is the throughput?"

"In this wee beastie? Around twenty-five kilos an hour as it stands, but with a couple of modifications I'm going to make over the next ten days, I think I can at least double it."

"What's the theoretical achievable metal recovery?"

"Based on what I now know, I see 94% recovery of metal contained as achievable. Even with process tweaks it might be difficult to improve on that to any significant degree. My best guess is that, on a production unit handling 3-500 tonne of ore a day, yields will settle down at around 94-95%."

"How about energy consumption? Cancel that Jim, it doesn't matter."

"How come?"

"Our ore body is sitting on top of a natural gas reservoir, so our process energy would be free, apart from the costs of running the gas handling unit."

"That would be fantastic. It'll bring the basic recovery cost down to just that of mining and milling, with a bit of materials handling labour thrown in."

"What is your scale-up programme?"

"Depends on how much kit you're willing to let me buy."

"How do you mean?"

"Well, I doubt if we will be able to run at more than 50kg an hour with this kit. I would like to develop the process step-wise with 100kg per hour as the next step, then 500kg, then one tonne, 10 tonnes and finally 50 tonnes per hour, which equates to 1,200 tonnes in 24 hours - a full-scale production unit, in other words."

"How far can you go in this lab?"

"100kg max and only short runs at that, purely because of the logistics involved. Shovelling tonnes of ore around in here just isn't practical. We need to do this on a proper open-air site. How about doing it at Camp 25?"

"I'll have words when I get back to Cape Town and see what the implications are. Meanwhile I'll get the details from you before I go."

*

Back in the office, they sat down to a detailed discussion of the group's work to date and the inevitable setbacks as well as the successes. They discussed the forward plan and timetable, adjusting it to the point where Katya felt able to approve it. She told them not to worry about working themselves out of a job, as they would provide the process development input to the project on an ongoing basis once mining finance had been obtained.

CHAPTER 16

When the team left Adam's office, he made them both another cup of coffee and said, "After our chat last night, I feel a bit worried about security. Before you arrived this morning, I started to review our processes and practices. I'm happy about the team. Piet had them all thoroughly vetted before we employed them; you know the thing – money worries, gambling debts, drug or alcohol use, marital issues, mistresses, undesirable boyfriends, girlfriends and acquaintances, solid academic and employment history, etc. These four checked out 100% but I was amazed by the number of applicants who had skeletons clattering around their cupboards. Modern South Africa has spawned some seriously bad people and big problems.

"Physically, we have electronic access to the lab which could, I suppose, be hacked, but the master panel is in here. They would have to break down the main outer door first and that is alarmed with a radio link to a private security firm nominated by Luc. I think he owns it."

"Luc? I thought he was more into the kind of security offered by big muscle-men in camo clothing carrying guns."

"Yes, that too, but his real interest is mineral exploration and development. The security business is a bit of a hangover from his days providing security to mining and exploration companies in the DRC. It allows him to go off and explore for minerals with the certainty that no-one is going to spit in his beer when he's not looking."

"Having seen his 'security business' in action last week, I can only agree."

"Which brings me to my last concern, electronic security. We are not linked into the university's system but work instead with an internal server-hosted network here in the lab. I suppose that's pretty secure."

"And everyone just works off a terminal screen?"

"Yes."

"But I'm sure I saw a couple of laptops on desks in the lab."

"Oh, well, both Jasmin and Ravi use their laptops for work in progress, entering it up on the network when they're finished."

Listening to his response, she felt uneasy. Surely a man as bright as he undoubtedly was would see this as a potential risk.

"Can I assume they leave them here at the end of the day?"

"Normally."

"Normally! Normally! I don't believe it! Leaving staff with free access to laptops at work and then allowing them to take them home drives a main battle tank through our security screen."

"But they keep them secure."

"That is 100% not the point. Future Metals owns the process and all, yes all, of your group's research output. We're operating in conditions of total secrecy. Between my thesis and your work, we are creating new, unique and potentially extremely valuable technology. I know for a fact that people out there know what we're trying to achieve and are desperate to know how we're doing it. They're willing to bribe staff for information, blackmail them if they can and will steal things like laptops and memory sticks given the chance. From what I saw at Camp 25, some of them will even commit murder in pursuit of their aims

"In my trading business, no-one can bring any electronic device into the office or take any of our kit home. All our data is stored on secure servers off-site. There is no way that an outsider or employee can transmit any of our confidential information to a third party. There are no USB ports, printers or DVD writers accessible to the employees so that anyone trying to steal confidential data must have a photographic memory.

You are not running a secure operation and I need that remedied forthwith."

She stopped speaking and found she was breathing heavily. How could he be so blind to computer security? It was unbelievable.

Adam sat silently until she stopped speaking. "OK Katya, I'll deal with it and let you know what we're going to do."

At that moment, her satellite phone rang. She pulled it out of her briefcase and answered it. "Hi Marijke, how's things? Just a moment till I go somewhere where I can talk."

With that, a white-faced Adam stood up and silently left the room, closing the door firmly behind him.

*

"Yes, Marijke."

"Do you want the good news or the bad?"

"Start with the bad, then things can only improve."

"Over the last week, the procurement VPs of our American, Korean, Taiwanese and European customers have been on to us, worried about their future security of supply. They've heard the Chinese are rationing REE exports as part of a programme to clean up and concentrate their mining and refining industry. While this would appear to be true, one or two have been told via their local contacts that the best way to guarantee future supplies would be to establish manufacturing plants in China."

"Bloody hell! If they were to invest in China, that would be the end of our business. What have you advanced as an argument for not doing that?"

"Mark has been talking to everyone he can get hold of to say that we are and will remain a reliable and competitive supplier for their needs. After all, don't forget that setting up these manufacturing plants means a capital commitment running into billions of dollars, putting them at the mercy of Chinese industrial espionage, Politburo whims and changes of policy."

"Do they believe him?"

"He says most are receptive to his spiel, but he thinks they'll be hedging their bets in case we end up being unable to honour our promises."

"Hmmm – I don't suppose we can expect anything else. We just have to bloody well make sure we don't let anyone down. Mark must keep hammering the message home that when others fail, KF Trading delivers – and we have to make damn sure we do. But what's the good news?"

"As of this morning, I am down to final negotiations with both the Canadians and the Australians on future supplies and expect us to be able to ink the agreements by the end of the week."

KATYA'S CHALLENGE

"Well done! What are the key terms?"

"Volumes match our current offtake requirements, delivery commencing 60 days from signing, pricing as per the Metal Pages quotes, plus 5% from Canada, plus 6% from Australia, settlement 60 days from Bill of Lading."

"That'll knock our margins."

"Yes, but there's so much volatility in the market just now that we should be able to cover ourselves by stockpiling when the market is low to meet demand at higher prices."

"Hmmm, I don't like it. It ratchets up our risk. What is David's view?"

"We worked through it in detail and he says we can afford to cover nearly three months' requirements and would only run into trouble if we couldn't meet the interest payments, which would not be large. The banks will accept our stock as collateral at 80% of in-warehouse value."

"Look, I need to think about this, so don't sign anything until we have another chat. I'm flying up to Delft tonight and I'll call you from there tomorrow or Wednesday morning. I want David on the call as well, so have him on standby. 'Bye."

She put her phone away and went to find Adam. He was talking to Jasmin and Ravi.

"Excuse me, Adam, can we talk?"

He followed her out of the lab and back into his office where he sat down, a closed expression on his face.

"Look Adam, I apologise for blowing up just now. If you had been with me up at Camp 25 last week you would have seen for yourself just how aggressive the Chinese are. It looks as though they're trying to disrupt, close down and possibly steal our operation. To quote the Americans, they are 'a clear and present danger,' so please forgive my outburst but understand my concern."

He visibly relaxed and said, "OK, I understand. I was actually in the process of telling Jasmin and Ravi that we would have to beef up our security and that their laptops would have to remain here, as would they if they wanted to do any work out of hours."

"How did they take it?"

"OK, once they digested the reasoning behind it. I've contacted Luc's security company and they're sending someone over tomorrow to assess our systes and recommend a course of action."

"Good. Is there anything further we need to discuss?"

"No."

"In that case, can you get your driver to take me back to the hotel? I have some work to do before I fly up to The Netherlands this evening. I'll be back here before the end of the year, but we can keep in regular touch via Skype and email. Please send me weekly updates on Jim's work and let me know immediately if anything suspicious occurs that you think might be related to our friends from the east."

"Will do."

"Be alert – it matters. Meanwhile, 'ziens."

CHAPTER 17

As the plane climbed into the night sky heading north over Africa, Katya reflected on her suddenly complicated life. *It had all sounded like a fun extension of the 'day job' when she'd met and had lunch with the team in London a month ago. Even better, if they managed to turn the project into hard business, KF Trading would become one of the largest players in the market. But and this was a huge but, she could now expect that the Chinese would soon be taking a direct interest in her affairs, which could make life very difficult. It wasn't the first time she'd found herself in the cross-hairs of a political intervention in the metals market. When she'd been working in Belgium, one of her directors who had been on a fact-finding trip in the DRC and had probably asked too many questions, was dragged from his hotel room at three am and locked up in the local slammer. It had taken nearly six months to get him out, with the help of the Belgian Foreign Office, The company's president and a lot of unattributable dollars. It had all been driven by a failure to identify and pay off the government minister who considered this part of the DRC's assets to be his personal piggy-bank.*

*

The Gulfstream G550 landed smoothly at Rotterdam Airport at precisely 08:00 CET after nearly 12 hours in the air. It had been fitted out with fully reclining seats that converted into remarkably comfortable beds. Katya had managed to sleep for most of the trip and felt quite refreshed, especially after using the plane's fully fitted bathroom to shower and change prior to landing.

Clearing immigration and customs, Katya dumped her bags in left luggage and headed for the taxi-rank. She was driven the 10km to the Technical University Delft and dropped off in front of the Chemical Technology Building. She'd rung ahead to tell André Ten Berg of her imminent arrival and he came out of the main entrance just as she was paying off the taxi.

"Professor André Ten Berg?" she asked, looking at the tall, blonde and fit-looking Dutchman who smiled at her as she spoke to him. He wore a white lab coat over an open-necked checked shirt and smart jeans teamed with brown safety shoes.

"Yes, Dr Stevens?"

"Yes but call me Katya; we're working together now." She smiled back at him.

"And Katya, please call me André."

"Good, now I know Piet de Bruin will have told you I'd be here this morning, and here I am, all ready to see what you've been able to achieve with the mixed metal melt from the Wit."

"Come with me and I'll show you. I think you'll be quite impressed with what Drs de Rijke and Hegt have achieved."

Making small talk, they walked inside and over to the lifts. Nothing seemed to have changed in the years since she'd completed her doctorate, except that the paintwork looked fresher and there were more health and safety notices everywhere in evidence. She turned to André and said that it looked as if the Health and Safety Police had taken over. He grinned ruefully and shrugged his shoulders.

"We need to be insured to do anything nowadays and the insurers insist on all these notices, records and procedures."

"Bureaucracy! I don't believe it contributes a damn thing to our safety or that our experimental practices are any less likely to go wrong than they ever were. Well-trained staff and sound experimental protocols are all you need."

"You're right. Call me old fashioned but I have always studied experimental protocols in the same way since I, too, took my doctorate. The only difference now is that I must record my thought processes in case something goes wrong. As you say, it's just bureaucracy, adding to administration and cost, nothing to productivity."

They rode the rest of the way to the fourth floor in silence and walked along the corridor to the Future Metals Laboratory. André stood at the side of the door and looked into an iris scanner. Seconds later the door lock clicked, and he pushed it open, letting them in.

"That's neat, no keys or key cards to get lost or stolen."

"Luc and his guys came up when we took possession of the lab and installed the security, along with a clear set of procedures for the recording, handling and storage of confidential data. I thought it was all a bit over the top at first but in the light of what I have heard about your fun and games up in Mozambique, I'm a convert."

"Glad to hear it. I was in Mozambique when the camp was attacked and believe me, it wasn't funny. These goons meant business and if Luc hadn't fortified and equipped the camp, I wouldn't be here."

"Is it really the Chinese who are behind it, then?"

"No doubts. The group who attacked us were Chinese-led and their assault was organised from a Chinese compound in the Marange Diamond Fields area of Zimbabwe. Luc was injured when we took them down."

"How is he anyway?"

"On the mend. I'll be seeing him in London in a couple of weeks when we meet up for a detailed project review."

André preceded her into the lab suite and into their conference room, which was decorated with graphic models of the chemistry they were working on.

"Coffee?" asked André.

"Graag – zwart met 'n klontje suiker alstublieft."

"Uw spreekt Nederlands?"

"Ja, zeker."

"Can we please speak English? I really need to practice."

"OK, then English it will be," she said, taking the proffered cup and sitting at the head of the conference table. "Now, I understand from Piet that you're making real progress."

"Ja - I mean yes. Starting from your thesis, we've worked on your basic theory of separation, synthesising metal-specific zeolites. We now have one for each of the different rare earth metals in the mixed metal samples coming from the Wit. We can achieve 99.9% purity here in the lab and we're now working on scaling it up to an industrial process."

"Ah! It really does work. I thought it would but didn't have the resources needed to synthesise the zeolites. Very well done."

"Thanks, but it has been pretty painstaking work. The difference between one zeolite and another is both miniscule and critical. Anyway, we've cracked it and the separation setup is a cascade of zeolite columns. As you know, the ions of each rare earth metal have slightly different properties. So a cascade of these zeolites acts like a cascade of different-sized sieves and separates the individual metals from the mixture. Anyway, come and see for yourself. We have a bench-top installation running through in the lab just now."

Ten minutes later, having been introduced to the team, Katya stood in front of a row of glass columns filled with brown granules of the different, metal-specific zeolites. Electronic 'eyes' at the top and bottom of each column read the concentrations of the various metals in solution, displaying the results side-by-side on a large monitor. Following the cascade through, she could see that the individual metals were being successively stripped from the solution. Smiling, she turned to them and said, "That's brilliant, very well done everyone. Now guys, can you take me through the chemistry in detail?"

They spent the rest of the morning in the conference room going through the research notes point by point. Katya felt the years slipping away as they covered much of the ground she had sweated over on the way to gaining her doctorate but sat up and paid very close attention when they moved on to the work of the last few months, asking many detailed questions. She could see the change in the team's attitudes as her questioning went on – metamorphosing from the remote and peripatetic boss lording it over them to the academic supervisor, challenging every assertion and only being satisfied with hard evidence.

At the end of the morning, as Katya looked around the table, they all looked so proud of their achievements to date and were champing at the bit to move on and complete the job. Turning to André, she said that congratulations were in order all round and that he should buy them a celebratory dinner on the company. Meanwhile, she said that she'd buy him lunch somewhere local and nice, as she still had a few business details to discuss with him.

They walked in the sunshine to a nearby Italian restaurant and were shown to a table on the terrace. As Katya sipped her Campari Tonic and looked at the passers-by, she thought that Delft had maybe changed, but it hadn't really, and she began to feel more at home. There was the usual stream of students on foot or on bicycles, punctuated by some older men and women. Probably academic staff, she mused, as the campus wasn't really a tourist destination and it was well away from the picturesque centre of town. Just then, a Volvo police car drove past and Katya thought, *Police in a Volvo? Remembering that the Rijkspolitie with their paramilitary uniforms of jackboots, riding britches and white leather jackets, accessorized with sun visors and black crash-helmets and driving Porsche patrol cars, were being disbanded as she finished her studies. Typical greying down of anything that stood out in society in the name of inclusion and diversity. They had been awe-inspiring and certainly kept order on the motorways. But police in a Volvo – eeugh!*

A waiter came and took their order of grilled Dover Sole 'met frites' and a bottle of decent Pinot Grigio. He smiled and left them with Katya staring into space.

André interrupted her reverie. "What do you think?"

"I'm extremely impressed by your results. I was sure my theory was correct, but I was unable to synthesise the range of molecular sieves necessary. You and your team have taken my concept and made it a reality. So now we must patent the process - at least two patents I think, one for the controlled synthesis of the molecular sieves and one for their application in a cascade separation system."

"I've already started drafting them and I think I can possibly stretch our knowledge to three or maybe four patents."

"That sounds good. We're having a board meeting in London in a couple of weeks and I think it would be a good idea for you to come over and present your results at that meeting."

"Are you sure?"

"Look, the rest of the board know I haven't done any lab work in years. They will probably accept what I tell them, but nothing will convince them more than Professor Dr. André Ten Berg presenting his data, accompanied by the appropriate samples."

André smiled, preening himself. "If you really think so."

"I do. We have excellent assay data on our drilling core samples from the Alex Stewart labs in Zambia; we have similarly good data and samples from our smelting lab in Johannesburg. Your data and finished product samples complete the package. Along with Luc, I really want to be able to demonstrate that we have a project with an end-to-end process good enough to attract the level of funding necessary to commercialise it. Don't forget that success in this guarantees your future."

After a moment, he smiled and said, "I won't let you down – coffee?"

Later, as André settled the bill, she looked at her watch and said, "I have to go; there's a London flight I have to catch. Can someone get me a cab?"

With that, she said farewell and walked out onto the pavement to wait for the taxi.

*

Her mobile phone rang as she entered the business lounge in Rotterdam Airport. Fishing it out of her jacket pocket, she saw it was her mother.

"Oh Katya, we're in London for a few days to take in the sights and do a couple of shows. How about meeting up for dinner?"

"I'd like that, I'm actually in Rotterdam at the moment, waiting for a plane to London. As soon as we land, and I get through customs and immigration, I'll come right over."

"Would you?"

"Of course. Provided my flight lands on time, I'll be with you around seven or seven-thirty. I'll call you when I land. Are you staying at the Mandarin Oriental as usual?"

"Yes."

"OK, see you later, Mum."

*

Arriving at the hotel, she dumped her bags with the concierge and asked for her parents at reception. Told they were in the bar, she walked through, catching sight of them at a table near the back wall, a champagne bucket on the table

CHAPTER 18

Katya woke up late after twelve hours of dreamless sleep in her own bed. She got up, showered, dressed, grabbed a coffee and headed off to the gym.

An hour later she'd finished a really hard work out with Harry, who'd shown her some new self-defence tactics, showered again, dressed and headed to Nick's café for a full English breakfast. Orange juice, fresh fruit with yoghurt, sausage, bacon, eggs, tomatoes, mushrooms, baked beans, toast and marmalade, washed down with two large cups of coffee, and she felt ready to face the world again.

Returning to her flat, she made another coffee, grabbed the mail that had accumulated in her absence and went through it. Circulars, credit card offers, invitations to get into debt, special offers from the neighbourhood burger bars, pizza joints, Chinese takeaways and curry houses - all junk which went straight into her shredder. She then turned her attention to her phone answering machine, scrolling through friends' messages, none of which were particularly important.

KATYA'S CHALLENGE

That evening, Katya and her parents dined in a modern Italian restaurant near the hotel. Their conversation was rather subdued, and it was obvious that they were concerned for her safety. To lighten the conversation Katya mentioned that she'd been here in May to meet Piet de Bruin and gave them edited highlights of what had happened since.

"It all sounds a bit like the oil exploration business." Said her father.

"Yes, I guess so, but Piet and I and the rest of the team seemed to have attracted the unwelcome attention of the Chinese, who appear to want to take over our discovery."

"Isn't that dangerous for you?"

"Not with Luc on hand – now that is a real man."

"Oh! Kat don't say you've finally met someone that you really like. Who is this Luc? Tell me more." Asked her mother.

Katya described him and, responding to her mother's prompts, said, "No, he's not just an action man. He was certainly a decorated Special Forces officer in the South African Army with a Honoris Crux Silver Medal to show for it, but there's much more to him than that."

"Such as?"

"Well, he's very bright and well-read."

"You mean he reads books that don't have pictures?"

"Stop it, Mum! I've seen him here in your hotel and I've seen him in what you might call difficult circumstances in Africa. Whatever is going on, he rises seamlessly to the occasion. He seems to be able to turn his hand to most things, has excellent taste in wine, understands my trading business, makes me laugh, and I feel very safe when he's around."

"So - when's the wedding?"

"Oh Mum!" Katya felt herself blush as her mother smiled.

*

Wednesday morning saw Katya rise at six-o'clock, make coffee, eat a cereal bar and head for the gym. By 7:30 she'd had her workout with Harry, showered, dressed in her office clothes and was ready to face the day.

Letting herself into the offices of KF Trading, she was surprised to find Marijke, David and Mark already deep in conversation in the conference room around a pot of coffee and a plate of doughnuts.

"Morning all."

"Morning Boss," they chorused back.

"Well – are you ready to show me what clever people you are and dazzle me with the brilliance of your plan to manage the market?"

"Yes and no. We've got continuity of supply lined up but I'm not sure about our ability to manage the market." said Marijke.

Mark chipped in: "Heinz Henning of German Magnet rang me last night to say that he was rather confused. He said that he'd taken a call in the afternoon from a Chinese man who'd said that while he could understand his REE supply concerns, he shouldn't worry, that things were moving back in China and he would have some concrete proposals to discuss in a few weeks.

Henning wasn't sure what to make of this and asked me if I had heard anything. I told him that it was probably a typical Chinese 'snow job', that he'd get an attractive offer of a contract and that their first delivery would go to plan. The second and subsequent deliveries would all require completely new negotiations which would get progressively more difficult as they worked out who your end customers are and then stole them from under your noses.

I definitely rattled him and stressed that we could be relied on and wouldn't mess about with his customers. He sounded a little happier and promised to let me know what the Chinaman did next."

"I guess cautious optimism and close contact with our customers is the order of the day." Said Katya as they then went on to flesh out their plans.

*

KATYA'S CHALLENGE

As she locked the office door at the end of the day and walked downstairs, she thought that their plans had a fair chance of success. They had access to all the cash they would need to fund their procurement plan, and Marijke had been successful in setting up forward supply contracts with the Australians and the Canadians. These should guarantee them continuity of supply by the middle or end of December. The call from Henning was concerning, though.

Stepping out on to the street, she thought she'd walk home, as she hadn't had enough exercise while she'd been away. As she walked on, she had the sudden feeling that she was being followed - nothing concrete, just a feeling. She turned around sharply but saw no-one suspicious, so she walked on. Still feeling uneasy, she flagged down a passing taxi and took it the rest of the way.

Paying off the cab in Ranelagh Gardens at the door of her apartment block, she looked up and down the pavement, seeing a couple of young men walking in her direction. She walked over to the door and, as she reached for the entry keypad, she saw movement behind her reflected in the glass. Dropping her briefcase, she spun round to see one of the men lunging at her with a knife. Ducking under his arm, she continued turning until she was facing him again and planted a hard kick in his crotch. He let out a yelp and fell to the ground, dropping his knife and curling up in a self-protective ball with both hands nursing his injured privates. She turned again to see the second man advancing on her with his arm outstretched, holding what looked like a carving knife. She stood upright for an instant before spinning on the ball of her right foot and delivering a straight left leg kick right on the point of his chin. She heard the sharp crack of breaking bone and he too went down. She looked quickly round and saw that the street was clear.

With that, the pavement lit up as the entrance lights were switched on and the doorman came rushing out. Katya turned to evaluate this new threat, saw who it was and relaxed. "Are you all right, Miss Francis?" he asked with a tremor in his voice.

"Yes, thanks Joseph, you need to be a lot tougher than these bastards if you're going to beat me. Have you any duct tape handy?"

He looked at her in amazement before stammering, "Y-y-yes, there's a roll in my desk inside the door."

"OK, go and get it and a couple of largish poly bags while I keep an eye on these turds."

She walked over to her groaning assailants; her first attacker had rolled over onto his knees and seemed to be trying to get up. She waited until he was on his hands and knees before walking round behind him and delivering a second, very deliberate and very hard kick to his crotch. He fell over on his front without a sound and just lay there. The second attacker was still lying there without moving, making a moaning, burbling sound as he breathed, blood running from his mouth.

The doorman returned bearing tape, poly bags and a box-cutter. Still in awe of what he had just witnessed, he looked at her wide-eyed. She kept the initiative and told him to pick up and bag her two assailants' knives using a tissue or handkerchief to make sure his own prints or DNA did not contaminate them. He did so and showed her the two bags.

"Good, will you now please call the police and an ambulance while I tape them up, so they can't get away?" Grabbing the tape and box-cutter she set to work on the unconscious one with the almost certainly smashed jaw. She began by binding his ankles together before turning him on his front and taping his wrists together. She then ran more tape between his wrists and ankles before pushing him onto his side in the recovery position. With number two safely tied up, she turned back to her first attacker to repeat the process, but as she pulled his legs out, he pulled back and launched a kick which caught the side of her head. Still holding his ankles, she fell sideways, momentarily dazed, before she clamped her hands around a foot, wrenched and twisted it, dislocating his ankle, at which point he screamed and appeared to pass out.

She was just getting on with taping him up when the street was bathed in blue flashing lights and the shriek of sirens as two police cars and an ambulance drew up beside the door. A sergeant and two constables rushed over to Katya and her attackers. The sergeant took in the scene with some amazement.

"They went for me as I was trying to get into my apartment – I think Joseph here saw the whole thing."

The sergeant turned to Joseph and asked him what had happened. Joseph said that he had seen Miss Francis step out of her taxi and come to the door when these men attacked her with knives. "These knives," he said, lifting the two bagged knives and handing them over.

"Are you telling me that she disarmed and overpowered these two men herself?"

"Yes, I've never seen anything like it outside a Jackie Chan film."

At this Katya spoke. "Sergeant, I am a black belt kick-boxer; it's how I keep fit, and my personal trainer used to instruct special forces on unarmed combat. He taught me a few moves. Anyway, these thugs came at me with knives as I was trying to get into my apartment and I simply used my training to protect myself."

"Were they muggers?"

"I am pretty sure they weren't. Neither of them said a word; they just came at me with knives and if I hadn't seen the reflection in the door glass as the first one came at me, I think that ambulance would have been for me."

With that, one of the ambulance men came over and said to the sergeant, "You should see these." He handed him two packets of white powder. "They were each carrying one of these packets. And they don't seem to have any ID or anything else with them. The one with the dislocated ankle had this mobile phone."

Turning to the two constables he said, "Go with them in the ambulance to the hospital and make sure they have no contact with anyone but medical staff until we have the all-clear to interview them." Turning back to Katya, he said, "I need a statement from you."

"Can't that wait 'til tomorrow? I've had a very busy day and now this . . . to be honest, I just want to have a bath and go to bed."

"OK. I'll send someone around tomorrow morning to take your statement."

"Could you send him round to my office? I have been travelling abroad for more than a fortnight and I've got a mountain of things to do. Here's the address." She handed him a business card.

"My colleague will probably be round about ten-o-clock." He turned and left.

As she entered the apartment block lobby, Joseph came over to ask how she was.

"Pretty OK actually, if a bit shaken, but I just want a quiet night now."

"Are you seeing the police tomorrow?"

"Yes."

"Then you should give them this." He handed her a DVD in its case. "It's a copy of the front door CCTV recording which shows the whole thing - the attackers, your counter-attack and the police arriving. You shouldn't have to make much of a statement with this in hand. Your attackers are fairly recognizable, so it should be an open and shut case."

"Thanks for all your help, Joseph, and good night."

CHAPTER 19

Once upstairs in her apartment, Katya started her bath running, poured herself a brandy and undressed. *Lying in the bath, she replayed the attack in her mind, realizing that only her workouts with Harry and his unarmed combat training had saved her from serious injury or even death. Who were they? This wasn't a mugging; neither of them had said anything. They had come at her with knives poised. They were on a mission and that mission was to put her out of action, even kill her.*

The bath was starting to cool down, so she got out, drained her brandy, dried herself off and put on a comfy bathrobe. Walking through to her living room, she poured herself another brandy, picked up the phone and sat in her favourite chair.

"Mum, it's me, Katya, are you free tomorrow evening?"

"We were going to a concert at the Barbican, but the office called your father this afternoon and we need to go back home tomorrow."

"That's a pity, I was hoping we'd have tomorrow evening together, but I guess when you've got a job like Dad's, it goes with the territory. I've got a project running in Delft so I will be over fairly soon to see you."

"Great, look after yourself dear. 'bye"

She replaced the handset, picked up her brandy and went through to her bedroom, but before going to bed she thought she'd look at Joseph's DVD.

Looking at the screen she watched herself approach the door, then stop suddenly before spinning around and dealing with her attackers. The whole scene could only have lasted for five or six seconds before the entrance lights came on and she saw Joseph coming to her aid. The video ended with the appearance of the three policemen. Not much doubt there about who did what to whom, and the attackers' knives were clearly visible. Good, that should satisfy the police.

She was surprised to find that she didn't seem to have any after-effects, apart from what was going to be a bruise on her cheek from the first attacker's shoe. Who the hell were they? Was this a continuation of the trouble in Mozambique? Tomorrow morning, she resolved, she'd call Piet and tell him about this evening's little excitement. With that, she climbed into bed and was asleep in minutes.

*

The following morning dawned cold, wet and windy, the sort of day that made Katya think longingly of last summer's holiday on Damian's yacht in the Aegean. Cruising idly between the Greek islands, stopping here for a swim, there to water-ski and mooring at night near a taverna for dinner, wine and dancing to frantic bouzouki music with the sound of smashing plates as a counterpoint – touristy – but so what, it was great fun! Coming shudderingly back to the present, she paid off the taxi outside her office block and went in.

Moments after she put her briefcase down, Jean came in, cup of coffee in one hand and a folder in the other. "Morning boss, here's the overnight stuff - nothing urgent but the top two will bear a careful reply. They're offering to supply us but some of their conditions are a little strange."

"I'll get to them in the course of the day but first, there will be a policeman from the Met here around ten to take a statement from me."

"What?"

"A couple of thugs tried to jump me last night when I got home. They chose the wrong target and now they're both in hospital. The whole thing was captured on the apartment block's CCTV." She pulled the disk out of her briefcase and put it into the player in the corner of her office. Pressing 'play,' she turned to look at Jean.

As the scene on screen unfolded, Jean turned to her, eyes wide. "You did that?"

KATYA'S CHALLENGE

"Keeping fit brings some benefits. Can you make a copy of this? The police will want to take the original away. Oh, and can you do me a big favour and type up my 'statement' for them? Just a description along the lines of: 'I got out of my cab at the door of my apartment block and as I started to enter my code into the keypad beside the door, I saw movement behind me reflected in the glass of the door. I turned, saw a man armed with a knife coming at me and stopped him with a kick to the groin. I looked round and saw a second man, also armed with a knife, coming at me and brought him down with a kick to the jaw . . .' something along these lines and finish off with the concierge bringing me a roll of duct tape and a box cutter."

"OK – remind me never to pick a fight with you." She smiled and left the office.

*

Katya picked up the phone and dialled Piet de Bruin. When he picked up, he said, "I didn't expect to hear from you so soon. Did you get home OK?"

"I got home all right, but last night as I got home from the office, I was jumped by a couple of knife-wielding thugs at the door of my apartment block."

"My God! Did they hurt you?"

"I got a bit of a bruise on my cheek, but they are both in hospital under police guard. They didn't know about my keep fit regime."

"You continue to surprise me – in a good way. I knew you were academically smart and a good trader, but I didn't expect to see you behaving like one of Luc's merry men."

"Talking of Luc how is he?"

"He seems well enough, he's a bit pale and his left arm is in a sling. In fact, he's sitting opposite me right now. I'll hand you over and you can tell him the details yourself."

"Hi Luc, how are you doing?"

"Convalescing like crazy. Seriously, what's been going on? I heard most of your conversation with Piet. You've been attacked?"

She gave Luc the details and told him she'd be interviewed later in the day by the police.

Luc listened carefully before asking, "Our Chinese friends again?"

"They were both English low-life thugs, but someone must have paid them to attack me. And I can't think of anyone else who'd want to do me harm. Commercial harm maybe; KF Trading has made a few waves in the market, but that kind of trouble is usually resolved over dinner somewhere abroad outside the reach of the EU Competition Directorate or in extremis by lawyer's letters, never by physical violence. I may get more information from the police later today."

"OK then, your security is a real issue, I'll send a couple of my men over to London as bodyguards for you and until they arrive, please, please do not go walking about in London. Always take taxis and make sure it's safe before you get out of them. It's lunchtime here so I'll mobilise the men and get them on the overnight flight to Heathrow. They'll come straight to your office in the morning. Can you arrange accommodation for them?"

"No Luc! I'm not going to wander around London like some dodgy Russian oligarch's poulet deluxe with a couple of bodyguards in tow. In any case, I am now on the alert and I can look after myself. The only real risk would be a shooting and I don't think that's likely, not in London anyway, given that the police would be all over the case like a bad rash. Thanks, but no, I'll be OK."

"How secure is your apartment block?"

"Well, my apartment is on the second floor and the main door is controlled by a keypad. Joseph the concierge is a retired paratrooper sergeant. A bit out of condition but he can be relied on – especially after last night's fun and games."

"Good. Meantime, I'll be thinking of you; keep yourself safe."

"You too; when you were stretchered from the Chinook I was so afraid you'd been really badly shot up."

"Wim told me you made an excellent theatre nurse and helped him patch me up until I got into hospital in Beira. Anyway, the doctor who finished patching me up told me that the pair of you had done a good job, especially in cleaning all the garbage out of the wound and sterilizing it so that it didn't go septic. I expect that the IV antibiotic helped too."

"How long before you're fit for service again?"

"Brainwork from today, but it'll be around three months before my arm is back to full strength."

"Oh Luc! At least the bullet didn't hit your heart or your shoulder."

"If it had been my heart, we wouldn't be having this conversation."

"No – but take care and get fit soon. Are you still coming to London with Piet in the middle of next month?"

"Sure thing, I really want to see you again and continue the conversation we started at Camp 25 – before we were so rudely interrupted."

"See you then. I'm really looking forward to it too."

As she put the phone down, she realised that her pulse was racing, and she was actually blushing.

KATYA'S CHALLENGE

*

As Luc broke the connection he turned to Piet. "There's something seriously wrong here. I've been totting up a number of unexplained facts, beginning with the trouble at Camp 25. How did the PLA, for I'm sure they're behind this, know where our camp was or that we had more or less scoped out our deposit, or that our results were so good? Then there's the attack on Katya - how did they know she's a part of the team or where she lives? I'm sure our staff are loyal and that there haven't been any leaks, which points me towards the only feasible conclusion, your computer system has been hacked and the sods have been reading our files and communications.

I cannot think of any other way to explain it unless we were actually employing Chinese agents here in Cape Town, Mozambique, Zambia and London."

"Agreed. I'll get Benny to look over our system and see if he can find any evidence that we've been hacked."

"OK, and while I don't wish to suggest that Benny isn't up to this, but I have a couple of real whiz hackers on my security team and I'd like them to have a look as well. If you don't mind, I'll get them to have a look to see just how secure the De Bruin Investments computer system is."

"Fine by me, the more eyes on the system, the better the chance of finding any problem."

*

Katya's intercom buzzed and Jean's voice came through. "Detective Inspector Harris to see you."

"Send him in." The door opened and a smart, thirty-something policeman came in. Katya stood up and walked over to greet him. "Morning Inspector, I wasn't expecting a senior officer. I suppose you've come for my statement about last night's little unpleasantness. Have a seat. Coffee?"

"Yes please. My sergeant said you beat up a couple of knife-wielding thugs. How on earth . . .?"

"I'll show you." Buzzing Jean on the intercom, she asked her to bring a couple of coffees, her statement and the DVD into the office. "By the way, how are my erstwhile assailants?"

"The one with the broken jaw hasn't said anything at all while the one kicked in the crotch has just kept repeating, 'They didn't tell me; they didn't warn me.' However, we have been able to identify them from their fingerprints. They've both got form: GBH and knife crime and have served time in Wandsworth. They seem to be rent-a-thugs tied to the Reid family."

Jean came in with the coffee, a typescript and the DVD. Handing the typescript to Katya, she put the disk into the player and set it running. While the

KATYA'S CHALLENGE

DVD was running, Katya scanned the typescript, signed it and put it to one side. Harris watched the events unfolding on-screen without saying anything. "Can you run that again in slo-mo?" As he saw his colleagues appear on screen again, he turned to Katya. "Where did you learn that?"

"I like to keep fit and running and gym machines are terminally boring, so a friend suggested I took up kick-boxing. It's a fabulous exercise and the Kung-Fu element has certain benefits, as you can see."

"Yes, and more to the point, the video demonstrates beyond doubt that you were innocently trying to get into your apartment block when they jumped you. Self-defence without a doubt, although a defence lawyer might try and argue that you used excessive force."

"Excessive force by an unarmed woman against two knife-wielding male thugs? I don't think so; I didn't use any weapon at all. Anyway, who are the Reid family?"

"A fairly nasty bunch of criminals organised so that we only ever seem to catch their foot-soldiers. Joe Reid is the head of the family, that we know, but everything is done at one or more removes. Be it prostitution, money laundering, drugs or arms, every time we raid one of their operations, I get the impression that they know in advance and all we get is a sacrificial goat or two. I'm sure someone in the force warns them. They've also been in the rent-athug business for some time, so I wonder who paid for last night's street theatre."

"I might have an idea, but I need to do some checking first."

"Miss Francis, I think you should tell me. We don't appreciate civilians going off at half-cock and tramping around our criminal investigations. It always ends badly."

"Not really. I think this is the tail-end of some trouble our company is having in Africa over the exploration and development of a new mineral deposit. You would have to go through official channels; my colleagues do not."

Katya stood up, ejected the DVD and gave it to him. "Look, my checking is all going to be done outside of the UK and I promise you that if I lay my hands on any useable evidence, I'll pass it on to you. Oh, and by the way, here is my statement. I assume you want that as well as the DVD." She smiled and held out her hand. He looked hard at her and, realising that she wouldn't say any more, he shook it, took the DVD and her statement, said his farewells and left.

CHAPTER 20

General Tang called Colonel Wu to his office, laying out the Chengdu Unit's officer lists and service records as he did so. When Wu had taken a seat at the table, Tang relayed the conversation he'd had with Colonel Hsiu and asked him, "You hear things I don't; which of these officers would you trust for this Mozambique operation?"

"Either Major Huang or Liang would be my choices, Sir. They've both distinguished themselves recently in covert actions in various parts of Africa."

"Wasn't Liang responsible for the coup that replaced General Adoula last year?"

"Yes, that was a textbook operation. There were no Chinese fingerprints left behind at all. It was all ascribed to rebellious senior army officers."

"He didn't use any local troops?"

"No, he only used our own cadres and suffered no losses or injuries. And in General Tshombe we now have a very pro-Chinese head of state."

"Good, then he's the obvious man to sort out these South Africans. Send him to work with Colonel

Hsiu, giving him a preliminary briefing – covert entry into Mozambique, crushing attack and swift withdrawal – and have the pair of them come and see me tomorrow morning with their outline plan."

*

"Piet, I've been thinking over the events of the last couple of weeks and irrespective of what Benny and my lads find, or don't find, I am sure of two things. Firstly, we have been hacked; there's no way these PLA types could have located our camp in Mozambique and targeted Katya in London in that time-frame without inside knowledge. Secondly, the fact that we destroyed the squad that attacked the camp and their base will not be the end of the matter. I'll bet that there's a high-ranking PLA officer sitting at army headquarters in Beijing plotting a follow-up and probably more lethal raid. We need to reinforce the camp's defences; you should have seen the damage a single RPG round did to one of the watch towers. A better-armed squad with RPGs could sit 1,000 metres away from the camp and knock out all of the towers in short order.

Fortunately, the Brownings have an effective range of 2,000 metres so the key will be our early warning system, giving us the chance to take out an attacking squad before it gets close enough to do any damage. Personally, if I was planning it, and had the resources of the PLA at my disposal, I'd put an attack squad in one of their battlefield helicopters. I'd figure out a way to get it to within range of our camp, fly a three-a.m. mission to the camp and destroy it from the air - not so different from what we did to their camp in Marange.

Whatever happens, we need to strengthen the defences of the camp against a broader range of attack threats. Hennie is here in Cape Town now, so we'll have a council of war, scope out the possible ways the Chinese could get at the camp and prepare to help them fail to succeed, as Katya would say."

*

Colonel Wu led Colonel Hsiu and Major Liang into General Tang's office. As the four men settled round the conference table, the general began: "I don't need to tell you how sensitive and important this operation is. I just hope you have come up with a better plan than Captain Xiao's disastrous attempt. This time around, failure is not an option. What do you propose?"

Hsiu started off by saying that they proposed a purely Chinese operation with no involvement of Zimbabwean or Mozambican troops.

"So how can you attack without the extra soldiers?"

"Major Liang, the map please." With that, Liang stood up, unrolled the map of East Africa he'd brought into the meeting and attached it to the wall opposite Tang's seat and began.

"Simple, from what we now know, our camp, here, at Marange, was attacked from the air. The

South Africans seem to have a helicopter at their disposal, and we propose to return the favour. We want to use a Harbin Z-9 battlefield chopper and ship it disguised as deck cargo on a Chinese-owned, Panamanian-flagged freighter that will cruise down the east coast of Africa. Once it is off Beira, here, it will stop, and the helicopter, armed with air-to-ground missiles and cannon will take off and head for the South Africans' camp, there, where they will destroy it. It will then land and a squad of our men will deplane, kill any survivors, search for anything useful and then return to the ship for the voyage home. We can tranship our soldiers in Egypt and fly them home from there as civilian technicians."

"One problem." said Tang, "It will take a month to sail the Z-9 to Beira. That's far too long."

"Are we friends with the Russians at the moment?" asked Hsiu

"Yes."

"In that case, why don't we borrow one of their huge Antonov AN-124-100 cargo transporters and use it to air-lift the Z-9 down to Beira from Zhanjiang airport? These monsters can carry the helicopter, together with the troops necessary for the mission and all their equipment. They have the range to make the flight from southern China in one hop, so we could fly into Beira, unload the helicopter at night, fuel up and fly the mission to the South Africans' camp. While the mission's in progress, the

Antonov can be refuelled ready for the return journey.

When the Z-9 returns, it can be loaded back into the Antonov and flown back to China with our troops. Depending on the weather, the flight duration to and from China will be 10-12 hours, say a maximum of twenty-four hours for the round trip. Add eight hours to prepare the Z-9 for its mission and to stow it aboard the Antonov for the return trip, plus three to four hours for the mission itself and you are looking at no more than a day and a half from take-off from Zhanjiang to landing back there.

A nice tight mission, the only pressure point being Beira Airport, where our Embassy will have to come up with a way of getting permission for the Antonov to land. Maybe we should give them a cover story like: 'we're testing a new aerial scanner for mineral deposits."

"Worth exploring – a month is far too long for us to wait. Check out the details and let me have your revised timetable this evening."

*

Luc, Hennie and Piet were sitting together in Piet's office holding a council of war.

"We now know the Chinese are not going to go away and our best guess is that they'll try an airborne attack," said Luc. "Do you think you've enough weaponry to hold out against one?"

"Not without us taking a lot of damage and casualties ourselves." said Hennie. "What we really need are some MANPADs.[6]"

Piet said, "That makes sense. If they attack us from the air with rockets and cannon, they could reduce the camp to smoking rubble in seconds and that would be that. Any ideas on sourcing, Luc?"

"I still have pals from my time in Angola and some of them now work for the SASS.[7] I know that we got some French Mistrals[8] for use in that fight, mainly to take out helicopters, but I don't think we used them all. I'll ask around and see what I can find out."

"Do you think they'll cooperate?"

"I don't see why not. After all, our project has strategic significance for South Africa and there is no love lost between us and the Chinese."

"On the assumption that you can lay your hands on a couple, I think Hennie should head off to Camp 25 and beef up our defensive earthworks, just in case. As soon as you get hold of the Mistrals, Luc, get them to Jo'burg and have them air-freighted into Beira and thence to Camp 25. We'll pack them up as drilling spares and hand out the odd Krugerrand

---

[6] MANPADS – Man Portable Air Defence Systems or portable anti-aircraft missiles

[7] SASS - South African Secret Service

[8] Mistral – French-made 'fire and forget' anti-aircraft missile

where necessary to smooth their passage. How long do you think this all will take?"

"I should get a definitive yes/no decision tomorrow, more likely to be yes if you can pull the odd diplomatic string, Piet. And you can guarantee that no Mozambicans will be hurt if and when our anticipated scenario plays out."

"Hmmm, you're sure?"

"Absolutely."

"Then let's get to it."

CHAPTER 21

The Chinook sank slowly onto Camp 25's helipad. As the rotors wound down to a standstill and the engines died away, Jan van den Heuvel drove up in a fork truck, pulling a trailer and accompanied by a small squad of soldiers. Hennie opened the main fuselage door and, kicking out the ladder, climbed down.

"Hi Jan, I've got some nice new whizz-bangs for you."

"Whizz-bangs?"

"Ja, Luc has managed to get his hands on a couple of Mistrals for our air defence and we need to get them out of their boxes and checked out ready for use."

"Air defences? What the hell are we in for now?"

"Luc and I have been looking at the facts; the Chinese attacked us, we then counter-attacked them and we are 99% certain that they'll have another go. After all, the failure of their raid will have caused considerable loss of face up the chain of command to whoever gave the order in the first place. So you can bet your last brass cent that they will have another go and that this will probably be an airborne attack. Our embassy in Harare says that relations between the Zimbabweans and the Chinese are sub-zero now so they'll get no support from the Zimbabwean army. We reckon instead that they'll ship a battlefield helicopter down to Beira and try and obliterate us in a night-time raid, so we'll use these little babies to obliterate them instead."

"How the hell would they get a battlefield helicopter down here?"

"Luc reckons they'd charter one of the big Antonov freighters and fly it down to Beira with the attack chopper in its belly, ready to fly, destroy the camp and sod off back home the way they came – job done. That's why I've brought you the Mistrals, so that we can blow them out of the sky before they can get to us. Were you ever trained to use one?"

"Yes, about six years ago, so I'll need a bit of a refresher on the SOP."

"You shouldn't need much; after all, they're pretty much 'fire-and-forget' missiles. They lock on the exhaust plume of an aircraft and a few seconds later it's 'good night Vienna.' They travel so fast that the aircrew can do little or nothing to avoid them."

"But if they come at night we won't see them."

"Doesn't matter; there's no engine noise round here at night apart from our generator so you just need to point it in the general direction of an approaching aircraft engine noise until the IR sight lights up and pull the trigger. It looks for a heat signature and it travels at Mach 2.6, so there isn't any time for aircrew debates about what to do next."

"Do we have to be ready for an air attack from here on in?"

"I've spoken to our handling agent at Beira airport and asked him to let us know if and when a large freighter lands and disgorges a helicopter. If he calls us, we can then go to anti-aircraft defence stations."

"Are you certain he'll let us know if the Chinese come in?"

"He's OK, and I'm sure he will. After all, why would he risk steady, ongoing business from us for a one-off bribe?"

"I'd feel a lot happier if one of our guys was down there. The Chinese might just put the handling guy out of action and we would never know."

"Hmm."

"Go on, Hennie – you want the security of having our own man on the spot rather than relying on someone else."

"OK, pick a couple of the lads to keep a watching brief on the airfield, but to stay out of sight themselves, and send them down there with a satellite phone."

"Will do."

*

The giant Antonov 124 approached the airfield from the east, settling onto the runway like an enormous bat, shattering the late afternoon peace with the thundering roar of its reverse thrust. It came quickly to a halt before being directed away from the terminal towards the maintenance workshops. Once on its stand, the captain shut down the engines and the silence after twelve hours of roaring, whining, engine noise was almost palpable.

Up on the flight deck Major Liang issued his orders to the captain - he should ask for a specific immigration officer, Major Neyma, who had been briefed to expect them and offer refuelling facilities. The 70,000 gallons of jet fuel necessary for the return trip had been organised and paid for in advance.

The captain unbuckled his harness, picked up a small backpack and went down the stairs to the crew hatch and then opened it. The A jeep carrying two uniformed officers pulled up in front of the Antonov, and one jumped out and walked over to the hatch.

"Major Neyma?" queried the captain.

"Yes. I have been expecting you. I need to see your papers."

KATYA'S CHALLENGE

The captain handed the backpack to Neyma, who looked inside, took out a bundle of dollar bills and counted them. Moments later he smiled, put an arm through one of the straps and hitched it over his shoulder.

"Your papers appear to be in order. You are permitted to remain on stand here for 60 hours as agreed, after which time you must go. You can refuel your aircraft here on the stand; that manifold over there is connected to our Jet A-1 storage tanks and there are suitable hoses to connect to the plane."

"Thanks, we will be testing an aerial survey helicopter over the next couple of days and we'll then be gone. Thanks for your help, Major." The two men saluted each other. Neyma returned to his jeep and drove off. The captain returned to the flight deck and told the engineer to refuel the plane.

*

The Antonov's arrival was observed from across the airfield by Hennie's men, who immediately called him back at the camp. "You were right, Sir. A bloody great jet freighter landed about half an hour ago. It is definitely an Antonov and it has been parked over by the maintenance area, and it looks as though they've started refuelling. It's getting dark now, so we'll be able to move in closer and keep them under observation with night vision goggles."

"Well done, so our suspicions were correct. Look, that plane is almost certainly carrying an attack helicopter and a bunch of Chinese soldiers. If their plans are what we think they are, they'll open up the Antonov around ten o'clock and unload the chopper. Give them two or three hours to prepare it for its mission and they'll probably climb aboard around one a.m. and set off for our camp with an ETA of two to three a.m and death and destruction in mind. We'll be ready for them. I've discounted a dawn raid, as they won't want to be seen flying a battlefield helicopter into a civilian airfield in daylight.

"What I need from you is a call when you can see a helicopter being unloaded and a second call when it takes off. If nothing has happened by 1:00 am, I'd guess that they're resting up after their long flight down from China and they'll go for it tomorrow night instead. Either way, I need you to let us know at any time, day or night, when you see any activity going on around the plane."

*

Hennie called Jan into the office and they sat down together at the table. "Well, the bastards have arrived, just as we feared," said Hennie. "The lads saw an Antonov fly in and park up by the maintenance area. I've told them to keep it under observation and give us a heads-up as and when they see any action around it and especially if they unload a helicopter and it takes off."

"If their battle plan conforms to our expectations, when do you think we'll be attacked?"

"My guess is between two and three am."

"How come?"

"Well, they'll work under cover of darkness so as to keep their activities away from the Mozambican authorities, and they'll want to hit us when they think we'll be fast asleep. If I had flown an attack helicopter into Beira, I'd want about three hours with the engineers to make sure it was mission-ready, add ninety minutes' flying time each way to the camp, up to an hour for the mission itself and you are talking about seven hours from opening up the Antonov's hold to landing back at Beira. To get back before dawn, which is around five am, they need to launch their attack by two-thirty at the latest, so I would expect things to start happening down at Beira between nine and ten this evening. The last commercial flight departs just after seven-thirty, so the whole place will quieten down soon after."

"So we need to be on full alert from midnight on?"

"Maybe - it all depends on when and what the lads report. Also, I'd better call Luc now and let him know what's going on."

*

Shortly after nine, the satellite phone rang. Hennie picked it up to be told that there was some activity round the Antonov. "They've opened up the nose of the plane and it looks like they're discharging a helicopter."

"Can you see what kind it is?"

"Not really, but it is an attack helicopter of some kind. It's got pods and pylons all over and looks kind of nasty."

"OK, keep your eyes on it and call me if it looks like it's going anywhere."

Turning back to Jan, he said, "It looks like we've second-guessed them correctly. They're unloading a helicopter from the Antonov's hold, so I imagine they'll set it up for flight now, test it, arm it and they'll be on their way. Meanwhile, you'd better get the Mistrals ready. I think we'll be using them."

*

The phone rang again shortly before midnight. "They've just taken off, sir, and they seemed to set a north-westerly course. They'll be with you in an hour to an hour and a half."

"OK, assuming everything goes according to plan, we'll call you up when we've dealt with them and aim to pick you up around mid-day on what will appear to be a routine camp supply flight. See the pair of you tomorrow."

Hennie sounded attack stations and, once the men were in place, told them what to expect. He and Jan carried the Mistrals to the top of the south-eastern watch tower, took them out of their crate and sat down to wait. It was a clear, bright moonlit night, which meant they could probably see the helicopter against the sky, above the bush, while it was still more than three miles away. A little more than an hour later they heard the approaching engine whine and metallic clattering roar of the approaching helicopter. Jan picked up the first Mistral, popped the end caps off, put his arms through the webbing harness, donned the safety goggles, switched on the sights and, holding the tube on his right shoulder, pointed the missile in the general direction of the engine noise.

Hennie, looking through night vision binoculars, suddenly said, "Just above the horizon at ten o'clock, coming straight at us!"

Jan ranged the tube left and right. The sight stayed black as the helicopter noise grew louder, until it suddenly started flashing pale green. "Target acquired, firing!"

*

In the Harbin's cockpit, the co-pilot called out, "Target ahead."

The captain responded, "Laser lock and fire missiles."

"Locked on the towers - three, two, fire!"

Eight air-to-ground missiles whooshed out of their launch-pod under the port stub-wing in sequence, picking up their laser guidance beams, locking onto them and tracking towards the camp's four watch towers.

*

KATYA'S CHALLENGE

The Mistral's gyroscope spooled up and a couple of seconds later the missile's booster motor ignited and it shot out of the launch tube. The main rocket motor kicked in as the booster cut out and the Mistral roared off into the night, trailing a tail of fire which rapidly shrank to a pinpoint of light.

Hennie cried out, "The sods have fired at us too; we need to get the hell out of here!"

A moment later the sky lit up as the Mistral's warhead exploded and sent a hail of tungsten balls ripping through the engines, airframe, aircrew and soldiers. Frozen to the spot, Hennie and Jan watched as the crippled and blazing helicopter corkscrewed across the sky, plunging to the ground with the sound of tortured metal. As it spun through the sky, the guidance laser beams span with it until they were extinguished. The incoming missiles twisted and turned, trying to follow the beams, before losing contact, shooting vertically into the night sky until they ran out of fuel, then falling harmlessly to the ground well past the camp, where their warheads detonated.

The crashed helicopter's fuel blazed up, followed by more explosions as the on-board munitions exploded in the heat of the flames.

"I think that was a bull's-eye," said Jan with a smirk. "Talk about fire-and-forget! God, that's some whizz-bang! Thank God I fired when I did, or we'd both be hamburger by now."

"Not bad, but that was a really close call. The Mistral was faster than their rockets – just - for which I am truly thankful. It's also an object lesson in never using semi-dumb munitions that rely on laser-lit targets. Let's take a squad over to the crash site and make sure that there'll be no further distractions tonight."

Jumping into a couple of Jeeps, Hennie, Jan and half a dozen soldiers roared out of the camp to the crash site. By the time they got there, the fires were dying down and the remains of the helicopter were a twisted mass of glowing red and fire-blackened wreckage.

"We can't get in amongst that lot until the fires are out and the wreckage has cooled down. What we do need to do now is scout around the crash site for survivors. We don't want anyone trotting back to civilization and telling them that nasty men were waiting for them at the target site and were very unkind. Drive slowly round the edge of the crash zone and use the spotlights to search the ground."

After making a couple of circuits around the crash zone, they concluded that there were no survivors and decided to come back in daylight to make a more thorough search. Back at the camp, Hennie called the men observing Beira Airport to tell them that they'd intercepted the helicopter and that it wouldn't be returning. He told them to keep an eye on the Antonov and see what they did when the helicopter failed to return and said he'd send the Chinook down to collect them around mid-day.

*

After breakfast, Hennie and Jan called Luc in Cape Town and brought him up to speed on the night's events. "Those Mistrals are quite something, Luc. Where did you get them?"

"They're left over from the Angolan war and I was able to get my hands on them via a friend of a friend in the SASS at a reasonable price. My only worry was that they might not function properly after all this time. Sophisticated weapons are not like fine wines; they really don't improve with age and these are more than twelve years old."

"Well this 'did what it said on the tin' - they really are fire and forget."

"Yes, good, aren't they? I thought they'd fit the bill. Did you use both of them?"

"One was enough, so we still have one in reserve if necessary. What do you think the Chinese will do next?"

"I think that they will now know that only a full-on land attack by properly trained troops will physically stop us. And I doubt that there is any way the Mozambicans would be willing to let foreign troops loose on their soil, so that option is probably off the table. However, there are other ways and I would imagine that good old-fashioned bribery and corruption will be their next step.

"I'll set up a teleconference for ten o'clock tomorrow morning with Piet, Katya and ourselves. You'll have had time to look at the wreckage today in daylight and recover the guys from Beira by then. OK Hennie?"

"OK, talk then, Luc."

*

CHAPTER 22

Driving round the wreckage of the helicopter, they could see that it was completely burnt out and that no one could have survived unless they'd been thrown from it on its way down. Even then, they would have been killed or very badly injured when they hit the ground.

"Let's increase the radius of our search," said Hennie.

By the time they'd increased the radius of their search to nearly a kilometre from the wreck it was obvious that nothing, other than a few fragments of metal, was lying on the ground.

"It might be a good idea to try and hide the wreck," said Jan.

"How?"

"The wreckage itself is restricted to a relatively small area. The ground here is very sandy, so we could use the backhoe to bury the smaller stuff and the evidence of the fire. We could dump sand and earth over the rest. Make a small hill over it. That way no one overflying the site would see wreckage or any evidence of a crash. Short of an overland approach and knowing precisely where to look, the helicopter will seem to have vanished into thin air."

"Good thinking - go to it."

*

When the Chinook returned from Beira, Hennie and Jan asked them to describe what they'd seen when the attack helicopter failed to return.

"The Antonov was waiting with its cargo door open from three o'clock onwards and as time went past, the plane's crew and what looked like a couple of soldiers paced around it, up and down, down and up, back and forth, looking more and more agitated. As dawn broke, everyone went back on board, the cargo door was closed, the plane's engines started up and they took off, heading north east."

"You don't think they were going to over-fly the route the chopper would have taken?"

"We can't be sure, but it looked as though they were heading directly out of Mozambican airspace for home. Anyway, you would have heard it if it had come anywhere near the camp. It's a noisy brute and we could still hear it long after it had disappeared from view."

"So it's quite possible that they've flown off without any idea of what happened."

"They would obviously be in radio contact and that contact would suddenly be lost. They will suspect anything from radio failure to engine failure and a crash in the bush, but probably not a surface-to-air missile. They were obviously not going to hang around and find out."

"Was there any other activity?"

"Nothing until the morning commercial flight from Maputo arrived just after eight."

*

A pale-faced and very upset Colonel Wu knocked on General Tang's door and came in clutching a sheet of paper. "Comrade General, The Mozambique mission has gone wrong! The Antonov has radioed to say that they lost contact with the helicopter around two am local time and have been unable to contact anyone from the mission since. The pilot waited until dawn, when the helicopter would either have returned or run out of fuel. He was worried that the locals would start to wonder where the helicopter was and then he'd be asked all sorts of difficult questions about its whereabouts and although he was contracted to us, he didn't fancy spending time in an African police cell facing questions he couldn't answer, while the plane was impounded, and his owners sorted out the legal niceties of the situation. So he decided to shut up shop and took off for Zhanjiang. He's currently still in the air and has two of our troops on board, the load-master and a guard."

"Get them on the radio." Standing up, he walked over to the window and looked out over the Military Headquarters Compound through the afternoon smog towards Tiananmen Square. "What the hell's happened to them? A modern, fully armed and operational helicopter, fitted with the latest avionics, driven by an experienced special ops pilot, and it just bloody vanishes? No signals, no nothing. Why no signal?"

With that, the radio beside his desk crackled. "Antonov XM200 to Army base Beijing, Antonov XM200 to Army base Beijing, do you copy? Over."

Tang picked up the microphone and pressed the 'transmit' button. "Army base Beijing here – General Tang speaking – put the load-master on for me."

"Wilco – stand by."

Less than two minutes later the set crackled into life again. "Load-master Chin speaking, Comrade General."

"Sitrep Chin."

"Sir, Major Liang and the troop took off in the Harbin at 23:50 on Saturday night, heading for the South African camp. Their instructions were to maintain radio silence for the duration of the operation, until they were within thirty minutes of landing back at Beira. Their ETA Beira was 03:00 this morning. By 04:00 we'd heard nothing and tried to make radio contact with them ourselves. We couldn't raise them even on the emergency frequency.

"The pilot was getting edgy and as dawn began to light up the sky, he said we'd have to go. I argued with him, but he said that the helicopter must have crashed and if the locals found it while we were still on the ground, we'd be arrested and put in the local prison. He said his job was flying planes, not sitting around in an African jail, and he was going to take off. We argued but he was obviously frightened and both he and the co-pilot started their pre-flight checks. I heard him talking to the tower, telling them he'd been recalled early and asking for clearance to take off, leaving Mozambique airspace on a heading of 030 degrees. He was given permission and we took off at 05:15."

"Couldn't you stop the pilots?"

"No Comrade General, they're Russians and only in it for the money. I think that they put the safety of their bloody Antonov ahead of any duty to us. I think I would have had to shoot the captain to change his mind, and I don't know how to fly this crate."

"Have you heard anything at all from Major Liang since take-off? Didn't you ask the pilot to over-fly the route the helicopter must have flown to look for it?"

"Nothing from Major Liang, Comrade General and no, the pilot flatly refused to re-enter Mozambican airspace."

"What is your ETA Zhanjiang?"

"17:00 hours Beira time, 01:00 hours Beijing time."

"All right Chin. When you land I'll have a plane standing by to fly you back here for a full debriefing. Over and out."

Wu and Tang sat looking at each other in silence for a few minutes, until Wu asked, "When are you going to talk to Director Zhang at the Ministry, sir?"

"Not until I have seen Load-master Chin in this office and got the full story. Meanwhile, get hold of Colonel Hsiu and have him here when Chin arrives. We need a convincing story for the Director and a robust plan to close down the South Africans. After all, we've just lost a troop of top-flight soldiers and a state-of-the-art battlefield helicopter with nothing to show for it – and the Russians will know all about it by now – the loss of face!"

*

Wu ushered Load-master Chin into Tang's office along with Hsiu. "Well, how do you explain this catastrophe?"

Hsiu cleared his throat and said, "Comrade General, the Chengdu team deployed for this mission failed catastrophically. Except for Load-master Chin and the soldier left at Beira on guard duty, the entire force and their equipment have been lost. It is a complete disgrace and I humbly apologise to you and to the army for my part in setting up this disastrous mission and bringing disgrace on our Special Forces and the Chinese Peoples Republic."

Tang sat silently for a moment.

"Return to your barracks Chin. Hsiu, I need to talk to you."

When Chin had left, Tang gestured to Hsiu to sit down at the conference table and sat down opposite him.

"What do you think happened?"

"Well sir, I would discount a crash, unless the pilot was trying to make a low-level attack. I also think that is unlikely as they were armed with air-to-ground missiles which could be launched some distance from the target. My best guess is that the South Africans were somehow expecting us to attack them from the air and had some form of anti-aircraft defence capability".

"How could they have known?"

"Not from us sir, but maybe they guessed that we might try an attack like this and bribed ground handling at Beira airport to alert them to any unusual traffic."

"But I thought they had a good, diversionary cover story."

"Not good enough, obviously.

Leave me now, I need time to think."

"Sir." Tang's office door closed behind him and he slumped down at his desk considering what to do.

CHAPTER 23

At five to ten, Benny Kim joined Luc in Piet's office and set up video conference links with London and Camp 25. With everyone on-line, Piet began by asking Hennie to bring everyone up to speed on events at Camp 25.

"Well, our guesswork was correct. The Chinese flew an attack chopper into Beira, tooled up and headed for the camp. I had put a couple of men down there to keep a lookout and let us know if a big freighter turned up with hostile intent. It did, they told us, and when the chopper was airborne, we went to battle stations with your Mistrals on top of the south-east tower. We picked the chopper up when it was a little over three miles away. Jan lined it up and pressed the button. Just as he did so, we saw the chopper fire rockets at us and I wondered if the Mistral would be diverted and go after them. But it didn't and a few seconds later it hit the chopper which blew up and crashed in flames –goodnight Vienna! The chopper's rockets must have been laser-guided because when the helicopter went, the rockets shot up in the air between our guard towers and detonated harmlessly behind the camp, thank God.

"The chopper crashed in a sandy clearing a couple of miles from the camp; presumably the pilot tried to put it down there after the missile crippled it. We inspected the wreckage and it was definitely the remains of a Harbin Z-9. There were no survivors, the wreck having been blown apart, presumably by the munitions it carried. We were actually only able to identify it from the remains of the tail rotor, which was the largest remaining piece of wreckage. Jan and a squad took the backhoe out to the crash site and buried the wreckage yesterday afternoon. It shouldn't be possible to see anything untoward from the air, be it an aircraft or satellite fly-past."

"What happened to the transport freighter?"

"They shut up shop at dawn and took off shortly after, heading north east away from Mozambique air-space."

"Didn't they overfly the route the chopper would have taken?"

"We don't think so. They took off and flew on a north easterly heading after take-off, not north-west and no-one heard aircraft engines at the camp. If they had overflown the crash site, we would have heard something."

"Well done," said Luc. "A nice, clean defensive action with a positive outcome. I'd like to be a fly on the wall when the news gets back to

Beijing. You've just wiped out more than ten million dollars' worth of helicopter, to say nothing of a Special Forces platoon and their assorted weaponry. I imagine a bunch of senior officers are working extremely hard at trying to avoid carrying the can for this one."

"What now?" asked Katya. "We've shown them that we're pretty good at self-defence, but I'm not happy. We need to figure out what the sods will get up to next, get ahead of the curve and take the battle to them. What do you think, Piet?"

"You're absolutely right. We knew from our contacts in the SASS that the Chinese had got wind of our Mozambique claim and had decided to shut us down as a preliminary to taking it over. We also know why; they think that our in-house refining, purification and separation technology will put us way ahead of them. Benny reckons that they only hacked us to a limited extent and did not get any of the data from Delft, so yes, they know we've got something but not what that something is. There is also the fact that our deposit doesn't contain any thorium, a geological quirk that makes our operation relatively clean.

I've seen some of the Chinese facilities and in addition to mine tailings, leaky effluent lagoons and river-polluting effluent streams, they generate around a tonne of radioactive thorium sludge for every tonne of rare earth metal extracted. This is not good; thorium^{232} has a half-life of more than 14 billion years. In other words, there is no way that you can leave it lying about. It isn't nearly as dangerous as uranium or plutonium in that it only emits α and β radiation, which can easily be stopped by lightweight shielding. The real problem is containment. If and when the lagoons holding the sludge leak, then harmful radiation spreads with the sludge.

I think that we should be taking a more political view of the fight, talking to the Mozambican authorities and demonstrating that granting a mining and refining license to us, rather than anyone else, ensures 'best practice' and leaves their lovely country unspoiled. It is one thing to develop a country's natural resources, but if you want to attract tourists, you don't turn the country into an industrial zone peppered with fuming acidic slag heaps and radioactive lagoons."

"I agree. Our lab work has demonstrated a clean and efficient way to extract the rare earths, and as we know, there's natural gas under Camp 25. This lets us beat the Chinese at their own game in terms of manufacturing economics. Their tactics seem aimed at hollowing out the Western electronics industries; Phase one is about restricting the flow of REEs to the West, then offering the Samsungs, LGs, Intels, IBMs and AMDs of this world access to as much product as they want, but only if they're prepared to set up manufacturing plants in China.

Phase two will be all about industrial espionage, the theft of the technology and the establishment of Chinese-owned plants making exact copies and selling them at prices below manufacturing cost, making it impossible for Western manufacturers to compete. Phase three will see the closure of the Western electronics industry and the global supremacy of the Chinese electronics industry.

Now if we can get our discovery up and producing, at the very least we could have enough product to frustrate the Chinese' ambitions. I know they have dollar reserves of more than $2.5 trillion and I guess they'll be prepared to spend a fair chunk of that in advancing their policies, but from what I hear from our key customers, the Western manufacturers will support a Western producer ahead of the Chinese, if only for IP and supply chain security."

"So?"

"So we need to make the Mozambique Government our new best friends. Look, we're meeting up in London later this week to finalise our PEA and make a start on our Bankable Feasibility Study. With that in hand, I think we should head for Maputo as soon as your Foreign Office contacts can arrange a cabinet level meeting for us, Piet. The sooner the better, as I suspect that our little Chinese 'friends' will be making their own overtures in short order."

*

Colonel Wu knocked on General Tang's office door, opened it and stood aside as two military policemen brushed past him and marched over to the general.

"Comrade General," said the senior of the two, handing him a sheet of paper, "you are under arrest and will come with us."

"What! This is outrageous! I have committed no crime. I demand to meet with Senior General Li!"

"No, Comrade General you must come with us," said the senior MP, un-holstering his pistol and pointing it at the general. "Give me your pistol now and come with us!"

The MPs each took one of the general's arms and marched him out of the office past a blanched and quivering Colonel Wu, who turned to the general's secretary and asked, "What the hell's going on?"

"I'm not sure, sir. I got a call fifteen minutes ago from Senior General Li's ADC and was told to keep General Tang in his office, as special messengers were on their way over with a message for him."

"Well, he certainly got a special message; he's been arrested. I'd better try and find out what this is all about and what happens now. Can you get me Li's ADC on the phone, and I'll see what I can find out? I'll take it in General Tang's office."

He re-emerged a few minutes later, looking shaken. "The general's been taken back to his quarters and placed under house arrest. Li's ADC says he'll be tried for the 'dereliction of duty, criminal misuse of army property and for the loss of men under his command through inadequate supervision, planning and support.' He's likely to be found guilty, spend four or five years in a labour camp, be stripped down to the rank of Private and posted to do sentry duty on a guard post in Outer Mongolia. The Chengdu Special Forces commander has also been arrested and stripped of his command."

"Why?"

"Well, from what I've heard, the operation failed because the unit didn't carry out a proper reconnaissance of the South Africans' camp before they attacked. Civilians though the South Africans may be, they obviously have a military background and Major Liang should have picked up on that after what happened to our first raid on their camp. It seems he made the classic mistake of underestimating his enemy's capabilities and sailed in expecting an easy victory and glory when he got back to Chengdu. As the general in charge, Liang's boss should have made sure that the attack plan was sound. He obviously didn't and must face the consequences."

"What'll happen to us, sir?"

"Well, Special Forces Command still has a job to do, General Tang or no General Tang, so I guess we carry on and hope the general's successor likes us, or else we'll be redeployed somewhere or other, possibly away from Beijing because of Tang's disgrace. We need to be really nice and helpful to our new boss. From what I've just heard, we will know who it's going to be in just a few days."

"And we had absolutely no role in planning the Antonov raid to Mozambique."

"No, absolutely not! We just did what the general ordered. But remember that that excuse didn't work out too well in Germany in 1945, so we'd better be really careful and make sure that the Chengdu command carry all the responsibility."

"What did you mean about Germany in 1945, sir?"

"When the Allied side were prosecuting senior German officers for so-called war crimes, their main defence was to say that they were just following orders. The courts didn't buy it and the officers were either hanged or put in prison."

"Oh, I see, sir."

*

CHAPTER 24

Piet, Luc and Ton flew into Heathrow on Thursday evening and went straight to their hotel. Katya joined them later for a nightcap. Katya thought Piet looked stressed and asked him what was wrong.

"It's these bloody Chinese again. Our man in Maputo says that a Chinese delegation arrived at the beginning of the week and have been cosying up to the local politicians. Knowing what we now know, it makes me uneasy. I'm not sure just how corrupt the Minister for Mineral Resources and Energy is and whether the Chinese might buy our claim out from him. I'm going up there next week to see him, and it would be good if you and Luc could come as well. I want to impress the Ministry with the environmental soundness of our scheme as well as its revenue potential for the country."

"It's the old joke, is it? 'A reliable politician is one who once bought stays bought' and you're not sure about this one."

"No, it's the typical sub-Saharan economy. Dirt-poor people run by a kleptocracy where access to the things we take for granted is only available to the people at the top, their family and hangers-on. I know they are trying to do something about it under pressure from individual aid donors and the international donor agencies and there are actually anti-corruption laws in place, although it's difficult to press charges and make them stick. Anyway, that's why I want us to go there and make sure the Chinese don't bribe our claim out from under us."

Katya told them she'd arranged for André Ten Berg to join them in the morning to demonstrate the effectiveness of their new metal separation technology. "It's a long time since I held a test tube and I thought it best to let an expert lay it all out for us. Besides, it'll allow me to develop my presentation for our meeting in Maputo, provided you can get us an appointment."

On that worrying note, they decided to head off for bed and agreed that they would come to Katya's office in the morning to put their accumulated data together in a PEA and see how far they could get with drafting a Bankable Feasibility Study. Luc escorted Katya to the hotel lobby and made sure she was safely ensconced in a taxi. They kissed goodnight and Luc stood on the pavement thinking about her as the cab dwindled into the distance. *A remarkable woman who doesn't seem to be fazed by anything and yet who is also gorgeously feminine. An attractive enigma I intend to get to know better over the next couple of days.*

*

The following morning, they convened in Katya's conference room to draft the PEA and start on the bankable feasibility study.

"Well, we have an excellent claim," said Luc. "The assays of our core samples, together with our geological mapping, give us at least 16 million tonnes of recoverable ores, maybe more. The ores assay at 20-33% metal oxides, conservatively a minimum of 3.2 million tonnes of oxides, possibly more than 5.3 million tonnes. We have the additional and unexpected bonus of a natural gas field sitting under the ore body. This gives us a free energy source for our mining, smelting and refining processes."

"How's the downstream technology shaping up Katya?"

"Adam Smith's group at the Wit have succeeded in recovering 94% of the metal contained in the ore at a throughput of 50 kilos/hour. Depending on the mill and calciner chosen, you are looking at a mining and smelting cost of less than $5 per tonne of ore or around $16 - $25 per tonne mixed metals. Separation costs come on top of that and we're still working on them, 'though I don't expect them to exceed $1,200 per tonne of finished oxide."

Jean interrupted to tell them that André Ten Berg had just arrived, so Katya asked her to send him in. Greetings exchanged, and once he was seated with a cup of coffee, she asked him to bring them up to speed on his group's progress.

André took them through the group's programme, complete with facts, figures and samples of the refined REEs. Piet, backed up by Katya, grilled him on the numbers and the work and probable cost of scaling the process up to production levels. He answered all their questions easily and in detail. Eventually, Piet sat back and said; "That's both impressive and attractive."

"Yes, isn't it, André's team at Delft have done us proud. With a 99.9% separation efficiency, 95% overall recovery and a reagent cost of $10.32 per kilo of oxide. If we put this all together, we're looking at less than $11.00 per kilo of metal."

"That's unbelievable."

"Don't take it from me. Ton, you've been doing the sums - am I right or am I right?"

"You're nearly there. My calculations suggest that with the usual safety allowances for the known unknowns and the unknown unknowns, we're better budgeting on $12.00 per kilo. It is still a fantastic cost profile. If we assume an average mix of metals in the ore at their current average market prices, you're looking at an average value of say $100K per tonne from the refinery, or a minimum total value of $300 billion. This makes the required capital investment a simple decision. Even if our assumptions are all out by a factor of 10, you are still looking at a project value well in excess of $30 billion."

"Talking of investment, are we going to do this ourselves or do we sell the deal on to a mining group?"

"Frankly, my life's greatest ambitions do not include running a mining and refining operation. I'm more of an explorer and prospector; besides, I'm not a mining or a chemical engineer," said Luc

"Me neither," said Ton. "I'm happy to look at this kind of operation, but only as an auditor and with an auditor's jaundiced eyes. You wouldn't want me in the operating team, I'd only depress them. What about you, Katya?"

"Ha! Ha! Ha! Absolutely not! My role, if there is to be one, would be to manage the process development team, that's you André, and Adam, and to sell the end products, but you wouldn't get me near the actual mining and metal production."

"So, we're agreed," summarised Piet. "We don't see ourselves running a mining and refining operation. Much better to sell it on to those who like doing that sort of thing while we take an up-front payment, consulting fees and on-going fees and royalties from its exploitation."

"Including my consultancy fee and appointment as the project's sole and exclusive Sales Agent."

"Yes Katya, that too. But if we're going to pull this off, we need to firm up our exploration license with the Mozambican government and convert it to a mining and refining one."

"Well, I think the strong points of our proposition are the total enterprise value, the cleanliness and environmental friendliness of our technology and the financial head-room to pay generous royalties to the Mozambicans, whether in cash or in infrastructure investment.

I believe the cleanliness of our technology is a huge advantage." said Katya. "I've had my man in Beijing visit some of the Chinese mines and refineries. He's sent me pictures of them which would make your hair curl, even yours Ton. Environmental standards and Chinese refineries are not even in the same book, let alone on the same page. When we go to Maputo to negotiate, I'll mount a presentation of our proposal, versus what the Chinese do at home and what that would mean for Mozambique. Any minister, no matter how venal, would have to approve our project over any offering from China.

And another point - our deposit does not contains any thorium. If you look at these photos, you will see horrible effluent lagoons beside their refineries. They are full of radioactive thorium sludge, about one tonne for every tonne of rare earth metal extracted. OK, it's only low-level stuff but it remains hazardous for more than 14 billion years –

imagine voluntarily turning a part of your country into a radioactive desert."

"OK," said Piet. "And to be honest, there is no-one sitting around this table who has the expertise to project manage this. Then a sale on the best possible terms it is."

"Agreed."

"Yes I agree."

"Me too"

*

The numbers in the PEA looked rock-solid and they were only waiting for the latest assays from Alex Stewart to complete the Bankable Feasibility Study.

André looked at his watch and asked if he could leave now as he'd given his briefing and could just catch the last flight back to Rotterdam if Jean would call him a taxi.

The team relaxed over dinner in the comfort of Scott's: oysters, grilled lobster with a tangy green salad and chipped potatoes, washed down with Krug Champagne.

Over the coffee and brandies, Katya came in for some teasing. They'd all seen the video of the attack she'd beaten off outside her apartment and started calling her 'Cat', short for Cat-woman. "But you've got it all wrong. Cat-woman is evil, and evil I am not - well, not really, and only when I absolutely have to be!"

Luc came to her defence, saying that she was gorgeous and although there were certain similarities, the only thing she had in common with Cat-woman was her ability to make life very difficult indeed for anyone who crossed her, and besides, he'd never seen her with a bullwhip! She blew him a kiss and the conversation moved on. Looking at him during a short lull in the conversation, she thought that he really was delectable and that she'd like to try him out for breakfast; lunch and dinner too. She smiled to herself and resolved to move things in that direction when they left the restaurant.

As Piet settled the bill, she asked Luc to see her safely home. Piet and Ton looked at each other, then back at Luc. "On you go," said Piet, "and make sure that our Cat doesn't need to use her claws again. We'll grab a cab and see you back at the hotel."

Sitting next to Luc in the back of their cab, she felt all warm and happy and snuggled up against him. "Pussycat, pussycat, what are you doing?" asked Luc with his arm around her.

"This!" she said, reaching up, putting her hand behind his head and kissing him firmly on the lips. He responded with matching enthusiasm and she felt herself tingling with desire.

When they got back to her apartment, she hammered the keypad urgently to get into the apartment block, and ignoring the lift rushed for the stairs leaving an astonished Joseph staring after them. She had her door key in hand as they reached her apartment door and she scrabbled to open the door as Luc held her from behind while nuzzling her neck. Once inside, she slammed the door behind them and threw her arms around him in a passionate embrace. As their urgency intensified, they ripped off each other's clothing and tumbled into bed. Rolling all around the mattress, they consumed each other in a blaze of lust until she suddenly went rigid, let out a howling yell as he roared and went limp beneath him.

When they came back down to earth and their breathing had returned to normal, she propped herself up on one elbow. Tracing his chest with her finger, she stopped at a scar that ran from under his right nipple almost to his navel. "How did you get that?"

"A little bit of trouble with someone wielding a panga."

"You obviously survived - did he?"

"No."

She tickled his left arm gently. "Your bullet wound has healed well."

"Down to the excellent nursing care I had - and regular workouts like this can only help."

He returned the favour, lightly tracing her breasts and pinching her nipples before moving on to her belly. "You've got an athlete's body – taut and strong."

"There's got to be some benefit from working out. Besides, it allows me to do this. . ." and pushing him onto his back she took the initiative, straddled and made love to him.

When Katya awoke, she found that Luc was spooned behind her with his hand on her left breast. The bed smelled of sex, overlying Luc's natural musky, masculine odour. She disengaged herself carefully, slipped out of bed and went into the bathroom to shower. As the hot water coursed over her body, she thought back over the evening and smiled to herself. That was the most intense sex – or was it pure animal lust – that she had ever enjoyed. Moments later Luc joined her and they enthusiastically soaped each other's bodies down, paying especial attention to their erogenous zones.

"Stop it," said Katya.

Luc turned her face to his and silenced her with a kiss. She found herself responding and, taking him in one hand and grabbing a towel with the other one, led him back to the bedroom and into bed for slow, measured and ecstatic love-making.

Later, she sat up and, looking at him, said, "I'm hungry; how about you?"

He reached for her breast and said, "Yes."

"I mean for food."

"Oh, yes, that too."

"I've got some bacon, eggs and croissants in the fridge. How about that and coffee?"

"Perfect. We can have another shower and I'll help you – prepare it, I mean."

When they were showered and dressed, they made breakfast and sat down to enjoy it.

"I'd better phone Piet and tell him where I am."

"Luc, I'm going to show you 'my' London this weekend, so tell him you'll be at Heathrow on Sunday in time for the overnight flight back to Cape Town, OK?"

"OK, what do you have in mind?"

"Well, there's a new Canaletto exhibition on at the National that has had good reviews and I feel the need of a bit of culture therapy after the events of the last few weeks. It won't do you any harm either to drink in scenes of 18th Century Venice. I just love his depictions of Venice and his ability to populate his paintings with busy gondolas and hundreds of people scurrying about among the magnificent buildings along the canals."

"I'm not an uncultured Colonial, madam; I too know and like Canaletto. But I also like most of the Renaissance artists and if we do make any real money, I intend to invest some of it in good art."

"Me too – so that's our first stop, and this evening we've been invited to a pre-pre-Christmas party at the Hurlingham Club. The folks giving it are

Dutch. He's a bond trader and pretty much what you'd expect a Dutch bond trader to be like. She's different, very artistic and has her own art gallery just off Bond Street. I bought that little Rodin bronze over there from her last year, a copy of 'The Kiss.' We keep in touch and Marietta, Bart and I sometimes go out for dinner together. Bart keeps trying to fix me up with one of his ghastly trader colleagues, but his heart's in the right place and they do know how to throw a party."

"What's the Hurlingham Club?"

"It's a private members' club just down the road from here. I joined it after I bought this place. It's got great sports facilities and there's a big polo match once a year when all the great and the good come to cheer the players on, drink buckets of champagne and generally have a pretty wild time. I do want to show my face but if you don't like it, we can go on somewhere and have dinner before going home."

"Sounds great. I'm sure we'll enjoy it."

CHAPTER 25

The party was in full swing when Katya and Luc arrived. Marietta spotted them and came rushing over to greet them. After the usual embraces and kisses, Marietta took Luc by the arm and, turning to Katya, said, "So this is your Springbok, Kat." Turning back to Luc she said, "I've heard lots about you. It's all good, so you can relax."

Luc smiled awkwardly at her. "We've only known each other for a couple of months and she keeps surprising me."

"Me too," said Katya, turning back to Marietta. "He's so different from Bart's colleagues and the guys I meet in business. More to the point, he doesn't call any man master and is quite happy to plough his own furrow. He and I have had quite a torrid time together recently, but it has only deepened my feelings for him."

"Stop it, Kat! You're embarrassing me."

"Embarrassing you? I don't believe it."

KATYA'S CHALLENGE

"Anyway, why doesn't Marietta dance with me? That music is getting my feet twitching."

She smiled and the pair of them walked onto the dance floor as Katya went over to the bar to say hello to Bart.

*

Later, as the party was winding down, Luc and Katya were dancing slowly, wrapped in each other's arms. Katya was thinking that she would like this moment to go on and on. She couldn't remember when she'd last felt like this, at one with Luc in a little private bubble on the dance floor. She stretched up and kissed him. He responded and as they swayed together, he whispered in her ear, "Let's go."

*

As they were finishing a late Sunday brunch in her apartment, Katya put down her coffee cup, looked into his eyes and asked, "Where do we go from here?"

"Where do you want us to go?"

"I'm not sure. It's a very long time since I've ever felt the way you make me feel. You excite me but you also make me feel warm, happy and secure – and I don't want to be apart from you."

"And you are the most complete woman I've ever met. You are strong, physically and mentally, you're pretty damn smart and you are gorgeous as well. You are my dream woman."

"Well, here I am in the flesh." She smiled and leant over to kiss him. "When I first met you with Piet and Ton back in September, I felt a deep-down tingle. Here was a real man who also knew his wines and could make me laugh."

"Go on – I like hearing how wonderful I am."

"Idiot, I'm serious. I only ever seem to meet so-called macho men, hard-eyed traders, or evil, lying buyers who just want a fluffy little blonde to soothe their fevered brows at the end of a difficult day and tell them how wonderful they are. Eughhh!"

"Well, a fluffy little blonde you are not, for a start your hair is auburn and despite our different backgrounds, Dr Francis, you are the Yin to my Yang. Somehow, I feel that when we're together we are much more than just a man and a woman - more like a force of nature, unstoppable."

"Well, what do we do about it? How do we build on it? My business is here in London while yours is based in Cape Town, twelve hours' flying time between us. Could you move here?"

"Not without starting over again. How about you?"

"Almost impossible. South Africa isn't a good base for my kind of business, and I'd have to travel all the time."

"Hmm."

They sat in silence, looking away from each other, until he checked his watch and said, "Hey, look at the time. I need to get going or I'll miss my flight."

"Let's go!"

They made the Heathrow Express and sat in silence with his arm around her shoulders. They found Piet and Ton in the check-in queue and when the formalities were completed, Luc hung back to give Katya a farewell hug and kiss.

"Travel safely and give me a call when you get home."

He smiled and turned to catch up with the others as they headed into security. Katya watched until he went behind the screen, then turned away and walked slowly to the station, sad at their parting but elated by the fact that she had at the very least fallen in lust with a man who was going to figure in her life. She'd broken her cardinal rule about not getting involved with anyone from her business environment. He was still a special forces officer at heart and tough as they come but he treated her as an equal and could be surprisingly tender and romantic.

*

In the departure lounge, Piet turned to Luc and said; "we need to talk about your relationship with Katya."

Luc looked hard at him for a moment before he said. "Katya is very special. I've never met anyone like her. She's gorgeous, bright and brave, and I think I'd like to spend the rest of my life with her."

"Let's go and have a coffee before our flight is called. I need to talk to you. You've got a bit of a problem to solve first. Katya's life and her business are centred in London, yours are in Cape Town. Finding a compromise won't be easy."

"No, it won't. Assuming our Mozambican venture is successful, money won't be an issue. Maybe we can both sell up and go and do something else together."

"A huge step - you'll have to work it through and come to a mutual understanding, otherwise either you or she will come to regret it, feel frustrated and have a disastrous bust-up. I've got skin in this game. Don't forget that I have followed her career since she was still a schoolgirl and been almost a second father to her. And you know our relationship - I feel that I am a second father to you as well. I don't want to see either of my kids hurt, so don't forget that you can come to me any time, even just to talk to yourself at me."

"Thanks Dad!"

"I mean it, Luc. As I said before, I do think you and she would make an excellent match. I just want to do what I can to make sure that it'll work for both of you. Anyway, enough for now."

*

The next morning Katya arrived at the office at 7:30, made herself a coffee and settled down to catch up on what she would have done at the end of the previous week had Luc and the others not flown into London. She felt really happy for the first time in a very long time and didn't notice the hour until Jean came in with the post.

"'Morning Katya had a good weekend?"

"Terrific! And how about you?"

"Oh, not bad but obviously not as good as yours. I've just had your chum Detective Inspector Harris on the line. He'd like you to meet someone."

"Oh – business, or is he trying to hit on me?"

"Business, I think. When he left after he'd interviewed you last time, he looked a little surprised. I don't think he expects us girlies to mix it with the bad guys and win. In fact, I suspect he's a little in awe of you."

"Idiot!"

"OK, I looked at your diary and have written him in for 11:00. Is that all right?"

"I suppose so. I'll deal with him as quickly as possible. Thanks."

*

Jean rang through just before eleven to say that Inspector Harris and Mr Smith were here to see her.

"Send them in, Jean, and ask them if they'd like a coffee."

With a knock on the door, she ushered them in and asked if she could take their coats.

Katya stood up to greet them and asked them to take a seat.

"What can I do for you gentlemen?"

"Good of you to see us at such short notice, Ms Francis. May I introduce Mr Smith?"

Katya wondered where this was going. Somehow a friendly policeman was more of a worry than a hostile one. What were they after?

"In light of our investigations, I've had to pass your case to the Anti-Terrorist Branch, and they've escalated it to Box 500[9] Mr. Smith is from the Foreign & Commonwealth Office and the ramifications of the attack on you at the end of October have come to his attention. What I have to tell you is in the strictest confidence: The men who attacked you were hired out from a London criminal gang by a Chinese national who fronts up a trading house, Cathay (UK) Metals, just down the road from here in Hill Street. Both Special Branch and the Drug Squad have had their eyes on him for some time but

---

[9] Police investigations that appear to have a national security component are forwarded to "Box 500," the central MI5 clearing house address for assessment and further action.

haven't been able to get enough evidence to charge him until now."

"Does this mean you have him?"

"Yes, but this is where Mr. Smith comes in."

"Yes, Ms Francis, you will be aware that the Chinese have invested massively in Africa in search of strategic raw material supplies, and this concerns HMG. Their tactics are unsavoury to say the least, and the native workers are treated as little better than slaves. We have spoken to our little Chinese friend and persuaded him to tell us why he ordered the attack on you."

"How did you manage that?"

"The threat of imprisonment here, followed by deportation back to China for criminal activities in the UK."

"But that surely wasn't much of a threat? I mean, this sort of punishment doesn't seem to worry them."

"In his case, yes. He turns out to be quite important in their scheme of things. With London as one of the major centres for global commodity trading, it turns out that Cathay (UK) Metals is their eyes and ears in this sector in Europe. They do trade legitimately, basically as a cover, but their true objective is intelligence gathering and a bit of undercover work to advance Chinese interests. His deportation would give us the opportunity to shut them down in London and that would set their intelligence operations in this sector back by at least two years."

"Why don't you then?"

"You've heard the old saying: 'Keep your friends close but your enemies closer'?" Katya nodded, and he went on, "Well, having our little friend under our control improves our understanding of their plans, and this is where you come in. We know that you and your colleagues are busy in Mozambique developing a rare earth deposit. We understand that the attack on you was intended to slow up your Mozambican activities and was part of a couple of unsuccessful attempts to destroy your operations there."

Katya sat still and kept her face impassive as Smith set out this information. "So?" she said.

"We're completely behind your project there. The development of a new source of rare earth metals is in the strategic interests of all Western nations. Given the level of the contacts you have in the Mozambican Government and the quality of your operations, you will probably find out what the Chinese are up to before we do. What I'd like you to do is give us a 'heads-up' on Chinese activity there so we can do all in our power to frustrate them and help you to succeed in your project on the way past."

"But the Chinaman?"

"We'll run him for a bit while your team are busy and then burn their operation."

"So you're actually from MI6."

Smith sat back and said, "You'll be doing your country a real service."

"Don't forget I have dual nationality, Dutch and English. Are your colleagues in the AIVD[10] in agreement?"

"We're all singing from the same hymn sheet, to use the trite phrase."

"You're assuming a lot, asking me to stick out my neck like this, and don't forget that this is a South African project, not a European one."

"Not a problem - between the Dutch and ourselves we have good relationships with the South African agencies and we all want your project to succeed. And regarding risk, really you'll be in no more danger than you are now and if you need help in Mozambique you'll have several helpful individuals to call on.

There is a further and more serious point, we don't think that the troubles you've experienced are Chinese Government policy. We think that someone high in the Chinese hierarchy has gone rogue and has decided to take over your project to boost his chances of advancement within the Politburo. He's using his status and connections to further his ambitions, but it's not official policy"

---

[10] Dutch Secret Service

KATYA'S CHALLENGE

She thought furiously *This is a lot more complex than I thought, the Chinese Government, rogue Chinese operators, western governments wanting our project to succeed and a heavy involvement with the world of spooks. Do I go along with this or do I tell him to sling his hook? Maybe I should agree, after all, it looks increasingly that we are going to need high-level support.*

"OK, I'll do it on one condition: if that Chinese trader looks like thinking about making another move towards me, you'll pick him up and put him away so fast his feet don't touch the ground."

"Harris?"

"We will. He's under close physical and electronic surveillance - all his communications are tapped."

"OK then, I'll do as you ask. Who should I contact if I've anything to report?"

"Inspector Harris will remain your contact point; he'll make sure that your reports get to the right people. Well, thank you, Ms Francis; we won't waste any more of your time."

Harris' parting remarks were: "Thank you Ms Francis, and one last thing, do be suspicious of any letters or parcels you receive that look odd or don't come from anyone you know of."

*

When they'd gone, Katya sat at her desk, thinking furiously. *Positive – they were looking out for her, or at least said they were. Negative - she didn't want to be involved in the spooks' world, although she confessed to herself that some of her business intelligence gathering came close. She decided to keep everything to herself in the knowledge that she could call on English, Dutch and possibly South African resources if necessary, knowing that the issues around Future Metals were known to all three organisations. Harris' parting shot stayed in her mind – letter bombs, parcel bombs? Whatever next? She gave an involuntary shiver.*

*

CHAPTER 26

Their planes landed mid-afternoon in Maputo within half an hour of each other and they met up outside the customs hall. Piet and Luc looked tense and unhappy. Katya asked, "What's up? You look as if your horse was still running after the cup had been presented in the winner's enclosure."

"Hmm, it's a bit like that. Our liaison at the embassy rang me just before we left the office to say he thought there would be some difficulty in getting our exploration license converted to a full-on mining and refining one. But look, don't let's talk about it here; 'walls have ears' and all that. Wait until we get to the hotel. He'll be joining us for dinner and we will get the details then."

Piet had organised a limo to take them into town and to the Radisson Blu hotel, a twenty-minute run from the airport and only two hundred metres from the beach. Luc and Katya were booked into a double room together; Piet saying that there was no point in pretending any more. They smiled at the news, Katya thinking that the trip wouldn't be entirely wasted, whatever the outcome. "Get settled in and then let's meet in the bar at six for a full debrief."

*

Luc and Katya's room had a sea view and with more than an hour to kill before they were expected in the bar, they got ready and went for a quick swim in the hotel's pool. Although the sun was setting, the pool was lit and after swimming a few lengths, they splashed around the pool in a light-hearted water fight, with Katya succeeding in ducking Luc when he least expected it. They returned to their room, showered, dressed and went downstairs to the bar, where they saw Piet and Ton huddled over what looked like a couple of gin and tonics.

"Those look good," said Katya. "I'll have one of those too."

"Just a beer for me," said Luc

The barman brought the drinks over and they raised their glasses to "Future Metals, may it survive and thrive!"

"So, Piet, what's the problem?" asked Katya.

"It seems that our good friend Minister Eusebio is not as good a friend as I thought he was. All kinds of objections have been raised to our request for the conversion of our exploration license to a mining and refining one. My guess is it's a matter of dollars and that the Chinese have topped our initial offer. Jim Palmer from the Embassy will be along shortly and fill us in on the details."

"But this was surely all sorted out, in principle at least, before you started boring holes across the countryside?"

"This is Africa, Katya, and although the ruling party dropped their Marxist ideology years ago in favour of a free market economy, the populace is so poor that there is bribery at all levels of society and I suspect that my good friend the Minister has been offered a contribution to his Swiss or Caribbean pension fund that he finds attractive and wonders if we will top it."

"Yes, but there's no way you can offer him more cash than the Chinese."

"Don't be so sure of that, Katya. There's more than one way to play your cards in a situation like this." His voice trailed off as he looked across the bar to see a stocky, weather-beaten man approaching them. Standing up, he waved to him and said, "Here's Jim."

Introductions were made, and a fresh round of drinks served. "Any developments?" asked Piet.

"I've been checking our friend's background and it turns out he was educated in Europe, at the Freie Universität Berlin, where he gained a bachelor's degree in earth sciences - whatever they are. In contrast to the usual African politician, he actually understands the true implications of the various mineral exploitation projects he has to pass judgement on. I suspect that's why he got this job, being one of the few men in government who has a scientific background. He's also a patriot and wants what is best for Mozambique as well as what's good for him personally."

"That's great," said Katya. "I've brought a scientific presentation and samples with me that will demonstrate how far our technology is ahead of anything that the Chinese can offer."

"Will that be enough?"

"What's to argue about? Go the Chinese route and turn the area of our claim into a toxic dump with lagoons of contaminated water that will leak into the surrounding area, destroying agriculture and poisoning the local populace, or go with us and have a non-polluting process whose by-products all have commercial applications, and which will enrich the country."

"Is it really that good?"

"The best! Our process development studies in Jo'burg and Delft have delivered a real 'gold standard' method for extracting and refining rare earth elements."

Piet chipped in, "Jim, you know I'm not an easy man to convince, but our R&D has delivered big time and if Eusebio is as smart as you say he is, he will understand that granting our license will not only make him rich but will also help develop Mozambique in an environmentally satisfactory way. I'm so pleased that Eusebio is an educated man, a patriot, and not just a political nodding donkey with an ever-outstretched hand. I think I see how we can play this tomorrow, Jim. Will you be coming to the meeting?"

"Yes."

"Great, your presence will add the weight of the South African Government to our proposal. Now let's go and have something to eat while we refine our strategy."

*

Later in bed, Luc asked, "Is your presentation really the 'killer' you say it is?"

"Yes, you saw the pictures I had in London that Tommy Chung took during visits to a couple of their rare earth mining and refining operations earlier in the year. I've also had a friend in London make a short movie of what our process would look like. When you see the two in sequence, they are pretty damn convincing. I've also brought samples of the ore, the clinker after the metals have been extracted, samples of the refined oxides and salts and also of the final liquid effluent."

"What's it like?"

"It's not quite perfect but it is pH neutral, clear, metal free and safe for washing in certainly, although I wouldn't like to drink much of it."

She felt him relax beside her and turned to him. Reaching across his thigh, she took hold of him, grinning that she could feel that they had unfinished business from earlier in the evening as she straddled him.

Later they fell into a happy and dreamless sleep.

*

He woke to find Katya leaning over him. "Time to get up. It's seven o'clock already and we're due at the ministry at ten. Bags me the bathroom first." She slid out of bed and ran across to the bathroom.

"Women!" exclaimed Luc.

*

Over breakfast they discussed their tactics for the upcoming meeting with Eusebio and decided that Katya's presentation should be given as early as possible in the discussion. "I think it'll be a game changer," said Piet, "and based on the project economics, we can afford to be generous on the royalties we pay the Mozambicans – however they distribute the cash among themselves."

Luc spoke up. "Don't forget we need to be certain that we can sell our agreement on intact to whoever we end up doing a deal with."

"Luc, that's up there top and front but first, we need to get him to commit to our deal in such a way that the Chinese can't weasel their way in. I think we can do that with the promise of jobs for the locals – just labouring at first – but we could also offer to build a school that would teach them literacy and numeracy and skill them up to handle the technical and supervisory roles in the fullness of time.

I also know that there is no way that the Chinese could or would match that. They see the Africans as little more than apes and treat them like animals. Workers' conditions are terrible, and health and safety is an optional extra – an option that is seldom exercised. I'm sure Eusebio knows that but there's no harm in reminding him."

With that Jim Palmer walked up to their table, ordered a coffee from the waitress and sat down. "'Morning all, are we ready for the meet?"

A chorus of 'yeses' was the response and Piet said, "We've run through what we want to say and basically what we need from you is a clear statement of support from our Government."

"I can promise you that, although not everyone in Pretoria will agree. We've been trying to build relationships with Beijing, and this might be seen as a bit of a fly in the diplomatic soup."

"Good, thank you. I would consider their attempts to destroy our operations here and the murder two of our men to amount to a damn sight more than a 'fly in the diplomatic soup.' This is our project on our continent, not theirs, and our project will benefit both Mozambique and our country and I can't think of any justification for us to bend the knee to China over it. Another thing - do you by any chance have any data on the maltreatment of African workers by Chinese companies?"

"Some, but you've spent time in the DRC and must have seen some of it for yourself."

"Yes, but although I've seen some, most of it is at second hand and no-one seems willing to speak out in case they lose what little livelihood they've got. The Chinese control their operations very tightly so far as the outside world is concerned."

Katya spoke up. "Some of the pictures in my presentation show workers in the Chinese mining areas operating under dreadful conditions. If that's what they do to their own, how do you think they'll treat the Africans?"

Jim interrupted to say that it was time they left for the Ministry, so they headed for the lobby, gave their bags to Jim's driver and got into the Embassy people-carrier, ready for the drive to the meeting.

*

From reception, they were shown to a lift and taken to the top floor of the Ministry building. Exiting the lift, they were met by a tall, slim secretary wearing an elegant flowery dress and shown into a modern conference room. The room had small windows covered with net curtains and with two Mozambique flags flanking a portrait of the president, Armando Guebuza, at one end of the table. Each place around it had a note-pad and pencil in front of it, an ice bucket full of water bottles and surrounded by tumblers stood in the centre. She said she'd bring them some coffee and that Minister Eusebio would be with them shortly.

"Great!" said Katya. "That gives me time to set up the presentation." With that she reached into one of the pilot cases she had brought in with her. She pulled out a laptop, projector and a number of labelled sample bottles, arranging them on the table-top, with the projector lined up on the wall opposite the bottom end of the table. She had just finished focusing the projector when Eusebio walked in, followed by the secretary carrying a tray of coffee cups.

Carlos Eusebio was very tall and built like an American footballer, with short, black wavy hair, a sallow complexion and features that reflected mixed Portuguese and Mozambican ancestry. His tan linen suit was well cut and was paired off with a sparkling white shirt and a yellow tie displaying the Mozambique star.

Smiling broadly, he began, "Good morning, lady and gentlemen. I'm pleased to meet you today and to have the opportunity to get to understand just what your proposition is."

He sat down as Piet made the introductions and said that he would like Doctor Francis to lead off with her presentation. Standing up, Katya began:

"Minister, I have put a presentation together that demonstrates our approach to the project - its inputs, outputs and the extent to which it is an environmentally friendly approach to what has traditionally been an extremely dirty and polluting process. But first off, I want to show you what the Chinese do." The pictures on screen showed a virtual moonscape: mounds of black earth and fuming lagoons of effluent. Nothing grew on the land and the labourers were bowed, obviously unhealthy and thin.

"Please ask any questions you have as we go along. These pictures were taken earlier this year in China at two of their largest production sites. The appalling environmental mess that you see shows what they allow in their own country and what they do to their own people. Knowing how they regard non-Chinese workers; I would worry about allowing them into your beautiful country. I know that you want to develop your country as a modern industrial base and as a tourist destination and I believe that the Chinese would destroy that ambition.

Now this is a run-through of our process, starting by crushing the ore and then calcining it in a reducing atmosphere to release the metals contained as a mixed metal output we just call 'mixed metal.' The liquid metals flow from the calciner at 1,700 Deg.C and are collected in these moulds. The calcined ore, once the metals have been extracted, looks like this - a clean grey granule, an ideal replacement for sand in making concrete, so no waste, no mountains of spoil to disfigure the countryside.

The mixed metal is then dissolved in nitric acid and the nitrate solution treated to remove entrained iron, calcium and magnesium. The purified solution is then passed through this column cascade, which separates the rare earth metals. Each individual metal nitrate is then crystallized out and calcined to convert it to the oxide. The NOx released during calcining is scrubbed and recycled into fresh nitric acid to dissolve more mixed metal. There are samples of each metal oxide here in these vials.

The energy for the process comes from the natural gas field we found at the site of the final test bore. There is enough gas there to process the entire ore body, and this is a jar of the liquid effluent from the process. It is pH neutral, non-toxic and can be discharged into the river without causing any harm to fish or other river life."

With that, she took the top off the jar, dipped her finger in the liquid and put her finger in her mouth. Smiling, she turned to Eusebio, saying, "It's OK in small doses but I really wouldn't like to drink large amounts of it.

There we have it: a clean process that delivers high purity metals and oxides, and only needs to bring in small quantities of concentrated nitric acid from the outside world. The calcined ore goes for construction, the calcium and magnesium can also be used in special cements and the iron can be reclaimed as DRI, a useful feed for your local steel industry, and you know the value of the rare earths. I'll be happy to answer any questions you have."

"You really can deliver that?" asked Eusebio

"Absolutely, Minister," replied Piet "In fact our technology is world-beating, highly efficient and non-polluting."

"Hmmm," responded Eusebio. "What about labour? I imagine that you'll want to fill all supervisory, technical and managerial posts with expats."

"Only in the beginning. Our intention is to train up our employees to the point where Mozambicans fill all technical, supervisory and managerial jobs in the plant. One of the buildings on the site plan you saw is a residential school for employees, where they would be taught the theory and experience the practicalities of the jobs they do. Good for us, good for them and good for your country, minister."

"Hmmm, you do know that there are other interested parties."

"Yes, but I also know that no-one can compete with us on technical or environmental grounds. I would also like to point out that the efficiency of our process allows us to be very generous when it comes to royalties."

"How generous?"

"What would you consider a generous royalty to be and how and where would you require it to be paid?"

"I can't answer that just now; I need to confer with my staff. Can you leave the samples with me, and a copy of your presentation? I want to show them the difference in approaches to the practicalities of mining and refining rare earth metals. Could we reconvene at the same time tomorrow and get down to details?"

*

CHAPTER 27

Back at the hotel they went into the bar to discuss the meeting. "What do you reckon, Piet?"

"Not happy about the overnight delay, Luc. I'm worried that he'll be having a Chinese takeaway tonight and we'll find ourselves left with cold noodles in the morning."

"So we've got more to come?"

"Yes, but don't forget he didn't bite on the royalty question."

"So?"

"My guess is that he would prefer to do business with us, rather than the Chinese, but he doesn't know how far we'll go. I imagine he'll press our Chinese friends to the point where they walk away, and then he'll give us a number to beat. Then if we do beat it, we've got it in the bag, but knowing the Chinese, they'll load their offer with extras as we have, and it won't be quite so simple."

"You mean 'are our extras better than their extras'?"

"Something like that."

They lapsed into silence for a few minutes until Luc asked, "Did you see that secretary?"

"Why?"

"When she bent down to serve my coffee, I could see down the front of her dress – all the way to the floor - and noticed she hadn't spent any of her wages on underwear."

"Trust you to notice that," said Katya.

"Well, she did make it kind of obvious."

Piet chipped in to say, "She was merely showing you what Eusebio was going to have for lunch."

"You men!"

"I'm serious," said Piet. "Ministerial secretaries in a place like this are chosen for their willingness as well as their secretarial skills."

"Strange to a European mindset, Katya, but normal here," said Jim.

"Poor bloody woman."

"She'd be a bloody sight poorer if she'd said no. This way she gets some of Eusebio's status, a reasonable salary and a job for however long she can hold his attention. Much better than scraping a living in a shantytown on the edge of Maputo. You don't know what this society is like, Katya."

"Obviously."

"Talking of lunch, let's go through and have some," said Piet, breaking the developing tension.

*

Minister Zhang was angry and upset. He'd just been handed a copy of a fax originated by the Chinese Commercial Attaché in Maputo telling of the South Africans' apparently friendly and positive meeting with Eusebio and that he'd been summoned to the Ministry to discuss up-rating the offer they'd made to take over the development of the South Africans' rare earth deposit and to demonstrate that they too had a clean process.

Watched by his solemn-faced and apprehensive staff, he paced up and down the office. Barking out his anger, he shouted, "If our incompetent, stupid idiot army colleagues had had the sense to reconnoitre their targets before attacking them, we wouldn't have this crisis. Project Golden Lion is vital to our economic future and thanks to their incompetence, the South Africans are threatening its success. By the end of next year, we should control more than 80% of global rare earth production and supply and be in a strong position to force Western electronic manufacturers to build manufacturing plants here, allowing us access to their technology and to be able to compete in the West on our terms. Their project must be disrupted, stopped, bought out!"

"Comrade Zhang," interrupted his senior assistant secretary.

"What?"

"Comrade Minister, even if they do a deal with Eusebio, it will be at least three or four years before they can produce any saleable product."

"And?"

"We will have many opportunities over the period, sir, not only to interfere with their operation as they go along, but also to find out just what their new technology is so that we can use it here in China."

"Haven't our security services been able to penetrate their computer systems and find out what they're doing?"

"Only to a point. We know what they are going to do but not how they're going to do it. They ramped their security up in the middle of October and now their Internet links are only seem to be via computers that are basically just dumb terminals with no local data storage, so hacking is a waste of time. Their communications are also heavily encrypted, and they change their encryption keys every week. We don't know what made them become so security conscious. Maybe they've been taking specialist advice."

"You think that we should just wait and watch and infiltrate their project on the ground and take their technology when they've developed it to production scale?"

"Yes sir, they will carry all the costs of development while we simply help ourselves to the resulting technology."

"But that leaves us with the fact of a competing rare earth deposit that we do not control."

"I have been looking at possible solutions to that, sir, but first we need to send instructions to our commercial attaché in Maputo. I suggest that we don't improve our offer by more than 5%."

"But if that's not enough?"

"It doesn't matter. We have a long-term plan to gain control and if we increase our offer by more than 5% now, it will look as though we were trying to rip them off in the first place. In other words, more than 5% undermines our credibility. Also, please do not forget that our process isn't exactly clean. We're working on improvements but can't demonstrate them yet."

"I see what you mean, Comrade Secretary. Go ahead with a maximum 5% improvement on our original offer and see how they respond."

"Yes sir."

"I also think that our colleagues working for APT1[11] in Shanghai should be targeting the South Africans as a priority, finding out exactly what they

---

[11] APT1 - part of China's cyber-espionage organisation operating from a complex in the Pudong District of Shanghai.

are up to and disrupting their business in any way possible. Maybe they are very security conscious, but they must surely have sensitive external links - banks, suppliers, customers, etc. - which can be disrupted"

"Can I authorise them to go to work on it in your name, sir?"

"Yes."

*

After he had left the room, Zhang returned to his office and sat behind his desk, thinking furiously. In one way, the man was correct; it would take a few years for the Mozambique project to come to fruition and this would offer numerous opportunities to steal the process and disrupt progress on developing the site, but even if the President was behind the long-game approach as stated, he still felt that if he went along with the proposition and the South Africans succeeded in bringing their project to fruition, the fact that he'd allowed a competitor to enter the market when he could have stopped it dead would count heavily against him. Time to take the initiative again.

He rang his secretary and asked her to connect him to the Commercial Attaché at their embassy in The Netherlands.

*

They met for breakfast early to discuss their tactics for the negotiation with Eusebio and decide what their 'walk-away' offer level should be. They were interrupted by a phone call from Jim.

"'Morning Piet, just to say I've had a call from Eusebio asking us to delay our meeting until two-o-clock this afternoon."

"Any reason?"

"None given, but my guess is that the Chinese know about our meeting yesterday and that Beijing have given their commercial attaché fresh instructions. This suggests that Eusebio wants to hear what extra goodies are on offer before he finalises anything with you – or not."

"Thanks for the cheery heads-up."

"Don't worry, an eleventh-hour offer does nothing for their credibility and your team gave an impressive presentation yesterday. It's just the numbers today. Anyway, I'll join you for lunch and run you over to the ministry afterwards."

*

Over lunch Jim turned to Katya and asked, "Something's bothering me. Did you really lick process effluent off your finger yesterday?"

"Of course! No, I used a trick taught me by a friend who was studying to be a vet when we were both at Cambridge. They had a lecturer on diagnostic skills who claimed that an animal's urine was one of the best diagnostic samples you could have: colour, smell and taste."

"Taste?"

"Yes, he said that sweet-tasting urine, for example, was indicative of pancreatic failure, like diabetes in humans. He had a beaker of horse's urine and did what you saw me do - claimed to taste sweetness and handed the sample to a student in the front row to try. The student balked but did as he was told and ended up with a disgusted face and a mouth like a cat's arse. It was all a bit of sleight of hand; what he'd really done was dip his second finger in the urine and then ostentatiously lick his index finger.

If you remember, I had a picture of a particularly disgusting Chinese mining operation on screen when I pulled the stunt. Eusebio was looking hard at the picture and not at me at the time. Anyway, had I actually tasted it, it wouldn't have done me any harm, it just has a weakly stale taste accompanied with ppb levels of metals. But all's fair. . . as they say."

They burst out laughing when she finished, and Piet clapped ironically. "Remind me to double check anything you send me in future."

*

On arrival at the Ministry, they were met by the same secretary they'd seen the day before and escorted to the top floor conference room. Eusebio joined them a few minutes later, accompanied by two other men who were introduced as Dr Matusse and Mr Simango, respectively the Ministry's chief chemist and mining expert.

KATYA'S CHALLENGE

After completing the introductions, Eusebio said that while he'd been impressed with yesterday's presentation, his technical advisors had come up with a slew of questions which he was unable to answer, and would Dr Francis be so kind as to run through it again and answer their questions. This she did and there followed an intensive hour of questioning. When she and Luc had answered all their questions, apart from the confidential data on their chemical technology, they turned to Eusebio and said they were satisfied with what had been an extremely professional presentation which answered all of their questions, barring the details of the chemical technology, which they understood to be confidential, and the subject of patent filings. They agreed that they would give the project their blessing and Matusse said that if the technology was to be replicated on an industrial scale, Mozambique would end up with a state-of-the-art rare earth mining and refining operation that would be both world class and environmentally sound. At that, Eusebio proposed a short break for tea before getting down to the details of an agreement, at which Matusse and Simango made their excuses and left.

*

Following a welcome cup of tea, they sat down again to begin their negotiation. Eusebio began by saying, "Mr de Bruijn, would you be so kind as to outline what your desired license would permit you to do?"

"No problem - we would like an exclusive license that allows us to mine the rare earth ore contained within the area of our exploration concession north-west of Beira as outlined on the exploration map and establish an extraction and purification plant to recover the rare earth elements contained."

"And what are you prepared to pay for such a license?"

"Difficult to say. However, we would point out that everything from mine development through to the export of finished rare earth metals and chemicals will take place in Mozambique, allowing your economy to benefit through supplies, taxes, royalties and local employment.

"Meanwhile, we must invest somewhere in the region of twenty-five million US dollars to get the project up and running and it will take at least three years before we see any return at all on this investment. We also note that the official license fees will come to between forty and fifty thousand US dollars, while the state will charge us around 32% in corporation tax and take a royalty fee of 3% on all shipments. We will also need to pay the costs of registering and operating a Mozambican company to manage the project. This doesn't leave us much elbow room when it comes to a signing fee, does it?"

"I don't know," replied Eusebio. "Some of these oxides you're talking about sell for as much as

$500 per kilo and if your process is as efficient as you say it is, then there is plenty of elbow room."

"So what we are really talking about is your 'signing fee'?"

"That's about it."

"How about fifty thousand US, paid to an account of your choice?"

"Fifty thousand US? That doesn't seem very much, given the scale of your project. I was thinking more in terms of two hundred and fifty thousand."

"Hmm, can you give us a moment?"

"Yes, just open the door when you're ready to continue." With that he got up and left the room.

"As I expected," said Piet. "And there's no way he's getting a quarter of a million just like that. I think that we go for $100K and a seat on our advisory board."

"What advisory board?" asked Luc.

"The one that'll be called into existence when we leave here. It's a perfect way of keeping up-front costs down, while tying his support into the project. He'll receive 'Advisory Director's fees' as we go along, while we'll have continuing governmental support for our project as it progresses."

"Smart," laughed Katya. "I like that."

"Yes, I've no problem paying out when I get value in return, but there is no way I will hand out a chunk of cash to someone who can then just walk away. Are we agreed?"

With nods from all around the table, Piet stood up, walked to the door and opened it. Two minutes later, Eusebio walked in and sat down at the top of the table. "Have you come to a conclusion?"

Piet laid out their agreed proposal, focusing on the Advisory Director position and how that would be a win-win solution with long-term benefits to Eusebio, the project and Mozambique. Eusebio seemed to be both surprised and flattered by the idea. After the expected to-ing and fro-ing on the level of the director's fees, he agreed. They discussed the timing of the granting of the license and agreed that the initial payment would be made on the day the agreements were signed. In the meantime, Piet would send him an Advisory Director's contract for agreement, while Eusebio would let him have his bank account details, so that everything would be done and dusted when he returned to sign off on the deal.

CHAPTER 28

They didn't get back to the hotel until the sun was setting and went straight into the bar for a celebratory drink, champagne all round. Toasts were drunk to each other, to Future Metals (Pty) Ltd, to Mozambique, to their technology, to the fast-developing electronics industry and to the gods of fortune who'd brought them safely to this point. Jim joined in the party to begin with but left for the embassy just before seven. He excused himself with the words, "Duty calls and I still have work to do this evening for a meeting with the Ambassador in the morning."

The others arranged a table for what was turning into a very merry dinner party. As they finished their main course of fat and juicy prawns, Katya looked at the faces around the table: a smiling, relaxed and resourceful Piet, a thoughtful Luc, presumably thinking of the challenges required to turn the license agreement into cash flow, and here was she at the start of what promised to be a real adventure in the company of a man she'd fallen in lust? love? with. What did she feel deep down? She examined her feelings as dispassionately as she could.

As a woman, Katya was hugely attracted to him, seeing his face whenever she shut her eyes, wherever she was. He was special, and she hadn't felt this way about anyone since her second year at Cambridge, when she'd fallen for Eric, a precociously sophisticated young man who had made her laugh and who embraced her experiences of the gypsy life she'd led as she and her mother had moved from place to place following her father's postings. That relationship had failed when he went to work in a London bank, and she went to Germany to work for Reacorchemie. Their career landscapes were just too different and points of common reference too few. She hadn't cried much then, and only in private, but it had taken four or five years before she got him fully out of her system.

And as a businesswoman, Katya had mixed feelings. She loved her business life, travelling the world, hearing about the latest advances in electronics before even the technical press, getting to understand 'breakthrough' technologies while building relationships with customers and suppliers. She knew she was good at it and she only had to look at the growth of her business accounts and profits over the last few years to understand just how good she was.

But . . . but . . . but . . . How could she work it with her business centred in London and his in Cape

Town? Wasn't that what had finished her relationship with Eric back in the day? Why couldn't she have fallen for someone who at least lived in the UK?

Luc broke into her thoughts. "You're looking very serious, Kat. What's up?"

"Nothing really, I was just thinking of the time and investment needed to turn that license agreement into cash in the bank. Meanwhile, I've got to replace my Chinese rare earth supplies in short order to keep my business afloat."

"Presumably you're well on the way to achieving that?"

"Yes, it's coming together but Marijke called me last night to see if I could detour into Kinshasa in the DRC on my way home and check out a certain Doctor Herman Mampata, who claims to be able to supply us with some hundreds of tonnes of good quality rare earth oxides. She said he'd only been on her radar for a few weeks, but she didn't feel like giving him a trial order without a face-to-face first, so I'll do that."

"You'd go to Kinshasa on your own?"

"Why not?"

"It's not a good place for a white woman to go on her own, especially if she's meeting people she hasn't met before. Kabila has only had limited success in pacifying and uniting the country so far, and kidnap and murder are daily hazards even in

Kinshasa itself. Europeans seldom travel without bodyguards. Have you got an escort organised?"

"Well no, do you really think I need one?"

"Kat, I would no more go anywhere in the DRC without bodyguards than I'd go sky-diving without a parachute. What do you know about this Mampata guy, anyway?"

"Not a lot. He popped up on our radar back in August as a potential supplier, but I think there's something a little strange about his operation. We think he's taking ores from some of the artisanal miners and processing them somewhere around Kinshasa. It has been very difficult to get hard information about him or his operation. None of my competitors seem to know anything about him either, which is unusual."

"Hmmm . . . I smell a large and rapidly decomposing rat here. Piet, do you think your contacts in the SASS or our pal Jim could give us a 'heads up' on this guy?"

"Yes, but I doubt I'll get much feedback before Monday evening. Can you postpone your trip until Tuesday or Wednesday, Katya?"

"I suppose so, and I'd rather go to meet him with more information than I have now. Up-to-date information is hard currency in the trading game."

"OK, I'll start the ball rolling in the morning and on the assumption that you'll be kicking your heels here until Tuesday, why don't we all head back down to Cape Town tomorrow and you can have a relaxing weekend at the beach with Luc. We can probably fit in a braaivleis[12] too."

Luc and Katya looked at each other, smiled and said yes.

*

Katya rang London prior to flying out on Friday morning and after speaking to both Marijke and David, she asked if they'd heard any more, either about or from Dr Herman Mampata. Marijke said she'd emailed him to rearrange his meeting with Katya for Wednesday but had only got back a bald acknowledgement.

"What do we know about this guy?"

"Very little," said Marijke, "I've been asking around but only one or two of our smaller competitors have even heard of him. It's very odd. I would have expected that the MMTA[13] Secretariat would have him on their books and would know all about him, but no."

"I'm inclined to smell a rat here. Luc and Piet seem to think that the guy isn't kosher, otherwise he would be known as a player already. Can you get

---

[12] Afrikaans word for a barbecue.
[13] Minor Metals Trade Association – a global trade association for companies whose business is centred on so-called minor metals, such as rare earth metals, which are not traded on open exchanges like the London Metal Exchange.

hold of Detective Inspector Harris, tell him about my upcoming meeting with Dr Herman Mampata, explain my misgivings and ask him to see whether his colleague Mr Smith has any useful information on Mampata and the current situation in the DRC? If they've anything to report, ask Harris to call my mobile urgently, day or night."

"Will do – and good luck!"

*

They were waiting in the departure lounge when Katya's mobile rang. It was D.I. Harris. "Ms Francis?"

"Yes?"

"Harris here. Regarding your enquiry, Mr Smith believes it would be a good idea for you to cancel your holiday. The chances of your catching yellow fever are too high."

Katya said nothing for a moment as she digested the coded references. "Thanks, that's what I was afraid of. Oh, by the way, can you tell him that the incidence of local yellow fever cases here is down to a new low. We'll have confirmation one way or another in ten days or so, well past the incubation time for an infection." She broke the connection and turned to the others. "Well, my sources in the UK are suggesting that Mampata is a front for, or is funded by, the Chinese in the DRC and that a meeting with him is likely to be bad for my health."

"That does it," said Luc and Piet chimed in with him.

"I didn't know you had contacts like that."

"They're the result of that attack on me in London. The police enquiry into the attack brought them to the door of a Chinese metal trader just down the road from my office. The foreign involvement brought them in contact with the Counter-Terrorism Branch and I then had a follow-up visitor from 'Spook Central.' They're now looking out for me both in London and here in Africa, in return for anything I can give them about Chinese activity here in the region."

"Well, well, well," said Piet. "You continue to surprise me. I had no idea you were plumbed into the world of international spookery. I thought my connections were good, but I must have spoken to my contacts around the same time as you this morning and yours has come back first. You must be highly regarded."

"I don't know about that, but I must be one of the few people carrying a English passport whose activities have put them in the cross-hairs of a Chinese operation. They're desperate to know what's going on in Africa just now and they claim that normal diplomatic channels are always behind the curve, hence my involvement."

With that their flight was called and Piet said, "Let's leave it 'til we get down to Cape Town and we can have a council of war at your hotel."

Katya then asked, "Where have you booked me into?"

"The Vineyard Hotel; it's got all the facilities and the food's pretty decent."

*

CHAPTER 29

Katya, Luc and Piet met up in the Garden Lounge of the Vineyard Hotel for pre-dinner drinks. Sitting in the evening sun, Piet reviewed the results of their negotiations with Eusebio.

"Not bad in sum. Although the deal isn't signed off yet, it looks as though we have got all the important stuff agreed and it doesn't look as though it's going to cost us too much. Based on Eusebio's body language, I reckon that the Advisory Board offer clinched it for us. I'm sure the Chinese would not make a similar offer, and this gives our project some real and ongoing political muscle in Mozambique."

"Where did that come from, Piet?"

"It's a tactic I've used before, Katya. It plays to the guy's vanity as well as his greed. It means that most of the money he gets comes out of profits instead of being an up-front charge, and we gain ongoing support from the local government. Highly recommended as a deal-maker in projects like ours. That is, provided we get the deal signed off in the next couple of weeks."

"Then what?

"That is what we need to discuss, but let's leave that 'til tomorrow when we can include Ton in the discussion. So, things are on the positive side of inconclusive. But first we need to talk about your projected holiday in the DRC."

"You mean the risk of me catching yellow fever?"

"Exactly. I've just had feedback from my contacts that also suggests you shouldn't go, reinforcing the information you got from London. They are certain that Mampata is a front man for the Chinese, running an under-the-radar operation to acquire both metals and intelligence for his Chinese masters. The fact that he's invited you to his offices suggests a line from the old nursery rhyme: 'Come into my parlour said the spider to the fly.'

I operated in the DRC with Luc's help for some years around the millennium and it is a terrible place to try and do anything. You must identify who in the government apparatus or the military 'owns' whatever it is you are interested in. You then must get them onside, usually by crossing their palms with gold – silver just doesn't hack it anymore - and then find a way of making sure that your exclusive rights remain exclusive, not easy in a country as unstable as that. More to the point, your personal safety is always at risk, which is why white people in the DRC all travel with bodyguards.

Our intelligence people said that if you went to Mampata's offices in Kinshasa, there was a fair chance that you'd either be arrested for the violation of some trumped-up trade or immigration regulation or kidnapped. Either way, you'd be taken out of circulation for weeks until we could get you released.

A French friend of mine was trapped like that a couple of years ago and spent six months in jail, emerging much poorer, much thinner and very ill. If you were to spend time in the local chokey your fellow prisoners would treat you even worse than the guards, and I can't imagine that being kidnapped would be any more relaxing. To cap it off, your freedom would have to be purchased, whether through bribes to your jailers or ransom to your kidnappers, and that could be very expensive.

For your sake, for Luc's sake and for my sake, please forget about going to Kinshasa. We need you out and about as part of the team, not kicking your heels in an over-crowded cell in a stinking jail - or worse."

"You silver-tongued charmer, Piet," said Katya with a fleeting smile before turning serious. "I'm sure you're right. Apart from the sheer damn inconvenience of being locked up, I don't have the time."

Luc had been listening without comment as Piet spoke, thinking, *Please God, let her decide not to go,* and remembering retrieving one of his men from a Congolese jail, five years earlier. He'd been put in a cell with about forty other men, no room to lie down and a tin bucket for a toilet. As the only white man, he'd been gang-raped several times, lost nearly half of his normal body-weight and was covered in sores. If he'd been there for another week he would probably have died. Luc had carried him from the jail and driven him straight to hospital where he'd stayed for five months before going home to South Africa, a broken man. No! Katya mustn't go to Kinshasa.

"You've been very quiet, Luc. What's up?" asked Katya.

"I was listening to Piet. He's absolutely right. This does look like a Chinese setup and I couldn't bear to think of what might happen to you. Even if I sent bodyguards with you, I'm not sure they could protect you in the circumstances. Don't forget, we've already had three serious brushes with them, and they'll doubtless be aiming to get lucky this time around. Please don't go; the risks are too great, and I really don't want to see you hurt."

"When a bunch of people tell me I shouldn't do something, I usually go right ahead and do it, but in this case, I'm listening and agreeing. If you, Piet and the English and South African spooks all say the same thing, it would be foolhardy of me not to listen. I'll go straight back to London when we're finished here. Now, can we please go and have something to eat? I'm famished."

"Off you go, you two; I'm going home to my wife and my own bed. Come around to my place around four tomorrow afternoon and we'll have a braaivleis."

"Great," said Luc. "I'll bring the wine."

"See you here around ten tomorrow with Ton. Bye."

*

With coffee and cognacs on the table, Luc took Katya's hand in his and looking into her eyes, said, "Thank God you've decided to abort your trip to Kinshasa. Piet was completely, absolutely and totally right. One of my men was caught up in a sting about five years ago and thrown in prison in Kinshasa. Even after paying out large sums of money, it took me three months to get him released. I won't detail what they did to him, but he spent the next five months in hospital and returned home a broken man. He'll never work again. The thought of anything like that happening to you makes me sick. We've only just found each other and although we have so much to learn about each other, I know from the bottom of my heart that I want to spend the rest of my life inside yours."

"Luc, once I got the 'yellow fever' warning I was 50% ready to cancel. With Piet's input that went to 100%. I too have heard horror stories about life in a DRC prison. For women, it is being raped, beaten up or having to become the plaything of the biggest bull dyke in your cell. None of these options are hugely attractive, so it's not going to happen."

Luc said he had an idea: "I know Hennie has some business in Kinshasa at the moment and we have a safe house as our operating base there. Why don't I get him to take a few of his lads round to Mampata's offices and find out what's behind his offer?"

"How do you mean?"

"Hennie's lads could turn up one evening when friend Mampata is shutting up shop, grab him and take him to the safe house. They'll then persuade him to tell us who or what is behind his sudden presence in the rare earths business."

"Will he tell them?"

"You bet! They can be extremely persuasive, especially when they've got him naked and tied to a steel chair bolted to the floor."

"Do they just beat the story out of him?"

"No! Nothing physical, they tend to use psychological techniques instead. Isolation, darkness, disorientation, sleep and sensory deprivation. It takes a little longer, say three or four days at most, but then they're happy to answer all your questions and are pathetically grateful for the odd cup of water."

"Sounds unpleasant."

"It is, but the target can be put back at the place from where they were taken, physically undamaged and with nothing to show to third parties about what happened to them. Plus, we get the information we want. I'll talk to Hennie in the morning and see if it is practicable.

Now we have a fairly clear weekend ahead, so let's take a gentle walk around the pool, then head off upstairs. I feel an itch coming on I'd like you to scratch."

She looked at him, winked and smiled. Standing up from the table and picking up her bag, she grabbed his hand and they walked outside. They walked slowly around the pool, with Katya snuggled up against him, then turned back into the hotel and took the lift to their room.

"I need a shower," she said and headed off into the bathroom. As the water cascaded over her she was suddenly aware that Luc had joined her in the shower, and they spent some time soaping each other down until they were each totally convinced the other was clean - everywhere. Grabbing towels, they headed for the bed and lay down side-by-side.

After a moment Luc propped himself up on one elbow and leaned over her, tracing the outline of first one breast, then the other, working in circles until he was tweaking each nipple in turn.

Katya giggled, then sat up, straddled him and with her hands firmly planted on his shoulders, began to make vigorous love to him, her hair falling like a curtain over her eyes. Coming to a noisy climax, she sat upright for a moment before falling forward onto his chest. "Oh! I needed that."

"Me too," said Luc as she rolled off him onto the bed, one hand on his thigh, before leaning over and kissing him deeply while he was wondering at this smart, tough and cool city woman who could suddenly shed all her inhibitions and enjoy pure, uninhibited sex. She was special and he wanted to hold on to her, no matter what.

Katya also lay there, tired and happy, thinking warm fuzzy thoughts about Luc and suddenly fell asleep.

*

Piet and Ton joined them on Saturday morning for a planning session, working through the list of potential buyers that they'd put together back in London who could take on the development of their deposit. Ton had pulled up the financial data and industry chatter on each one they'd selected. After some heated discussion and calculations, they agreed to concentrate on the four most promising prospective buyers: Corplan Mining, Ramontain Inc., Dycerb Resources and Devex Resources.

Piet then tasked them to put the various parts of the prospectus together: Ton to do the numbers, Luc to do the geology, assay results and mineralogy, Katya to do the extraction and refining chemistry, while he would write up the Mozambican political and economic scene and the legal agreements underpinning the project.

"Timing?" he asked.

"Given the data we have and the fact that we won't have the agreements signed off with the Mozambicans for a couple of weeks, then add Christmas and New Year into the mix, my view is that we should aim to have it in final draft form for the end of December, ready to sign off on and send it out in the middle of January," said Katya

"Agreed," said Luc. "Accuracy and completeness trump speed, although I don't think we should hang about. While everybody is running about like headless chickens complaining about the Chinese disruption of supplies, we mustn't forget that the material that is coming through is priced at such low levels that not only are outfits like Molycorp in the States and Lynas in Australia going to rack up huge losses if they are going to compete, they may even shut up shop.

"This is where your purification and separation technology comes in, Katya. It'll be an absolute game-changer. Your projected process costings would mean that if the Chinese still want to compete, then they'll effectively be paying their customers to take their products. My feeling is that we should commercialise the technology as a separate part of any deal, offering non-exclusive licenses under very strict secrecy terms."

Piet chipped in, "Good thinking, but let's return to the prospectus: everything in the final document must be legally bomb-proof, either demonstrably accurate or totally, utterly and absolutely unquantifiable. Buyers need to be able to rely on the data or we can find ourselves being comprehensively sued, which is not my idea of fun."

"How are you going to approach the target buyers?" asked Katya.

"I thought about going directly; after all, I've met all four CEOs, but something tells me we ought to use an intermediary at first. Our corporate lawyers have a lot of experience in the mining and metals industry and I believe that they could handle the initial approach better than I could. It also has the advantage of keeping us individually out of the firing line until actual negotiations start. Do you agree?"

All three nodded their assent and with that, the party broke up, Piet saying that he'd see them all that evening for a braai, and he and Ton headed off.

CHAPTER 30

"Have you ever been up Table Mountain?"

"No."

"Look, it's only ten-thirty. We can easily climb it in time for beer and a bite to eat before coming back down in the cable car to laze around my parents' pool for an hour or two before heading off to Piet's braai. Let's check out of the hotel and we can spend tonight at my parent's place."

"Sounds good. I'll head upstairs and get packed and changed."

Twenty minutes later the hotel's driver dropped them off at the cable car entrance, where they left their bags and walked over to the start of their chosen climb. Just before half twelve, they emerged onto the summit and headed over to the Café.

"I need some water after that," said Katya, "and I could murder a pizza just like that one over there." She pointed to where a couple were sitting in the sun.

"That's the local version of a Napolitano from the look of it, a good, nourishing and tasty pizza that'll put back what the climb took out of you. Grab a table and I'll order for both of us – water or beer?"

"Just water, thanks."

Ten minutes later they were tearing into their pizzas and bottles of water. "The view from here is just fantastic. The sun, the sea and a gentle breeze to keep temperature reasonable. It's absolutely idyllic."

"A good place to move to?" asked Luc.

"Not so sure, and I guess winter here can be as miserable as anywhere else."

"No, winters here are very mild, with highs of around seventeen degrees and lows of six or seven. Rainfall is limited too, so it's not a lot different from a decent European spring, although to be fair we have occasionally had a light dusting of snow. It sends the locals into a panic because no-one knows how to drive in it and the breakdown garages and body-shops make good money."

"But what about the security situation?"

"Not brilliant, to be honest. Old friends of my parents from their vineyard days were raided, robbed, raped and murdered three weeks ago. They were my Uncle David and Aunt Therese, lovely people who didn't deserve to suffer like that. That's why you see so many walled compounds and armed guards around the place.

Whites are an endangered minority now, with the ANC having been in power for what seems like an eternity. Like all long-lasting African governments, they've become lazy and corrupt, only working for their core voters and sod everyone else. We also have the typical African tribal loyalties which cut across society, class and borders. All too often, disputes are settled privately with knives, clubs or bullets, and all too often the perpetrator is never arrested, let alone prosecuted."

"So why do you stay here?"

"Well, our ancestors were amongst the Voortrekker families who came here in the early nineteenth century, which explains Dad's attachment to the wine business, and although my folks could easily get up and go, they have a visceral attachment to the land of their forefathers. After all, we can trace our family back to my four times great–grandpa, and that's a lot to put behind you when you go somewhere new. No old friends or connections and an unfamiliar society to cope with. It's not an attractive prospect when you're in your early sixties and actually have a great life here, the blacks and the government notwithstanding."

"What about you?"

"Well, my business is here but we operate all over Africa and are starting to operate in Europe as well but no, I don't see myself staying here forever. The politics of the RSA are not conducive to the kind of business we have. Yes, we get sub-contracted jobs from government agencies but usually only where our operations are distanced from government and thus deniable.

I don't believe that it has a long-term future here and the consequences of getting it wrong tend to be either acute lead poisoning or extended periods in unattractive jails. The difficulty is to find a liveable country that would accept our training base.

Israel was a hot spot for South African businesses seeking friends outside the country during the sanctions years. I know people who went to Israel in those years to set up procurement arrangements for European products wanted here but which could not be exported directly to us. Goods would be loaded onto ships bound for Haifa and their masters would receive instructions mid-Mediterranean to change course and make for Durban instead.

However, even Israel seems to have become unfriendly unless you are willing to be subsumed into the Israeli Defence Force and concentrate on defending Israel by fighting the Arabs in general, and Palestinians in particular, for them. Now I am no fan of militant Muslims, but I don't feel like adding them to my list of actual or potential enemies just yet."

"But the IT security business is truly international and that could surely be run from anywhere?"

"True."

"What about the UK or Holland?"

"Civilised, certainly, and I suspect I could bring enough references from here to open enough doors to establish myself in either country – but the weather!"

"Idiot!"

"C'mon, let's head back down and have a swim before we head for Piet's braai."

Grabbing their bags from the lockers at the bottom of the cable car run, they took a taxi and headed for Luc's parents' compound.

*

"We meet at last," said Marius. "You must be Katya. I'm Marius and this is my wife Nadine. Welcome to our humble abode." Kisses and hugs all round until Nadine asked, "Are you thirsty? Hungry? There will be plenty to eat tonight at Piet's braai, but it'll probably be on the late side of early, so just say if you want anything now."

"A glass of water would be great thanks," said Katya.

Lying out beside the Kruger's pool, Katya's mind was busy with two dominant themes, Luc and her increasing REE stocks. *Her future with Luc was the biggest question but not as urgent as dealing with the shock news that her best customer was transferring his magnet foundry operations to China. OK, they'd given her six months' notice, but that meant some serious crystal ball gazing. Which of her other customers would follow suit, when would they follow and what would that do to her inventories and would it depress prices across the board?*

As those questions went around and around in her head she saw KF Trading and Katya Francis in the bankruptcy courts, shunned by her former 'friends' and competitors, who would write her off as a cocky bitch who'd over-reached herself and got what was coming to her.

Nooooo! That wasn't going to happen. She was a trader, a gambler who only gambled when the odds favoured her, and she was sure they still did. Monday would allow her to assess her actual odds again and decide what to do. She couldn't do it here, not without all the information she needed - park it for now.

And so, to Luc – lovely man, strong when he needed to be, gentle when necessary. One of the few men she'd ever met who didn't feel the need to be in charge all the time. It was quite refreshing, but she could see that this sprang from the way his mother and father were with each other. How could they reconcile their lives in a way that would let them have a life together?

Her reverie was interrupted by Nadine saying, "We're leaving for Piet's in an hour, so if you want to freshen up Katya, now's the time."

"OK." She smiled, but she now had an idea that she'd follow up on later.

CHAPTER 31

On arrival at Piet's compound, two security guards checked both car and passengers before opening the gate to let them in. Once inside, they were greeted by Piet himself, who led them round to the west-facing rear of the house where his wife Molly welcomed Nadine and Katya to seats on the veranda alongside Ton's wife Sophie. Once the usual hugs and kisses had been exchanged, the women sat down around a table on the veranda while the men stood around chatting. Piet's butler came around with a Hamilton Russell Pinot Noir for the men and a Ken Forrester Chenin Blanc for the ladies. Katya broke with the implicit assignment of preferences and asked for the Pinot Noir.

Molly, Nadine and Sophie were fascinated by Katya and although Molly knew a lot of her history, they all focused on her like cats on a bowl of salmon. Katya answered their questions light-heartedly and soon the three women were listening raptly as Katya told them about the role Piet had played in her life at various critical points. Molly chipped in to reinforce her story from time to time and said that Katya was, in many ways, the daughter that she and Piet had never had.

As the focus on Piet and Katya's relationship over the years turned to her experiences in Mozambique and London in the last few months, she tried to play it down by telling them that she'd been in safe hands in Mozambique with Luc watching over her. She also emphasised that, even though he hadn't been there when she was attacked in London, she could look after herself. The women's lives could not have been more different from hers, so it took some time before she became one of the group, as opposed to some strange alien being.

Eventually the conversation became more general and the men wandered over to the barbecue and stood around, drinks in hand, talking about the meeting earlier in the week in Maputo. A maid appeared bearing a huge platter with raw steaks and a couple of large gutted and stuffed stumpnose fish, which Piet inspected closely before donning a vinyl apron adorned with a spectacularly bad taste depiction of a nude white woman with improbably large breasts. Picking up the fish, he put them on the grill while instructing the maid to bring out the salads and side dishes in about fifteen minutes' time, when the fish would be ready to serve.

*

The braai, or barbecue, was a success. The stumpnose was perfectly cooked and succulent. The steaks were tender and juicy with that unique barbecue flavour, and as the party started to slow down, Marius took Luc to one side.

"You're serious about her son, aren't you?"

"Absolutely, she's the best thing that's happened to me in a long time and I want it to keep happening."

"Your mum likes her too. The pair of them had a right girlie chat over dinner last night and she scored highly on the prospective daughter-in-law check-list. She seems pretty special to me too. Feminine, good-looking, and smart as anything. If the pair of you do take it to the next level, there'll be no objections from me. The pair of you are good together and I'd welcome her as my daughter-in-law."

"Thanks Dad. I didn't realise we'd been under the microscope, but then I know the pair of you, so I'm not totally surprised."

*

Over breakfast on Sunday morning Katya looked at Luc and said. "You've seen my business in London. Will you show me yours? I have an idea."

"Sure, no problem, although there won't be so much going on as it's Sunday morning."

*

A twenty-minute drive from the Kruger's' compound, Luc pulled up and parked beside about two dozen other cars in front of a featureless three-storey building with a small name board above a large security door that simply stated LKS (Pty) Ltd. "Looks exciting." said Katya.

"'Luc Kruger Security,' with a building made to look as nondescript as possible. Look at the top floor - it isn't a real floor; it's just four side walls without a roof. It's a shield for our satellite dishes and is covered over with camo-netting dollied up to make it look like a proper roof when seen from the air," said Luc. "We deal in computer security which, if widely advertised, would make us a target for all the bad guys in town. The only hint of our activity is the number of cars parked outside. We are in operation 24/7, which could suggest that something interesting might be going on inside. Our cover story is that we're working for the government, which isn't a complete lie as we do some work for the intelligence services. Anyway, it seems to discourage all but the most inquisitive and they don't get to hear anything important anyway. The whole building is RF shielded as well so no-one can sit outside with a scanner and see what's going on inside."

"I thought your real business was in camo-clad ex-special forces guys with machine pistols?"

"That's still an important bit of our business - the Executive Services Division, it's called, but it's centred about a hundred miles north-east of here, up near Ceres, where we have our training camp – a bit like Camp 25 to look at - but about twenty times the size, hilly and without a drilling rig. Hennie runs it on a day-to-day basis and we have the facilities there to train our men for everything from close protection duties through targeted extractions and covert operations, to perimeter defence, as you saw up in Mozambique.

"It's not nearly as profitable as computer security and there's a lot of serious competition. Our government has trained tens of thousands of combat-ready veterans but very few computer security experts.

"Let's go inside."

*

Luc lifted a matte blue flap on the side of the door to reveal the outline of a handprint on an underlying sensor plate and placed his right hand over it. The sensor buzzed and the door slid aside to let them into a holding vestibule about the size of a large office lift. The outer door closed behind them. Luc looked up into the lens of a camera facing them and spoke. "Luc Kruger with a guest." There was a pause for a few seconds before the inner door slid back to let them into a reception area.

"Very impressive," said Katya.

"If you're in the computer security business, it makes sense to keep your Operations Room secure. If any bad guys get past the outside door, we can knock them down in the vestibule."

"How?"

"We can just flood it with nitrogen gas. They can't smell it and they'd collapse within seconds. We then flush out the nitrogen and disable them as soon as they fall over and before they come to or die of suffocation. Cheap, non-toxic and very effective."

They walked over to the reception desk, where Luc signed her in and she was given a visitor pass. "All very official," said Katya.

"If I don't play by the rules, how can I enforce them on others? Let's go, and I'll show you round."

They went through a door behind the reception desk and came out on a platform overlooking a large, windowless air-conditioned room containing around fifty work stations, more than half of them manned, and with a large screen on the end wall.

"This is where we test out the security patches we offer for our clients' systems before we send them out. Downstairs is where our real specialists spend all their time hacking into people's websites and their enterprise software.

If you meet with a company and tell them that you don't think their systems are secure and that an enterprising hacker can get in and do them serious damage, the first reaction is usually disbelief. You then say that you can demonstrate their vulnerability and once you have done so and alerted them to what you have done, you can usually sell them a high-end security package."

"Isn't that a bit unethical?"

"Not really. We don't do any damage and we do prove their system really is vulnerable. If they don't buy from us, then at worst, we've given them a wake-up call. But nine out of ten companies approached like this will eventually buy a security package from us."

"Neat."

"Let's go down to the brains of our operation, or what I call Hacker Central."

He went through another door and down a flight of steps into a smaller but similarly styled basement room, with around a dozen workstations, all manned by young men. "Behold the South African criminal rehabilitation programme in action. Nearly all these youngsters have been referred to us by the courts. Our part of the deal is to reform them into IT-savvy assets for South African industry and commerce. What they all have in common is that they've all been convicted of hacking into important networks."

"Aren't you taking a bit of a risk?"

"Not really. They spend a week with Hennie up at Ceres before they come here, and they're suitably house-trained by then. After all, why should they complain? The Government pays for their pocket money, board and lodgings and gives them the chance to spend their days doing what they love - using high-end computers to hack into companies' computer systems without risking a prison sentence. It is impressed on them that going over to the dark side means an instant transfer to Pollsmoor Maximum Security Prison, where they'll spend their time as 'bitches' for the bigger and nastier gang members inside, until they either die of internal injuries or commit suicide. Pollsmoor has a hell of a reputation so we haven't had a single failure in the three years we've been operating."

"Isn't that where Mandela spent some time?"

"Yes, and he wasn't a great fan."

"How did you get into this anyway? It seems a long way from soldiering or prospecting."

"One of my officer pals ended up running part of the prison system and we were discussing a couple of beers one evening when he mentioned the difficulty they had in dealing with computer hackers. The prison system just couldn't deal with them; they were mostly nerds rather than thugs and the fatalities among them were unacceptable. If only there was a way of rehabilitating them and harnessing their skills profitably.

"That's when I had my light-bulb moment. Computer systems and the Internet were just taking off in South Africa and I thought that Internet security could be worth a punt. After all, you didn't need to know any of the technicalities; you just needed to recruit people who did. It was still security, just rather less physical. As you can see, it has worked out well for us with the financial support of the Government and the dramatic increase in hacking from all quarters, both domestic and foreign.

The government is getting worried as well: could hackers disable our power supplies? Could they interfere with police and military communications? Could they blackout air traffic control? All possibilities that keep our security chiefs awake at night"

As she was taking this all in, she had a sudden thought. "Could your guys here hack into the Chinese Ministry of Commerce in Beijing?"

"Probably, but I'd need a fluent Mandarin speaker."

"How about Benny Kim from Piet's operation?"

"Yes, he'd be ideal if Piet could release him for a few days. What do you have in mind?"

"It occurs to me that we might hack into their emails and keep up to date on their plans for the rare earths business."

"Have you any idea what the Ministry's email volume is?"

"No, is it a lot?"

"I don't know, but my guess is that the daily flow will run into the tens of thousands."

"Is that a problem?"

"Not in principle, but it means committing a lot of expensive resources to a single project without a client standing by to pick up the bill."

"What does it entail?"

"You basically hack into their main email server and save copies of all their incoming and outgoing mails to a hard disk in here. You quickly end up with terabytes and terabytes of data, at least 99.9% of which is irrelevant junk from our point of view. You then 'mine' it for relevant data. You need to write a program that looks through all the emails for key words or phrases such as 'Mozambique' or 'Eusebio' or 'rare earth' or 'neodymium' or 'de Bruin' and pulls these emails to one side for detailed evaluation later. Tedious, resource-intensive but usually revealing."

"Presumably you could run it backwards and use it to insert misinformation which would give us a real advantage in protecting our project?"

"Yes – not a bad idea at all. You are a devious lady. I saw what you arranged with the paperwork we retrieved from Marange, so I'm happy to go along with the idea, provided we can get hold of Benny Kim. I'll give Piet a call tonight, once I've seen you off at the airport.

"Now let's go and have a spot of lunch, followed by a sunshine session to top up your tan prior to flying back to a cold and wintry London to sort out your problems."

*

Luc drove them to a restaurant on Camps Bay called The Codfather, Seafood and Sushi. "Ignore the corny name; it does tremendous fresh seafood and the views are spectacular."

Seated at a table on the veranda, looking out over Table Bay to the South Atlantic, and sipping a chilled Cape Sauvignon while perusing the menu, Katya looked over at Luc and said, "This beats London on several counts, but what's it like in June, July and August?"

"Always nicer than a European winter. - not a bad place to live overall apart from the personal security issues."

Their waiter interrupted them with a plate of huge grilled langoustines, which stopped conversation until the last claw lay on a side plate. This was followed by grilled monkfish with a tomato salad and then coffee.

When the waiter had departed, Luc looked thoughtfully at Katya for a moment and then said, "How would you like to join my board?"

Katya looked surprised, but not very. "What would I bring that you don't already have?"

"Your mindset. You are a trader by instinct, which means you are also a bit of a gambler and always looking for ways to adjust the odds in your favour, to give yourself the advantage. By comparison, at LKS our personnel are largely linear thinkers, setting an objective and plodding towards it, bashing our way through, round, over or under the obstacles to get there. I sometimes think that your nirvana deal would be where a client falls over in excitement at being able to pay you a premium for the sheer, unadulterated pleasure of buying from you."

"True, although I don't see it quite like that. I just get upset if I don't succeed in squeezing the last cent out of a deal. I absolutely hate losing, don't you?"

"Of course, but you seem to have a laser-like instinct for the chink in an opponent's armour and the ability to press your advantage home without them realising what you've done until it's too late – if ever. I was watching you when we were negotiating with Eusebio You picked on his need to have a good technical and environmental story to back up his decision, while Piet used his vanity to get him on board for a relatively trivial sum of money – up front at least. The pair of you were like a good tennis doubles partnership, each seeing where the other was going before a word was uttered and moving to cover or reinforce as appropriate. These are skills we need to develop in LKS and that is why I would like to add you to my team."

"Who else do you have on your board?"

"Well, Piet is my non-exec Chairman – no surprise there then - and I have a banker pal of his, Jack Dupree, as my CFO, and I see you sitting in there as Commercial Director."

"What's Dupree like?"

"Fifty-ish and from the same school as Piet, rigorous when he needs to be but unlike most of his ilk, his view of business development isn't driven just by what he sees in the rear-view mirror. He's very forward looking, a strategic thinker and has helped me a lot. What do you say?"

"Thank you very much. I'm interested in principle, but I need to sort out what's happening in London before I can say yes or no. Can you give me a few days?"

"Sure. Let's get back to the pool while we've still got time."

*

As her 747 Jumbo reached cruising altitude and the seat-belt signs went off,

Katya accepted a glass of fizz, tilted her seat to a more relaxed position and began to review the events of the last week. *The news from London was worrying, especially as she didn't know the details of their exposures and liabilities on their forward contracts. That would have to wait until the morning. She just hoped that Marijke and David had acted to cover them, but no use worrying before she had the facts.*

Luc was the big surprise. They'd never discussed his business before, and it had turned out to be much bigger and more sophisticated than she'd expected. She might have guessed, as he didn't go around telling people how wonderful he was, but acted instead when necessary, and only then. She liked that.

But to join his board? That was superficially attractive, but she wasn't sure if she could deliver the kind of performance she thought he would expect, as well as running KF Trading. Maybe she should offer him a seat on her board? He would certainly be good at sourcing product, but she felt confused by the intermingling of her feelings for him as a lover and as a business partner.

Meanwhile, the Mozambique project seemed to be moving to a satisfactory conclusion. Her share of the eventual sale of the claim would mean that even if KF Trading were brought down by the current market turbulence, she wouldn't be left poor.

Pulling the airline blanket over herself, she shut her eyes and fell asleep.

*

CHAPTER 32

Arriving at a dark, cold and wet Heathrow early on Monday morning, she was pleased to see that someone, probably Jean, had arranged a limo to take her into town. Stopping first at her apartment, she asked the driver to wait while she had a quick shower, two cups of coffee and changed.

Dropped off at her offices, she walked upstairs and into reception. Jean was at her desk. "Welcome back, Boss. I hope you had a good flight because today looks to be very hectic. Marijke, David and Mark are already in the boardroom waiting for you."

"Hmmm – is there anything I should have a look at before I go and join them?"

"Not really. I think meeting with the team should take priority over everything else."

"OK! But I need coffee and something to eat. Airline food is awful. Can you rustle me up a couple of croissants, butter and jam?"

"Will do."

KATYA'S CHALLENGE

Walking into the boardroom she sensed gloom interwoven with pleasure to see her again.

"Feels like someone's just died," she said.

"Hi Katya!" they chorused before looking awkwardly away.

"Well, you'd better bring me up to date. My preference, as you know, is to get the bad news on the table first, in the hope that there might be some good news to follow. David, where do we stand?"

"Well, we're contracted to buy around sixty million dollars' worth of metals over the next three months and Mark tells me that the actual market for around a third of it has just disappeared or will have by the time we expected to sell it. So as of this morning we have an exposure of that amount, unless Mark can find another home for it in time."

"Well, Mark?"

"As of this minute the answer is that I don't know, and with German Magnets moving to China, I'll bet the Brits and French won't be far behind. What I will be doing as soon as this meeting ends is hitting the phones to see what their plans are."

"Do it! Now, Marijke, how much of our contracted metal can we cancel without penalty?"

"I spent yesterday afternoon going through the contracts with a fine-tooth-comb and we can certainly drop the German Magnets order without penalty. That leaves us with forty million dollars' worth that would cost us a contract cancellation penalty of around 10% of last months' average price, say four million."

"David, can we cope with that?"

"Not without the bank's help. As I see it, if they don't help us and if Mark can't sell the stock, we're going to go bust."

"But not immediately?"

"No, and it depends on Mark's skills as to whether we do or not and whether the prices hold up. If they go into a nosedive, we could be well and truly stuffed in short order."

"So much for our idea of trying to pull off a market squeeze. It looks as if there won't be enough market left for us to squeeze. We'd better unwind as much of that as we can without penalty. OK! Let's stop here. Without your input, Mark, we'll just end up recycling the gloom. Go and see what you can do. Let's re-convene at the same time tomorrow and see where we stand. Meanwhile, Marijke, will you please cancel our forward commitment on DM's metal?

"Good. Thanks everybody; we will find a way through, I'm sure."

As she left the conference room, Jean grabbed her, saying that Inspector Harris had been looking for her on Thursday and Friday and twice already this morning. "I might as well speak to him then. Can you get him on the line for me?"

As she sat down behind her desk, the phone rang. "Katya Francis here; is that you, Inspector Harris?"

"Yes, and am I glad to hear your voice. You obviously took my warning to heart. This guy Mampata is bad news and we are pretty certain that his invite was part of a plot to take you out of circulation. We're only not sure as to whether that would be temporarily or permanently."

"How did you find out?"

"You know your little Chinese trader friend down the road?"

"Yes."

"Well, we've been monitoring him pretty closely and there was an interesting exchange of emails between his office and Beijing where he was asked whether he thought 'the trader woman' would take up a sourcing invitation from the DRC, where they would be able to deal with her. He said he thought you would and that is why Mampata contacted you – and why we contacted you in turn."

"I liked the yellow fever touch, very creative, I'll always think of them now as yellow fever. But it wasn't just your warning I received. My friends in South Africa received a more urgent notice from their security people saying that no-one, absolutely no-one, from our group should be travelling to the DRC, as we were all on a Chinese shit list and at grave risk of being 'disappeared' if we went there.

Now my natural response to being told that I shouldn't do something is to go right ahead and do it, but I thought that two independent and serious warnings couldn't be ignored, so here I am back in London."

"I'm glad. This is turning out to be a complex business you're mixed up in."

"Fairly complex. We've beaten the yellow fever lot on the ground for the moment, but something tells me they haven't gone away and that we'll be hearing from them again. We're taking steps to find out just who is driving this and I expect to be able to tell you more by the end of the week."

"That would be very helpful of you. Well, we'll keep a watching brief over you. HMG would like your project to succeed."

With that he broke the connection and Katya called Jean into her office. "You'd better take me through what else has been happening in my absence."

*

Tuesday morning dawned with flurries of snow falling from clouds that looked like week-old bruises hanging over London. *Lovely,* she thought to herself, looking out of the window while getting dressed. She'd picked up fresh bread, orange juice, milk, eggs and coffee the night before and made herself an omelette with toast and coffee for breakfast. Putting the dishes in the dishwasher, she summoned a taxi, pulled on her overcoat, tucked her laptop into her shoulder bag and went downstairs to wait for it.

Arriving at KF Trading, she went straight into her office, with a brief "Morning" to Jean, to look at the overnight faxes. *Not much comfort there,* she thought before heading for the conference room.

"Morning all, where's Mark?"

"He'll be with us in a couple of minutes," said Marijke. "He was deep in discussion with someone as I passed his office just now."

"David, do you have anything that would cheer us up?"

"Not really, our current financial exposure remains covered, but I have a nagging worry that German Magnets is simply a bellwether of the coming storm. Let's face it, our volume customers operate in the magnetics and special alloys industries. Correct me if I am wrong, but these are not particularly sophisticated technologies and it would be relatively easy to relocate their manufacture to China. Mark said there wasn't much IP involved – after all a day's work in a decent analytical lab will let anyone identify the metals contained and their ratios. Anyone who knows a bit about metallurgy and knows what they're doing can make identical products."

"Mark! Do you have any good news for me?"

"Sorry guys, no. I've just come off the phone with Clarissa at Ingus Intelligence to see what she knows. She says they're getting strong signals from China to the effect that the authorities are working on an all-out charm offensive to get Western manufacturers to set up shop in China, or at the very least buy their rare earth-containing products like lasers and device screens from Chinese manufacturers."

"Does she think it's working?"

"Yes, she'd heard about German Magnets and agrees with you that this is perhaps the first of many."

"Well!" said Katya. "It sounds as though our business is really under threat and we need to batten down the hatches now, especially where our long-term contracts are concerned. We daren't let our forward exposures get out of hand. Marijke let's cancel every open order that isn't backed by a customer order. I know it may lead to some late deliveries, but our inventories should keep us going with the requirements of the customers who do remain loyal. Who would you put in that category, Mark?"

"Right now, I'd include the defence, chemical and aerospace companies, together with the clever end of the semiconductor, laser, and glass businesses. They're our 'bankers' in this because getting a new source of supply approved costs them a fortune and takes an age, so they'll stay with us – for now anyway."

"How much does that mean in business terms, David?"

"If our worst-case scenario unfolds, we'll be down around 40% on turnover but only 25% on gross profit."

"It's survivable?"

"Yes, Katya, if we're careful and work hard with our remaining key customers."

"I'd love to hold an open day schmooze fest for them, but I guess that's impractical."

"Too right! And it goes against all you've dinned into us about never letting two customers rub shoulders together if they know we supply them both. You only ever get grief that way, usually in terms of reduced margins. Why don't we put a "KF Trading Roadshow' together and tote it around our key customers to demonstrate what a wonderful outfit we are and why going elsewhere for supplies would be a high risk strategy?"

"Not a bad idea. Get together with couple of the traders and put a story-board together for me.

But back to our immediate problems, I think I'm beginning to see a way through this particular fog. Let's revisit our strategic plan over the rest of this week and work our way back to taking the initiative, rather than just reacting to events. Let's spend a couple of hours on it this afternoon and every day for the rest of this week. Same time tomorrow, then, for the next step."

*

By Thursday evening, they had the elements of a plan, and more importantly, letters of intent from most of the customers they'd identified as potentially being loyal.

"Well, that's as far as we can take things at this point," said Katya. "You know that we have a parallel activity around the discovery of a rare-earth deposit in Mozambique. The developmental work on extraction and purification of the rare earths contained is being carried out in our labs at Delft University. I'm going over to Holland tomorrow and will be going to the lab to see for myself what progress they're making. Progress reports are one thing but eyeballing the reality is always better. Reports can't answer questions. If this project comes off, it will solve all our problems, but it hasn't yet, so we need to stick closely to the game plan we have just agreed. I'll see you again next week, but please keep me up to the minute with developments while I'm away."

Walking back to her office, she stopped at Jean's desk and asked her to book her on the early morning flight from London City Airport to Rotterdam, open return, and book a hire car. "How long will you be gone?" asked Jean.

"I'm aiming to be back here by Monday lunch time, but it all depends on what I find out when I'm over there."

Back in her office she rang her mother. "Hi Mum, are you and Dad going to be around this weekend?"

"Hi Katya, yes, why are you coming over?"

"I'm coming over to check on our project's progress at the University and thought I'd take the opportunity to spend the week-end with you."

"Wonderful darling, what time will you be here?"

"I'm going to Delft first but should be in Wassenaar by late afternoon. Can you book us into a nice wee restaurant for dinner? We've a lot to catch up on."

Breaking the connection, she wandered out to Jean's desk just as the courier arrived with her tickets and car rental reservation.

"Perfect timing. I'm going to pack up for the day now, go home and get my things ready for an early morning start. Can you call me a taxi, please, and let me know when it arrives?"

*

CHAPTER 33

Pulling up outside the Chemical Technology building in mid-morning, she saw André Ten Berg standing just inside the main door waiting for her with a big smile on his face.

After the usual exchange of greetings, she asked him, "What's happened? You look as though you've just won the Lotto."

"Better than that - on our latest run we've been able to separate and purify all of the individual metals in the crude mixed metal sent up from The Wit to a purity of 99.9%."

"Better than I thought possible – but with what and how much effluent?"

"A dilute aqueous solution of sodium nitrate containing less than 10ppm[14] other REE metals, pH 6.8, very benign."

"Amount?"

"Around one litre per kilo of REE."

---

[14] 10ppm = parts per million, or 0.001%

"How does this fit with local effluent discharge regulations?"

"At that level, we can freely discharge it to sewer without penalty."

"That's wonderful. Very well done to you and the team."

André smiled and said, "Yes, it's a really good bit of applied science at the 100 gramme level."

"How about scaling it up to the one-, five- and 10-kilo levels?"

"I've no doubts about the process; it is simply a matter of being able to manufacture the mol. sieves in sufficient quantity under sufficiently controlled conditions to generate the required pore structure."

"Difficult?"

"Not really. It simply requires 100% attention to the process as it progresses, keeping temperatures and reactant concentrations precisely controlled and so on. So yes, we can do it, but it will take some time."

"How many cycles will the mol. sieves stand and how much can you manufacture?"

"Well, the test sieves so far have been put through nearly 1,000 cycles, with no loss of capacity and with our existing kit we can make around 100 grammes per day. Thijs has designed a larger version with a capacity of 2 to 2.5 kilos per day. We should be able to make enough sieve materials to run the process at the one-kilo level within a week, five kilos in four weeks and 10 kilos in seven."

"This means you could prove the process at the 10-kilo level within a couple of months?"

"If all goes to plan."

"Given what you have achieved so far, I have no doubt that it will. Now, let's go for a bit of lunch and then go over the patent applications."

"I have a better idea; why don't I send out for some finger food and stuff and we can lunch together with the team and answer each other's questions?"

"Good idea. I should have thought of that."

*

Over lunch Katya congratulated them on their progress to date and asked how long they thought it would take to scale the process up to treat one tonne of metal in an eight-hour shift.

Thijs looked reflective for a moment before saying, "If the small scale-up steps go according to plan, then we should be able to demonstrate a one tonne process within six months."

"And beyond that?"

"My advice would be to install as many one tonne lines as you need to match your throughput requirements. My guess is that scaling up to 5, 10 or 50 tonnes per day will take quite a while and with parallel lines installed and producing, you should be able to generate a big enough positive cash-flow to fund the project while the additional process development work continues."

"Good thinking."

"By the way, are you serious about offering us continued employment in developing the process once this laboratory programme is complete?"

"Absolutely, your acquired experience and your specialised know-how of the technology cannot be replicated easily, and you are an excellent team, as the last few months have demonstrated. Even if the commercialisation of the ore body were to be undertaken by another business, you would still be key to its eventual success, so don't worry on that score."

There were smiles around the table at that, and a relaxed and cheerful atmosphere as the remaining food was eaten.

*

Katya and André spent the afternoon going through the patent applications, tweaking them here and there so that although they protected their work, they also inserted sufficient misdirection to make it difficult or expensive for anyone trying to use the eventually published patents as a route to effectively copy their process. "Nothing like putting the odd bear trap on the paths your competitors may use," said Katya.

As they were finishing up André said, "Well, that's progress. We can go ahead and file them now. I think I'll ask Anneke to come in for an hour or so tomorrow morning to help me finish these off ready for filing with the patent attorneys on Monday."

"A Dutchman working overtime on a Saturday?" She smiled at him.

"Unusual, I agree," he said, smiling back, "but I do want to be able to shift the files from the 'pending' to the 'completed' tray."

"OK, I'm leaving now but I'm not flying back to London until Monday morning so please call my mobile if you need anything."

*

Katya arrived at her parent's house shortly after five o'clock and her mother opened the door and gave her a big hug.

"It's lovely to see you again, dear. How did it go on your travels? Oh, and what would you like to drink?"

"A glass of pinot noir if you have it, and how have you been?"

"Pretty good, but let's get the wine sorted and we can sit down and chat. Your Dad won't be home until later, there's apparently a bit of a flap on at the office. By the way, I've booked us a table at Mero's. You still like fish, don't you?"

"Absolutely, it's always my choice when travelling and usually when I'm not."

"Since we were over in London our social life has perked up. Last Friday we went up to Amsterdam for a night out. Your dad had booked us in for a gorgeous all Tchaikovsky concert with the Berliner Philharmoniker at the Concertgebouw, followed by a late dinner at the Oesterbar, which was wonderful, and overnight in the Okura. It was lovely to have breakfast served in our room again without having first to get up and make it. A bit like the old days, although your Dad used to say that the real downside of working in places like Nigeria was the total absence of European culture."

"But life's good?"

"Of course, dear. Now tell me, how's your attractive South African boyfriend? From what I remember you saying, you seemed to like him a lot."

"I do, and I haven't felt like this about any man since I left Cambridge. He's a real man but for some reason he doesn't act all alpha with me. In fact, he can be very romantic and allows me to take the lead when I want to. I think he's a keeper; the only difficulty is the way we each earn our living.

You know what my business is like in London and how I travel the world to pick up market knowledge and deal with customers and suppliers. Luc, on the other hand, is in the security business: tough guys in camos with guns on the one hand and a nondescript-looking, secure IT building on an industrial estate on the edge of Cape Town on the other. The tough guys are based on a training camp around 100 miles north-east of Cape Town run by Luc's number two, Hendrick Coetzee. The Cape Town building houses a bunch of convicted computer hackers who are being 'rehabilitated' by Luc on government money with the objective of turning them into highly capable IT specialists ready for employment by the big South African companies."

"Sounds interesting."

"It is, very. Now the tough guy side of the business is in decline - too much competition, too many freelancers, too little profit - but the computer security business is growing rapidly and very profitable. However, South Africa is a relatively small market with restricted international links. Do you know if the Dutch government spends cash in this area?"

"I haven't have a clue, but I can find out easily enough. Cyber-crime is mentioned nearly every day in the papers, especially in the Financiele Dagblad."[15]

"I didn't know you were into the stock market."

"I have suddenly realized that when your father retires, he'll want to go sailing, while I'm not

---

[15] Dutch equivalent of the Financial Times or The Wall Street Journal

quite so keen. With his retirement funds and our savings, we'll be quite well-off, and I've decided that I want us to stay that way. Your father always says that if you want to get the best out of your advisers, you needed to have a clear idea of your strategy and learn as much as you can about their speciality. So I read the financial press every day and I'm starting a course down the road on investment management in January."

"I'm impressed, and very well done."

"But to return to the matter at hand, if I understand my daughter correctly, you reckon the tough guy business is reaching the end of the commercial line while the cyber-security business is a real growth area and you are looking for an opportunity, either here or in the UK, that would persuade Luc to leave South Africa and come to Europe so that life together would be a practical proposition."

"As incisive as ever, Mother; you know me too well. There's a certain amount of urgency to this, as my business is under pressure from the Chinese and I can't spend too much time away from it."

Looking at her watch, Saskia said, "The taxi will be here in twenty minutes, so if you want to freshen up. . ."

"Thanks, I'll do that. Do I need to dress up?"

"Smart casual is the order of the day."

*

Over a lobster dinner and a bottle of Cape Sauvignon Blanc they talked about the way their lives were changing, with Saskia becoming an investment expert.

"Who knows? If I get good at it, I could maybe start a business as an investment adviser. There are lots and lots of wealthy people within a five-kilometre radius of where we're sitting. As you know, we Dutch like value for money, and I would be able to help them get it – for a fee.

"Given your business problems and the prospect of riches if the Mozambique deal goes through, wouldn't you be better served by changing the focus of your trading to another commodity? After all, it sounds as though you would have plenty of cash to cover the transition."

"I really don't know. Although I'm a professional trader, I'm still a techie underneath it all and the rare earths business is full of technical challenges which I delight in solving."

"Yes, but I remember your dad quoting a colleague in Shell Chemicals who used to say that the more technically interesting a bit of chemistry was, the smaller the chance of making any money out of it."

"Possibly, but I haven't done so badly so far, and I think we can weather this particular storm. I need to think about it."

As they were paying the bill and waiting for their taxi, Katya's mobile rang. It was André calling from the laboratory.

"Oh Katya, you need to come; there has been an attack on our lab."

*

CHAPTER 34

The taxi took them first to drop her mother off and Katya said she'd just take it on to Delft and see what the problem was. "I don't know how long I'll be so don't wait up. I'll see you in the morning."

"But Katya, will you be all right?"

"Don't worry, Mum, it's probably just some opportunist crooks and André says the Rijkspolitie are handling it. Nothing to worry about there then."

She gave the driver his instructions and asked him to go as quickly as possible, as she had an emergency to deal with.

Twenty-five minutes later the taxi tried to pull up in front of the Chemical Technology building but found the way blocked by a couple of police cars with their blue lights flashing. Paying off the taxi, she walked over to the policeman guarding the entrance to the building, identified herself and was permitted to go inside. To her surprise the first officer she encountered was a tall Koninklijke Marechaussee[16]

---

[16] The Koninklijke Marechaussee: The Netherlands' national para-military police force whose remit includes

Major built like a second-row rugby forward. He stuck out his right hand and identified himself as Major Janssen.

After identifying herself, she asked, "Major, what's happened and why are the Marechaussee involved and not the local police?"

"The local police were called out by campus security, who then called us when they attended the crime scene. As keyholder, we called Professor Ten Berg here to tell him of the attempted break-in. He told us that you were the Technical Director of the laboratory here and were staying locally and asked that you be contacted forthwith." André looked at her with a sheepish smile, shrugged his shoulders and looked back at the major.

Bloody wonderful! thought Katya. *Running to mummy at the first sign of trouble. It's not as if he isn't well enough paid, and he's supposed to be the man in charge of the laboratory. I shall have words with him later.*

"As soon as the name of Ms Katya Francis was entered onto our system, lights started to flash, and we were advised that the AIVD should be contacted if anything unlawful pertaining to you or your interests should happen. So there you are and here we are. What can you tell us?"

---

terrorism, cross-border crime and the policing of Dutch military units at home and abroad.

"Major Janssen, what can you tell me? I have no idea what has happened and am unable to tell you anything until I know what did happen."

"I can't tell you a lot, except that we have arrested a couple of Chinese men who were trying to break into your laboratories with the aid of an angle-grinder on the door."

"Did they succeed – in breaking in, I mean?"

"No, your door appears to be made of stronger stuff than usual and they seem to have burned out three grinder discs before they were caught."

"Well, our security company seem to have done a good job then. I assume that the noise, vibration and fumes from the grinder triggered the alarm and that's why we're all standing here."

"What goes on in those labs and why might they be the target of Chinese criminals?"

"Before I answer, can you tell me whether they've invoked diplomatic immunity yet?"

"Diplomatic immunity?"

"Don't worry, they will, probably as soon as you take them down to the police station and try and take their fingerprints."

"Look, come on upstairs with me, look at the damage and please tell me what the hell is going on here."

*

Walking down the corridor to the laboratories, they could smell burnt paint and resin, with an overlay of hot metal, hanging in the air. As they got nearer, it became clear that the door had been under serious attack. The areas around the lock and hinges were scarred and blackened while segments of broken grinding disc lay on the floor. The underlying door itself seemed undamaged.

"What kind of a door is that?" asked Janssen.

"It's a metal/ceramic composite that was developed around five years ago but never commercialised outside the military because it is almost impossible to drill, grind or cut – as you can see. This door had to be fabricated exactly to size, with all the necessary bolt, screw and handle holes in place. Outside the military, you'll only ever see it in high-value, high-security applications like this door."

She looked into the lens of the retinal scanner beside the door, which the would-be intruders appeared to have neglected. There was a whirring sound, followed by the thud of bolts being withdrawn. She pushed the door and it swung open with a slight creaking sound. She entered and looked around. Nothing appeared to have been interfered with or damaged. *Thank God for Luc's security obsession,* she thought. Turning back to André and a somewhat astonished Major Janssen, she asked them to come in.

"That is some security," he said. "What is this all about anyway?"

"The Chinese supply most of the specialised metals used in the manufacture of modern electronics and have started to squeeze supplies of these to the Western companies making everything from mobile phones to TVs, turbine generators and computers. We think their game plan is to tell these companies that supply would not be a problem if they would just set up manufacturing plants in China, at which point it would be almost impossible to protect their intellectual property and know-how. Wind the clock forward a few years and the Chinese would dominate the world market for electronics and have us all over a barrel."

"That doesn't sound good."

"No. Now my colleagues and I have discovered a new deposit of these specialised metal ores in Africa and are working on turning our discovery into a commercial reality using the ground-breaking, proprietary purification technology being developed in here, hence the high level of security. The Chinese have found out what we are up to and have made several attempts to disrupt our operations and steal our technology. Given the potential value of our work for the West, various intelligence agencies have decided to watch over us and that is why you are here and not the local police."

"Now I understand. Since the intruders failed to get in, all I can do is focus on the intruders and see what additional information I can get out of them."

"I wish you luck with that. As I said earlier, I am willing to bet that they will have claimed diplomatic immunity by breakfast time and your only sanction will be to have them declared 'persona non-grata' and deported by the middle of the week. There will obviously be some fluttering in the diplomatic dovecots, but your government will surely extract some minor concession from them and that will be that."

"Shit! I'd better get on with it then and see what I can get out of them first. In the meantime, are you OK?"

"Yes, I'm fine Major.

André, can you make sure that nothing has gone missing or been damaged?"

A quick check of the laboratory showed no evidence that the attempted break-in had succeeded. Nothing was damaged apart from the paintwork on the security door and everything was exactly where it had been that evening when the lab had been shut down for the weekend.

André then asked her, "Can I run you home?"

"If it doesn't take you too far out of your way, I'd appreciate it.

Major, thanks for your prompt action. I now have a lift home and will say goodnight."

"A pleasure and thank you for telling me what this is all about. Good night and good luck."

*

When André dropped her off at her parent's door, she told him she'd report the attempted break-in to Luc and that he could expect someone from his security organisation to turn up during the week and check that the door was still able to do the job for which it had been designed.

"I'm going back to the UK on Sunday evening, but I'll be in touch on Monday to let you know what's happening. Thanks for the lift and goodnight."

Fishing her keys out of her bag, she opened the front door silently, removed her shoes and tiptoed through to the lounge picked out a bottle of Armagnac, poured herself a large one and took it upstairs to bed.

*

"Morning Katya, are you OK? I waited up until after two o'clock but had to go to bed, as my eyes were shutting. What was all that about last night?"

Katya blinked at the morning sunlight flooding the room. "Yes Mum, I'm fine. A couple of intruders tried unsuccessfully to break into our laboratory, the alarm went off and I ended up having to explain things to a nice Marechaussee Major who had been called out to the scene of the crime."

"Marechaussee? How come they were involved?"

"It's all down to the fact that the government views our project as important to long-term national security and keeps a watchful eye on the comings and goings of anyone trying to interfere with our work."

"This is much bigger and more important than I thought. Do be careful, my dear.

I'm afraid you've missed you father again, he didn't get home until midnight, and was up and away first thing. There's apparently a big licensing deal going down and his input to the negotiations is critical"

*

After a late breakfast, she called Luc and brought him up to date on the night's events. "Your security door did a good job. The intruders broke several angle-grinder wheels trying to break into the lab and, apart from some scratches, only succeeded in damaging the paintwork."

"I told you it was tough."

"Yes, and now I believe it. The intruders were caught in the act and turned out to be a couple of Chinese - from their embassy, I think. My guess is they'll be claiming diplomatic immunity prior to being deported."

"So now they're using their own people rather than sub-contracted locals. It shows that they must be getting desperate. It also shows that they're inept. They attack Camp 25 without a proper reconnaissance, they attack you in London without realising who they're up against, they send a squad of soldiers up to Camp 25 in a battlefield helicopter which gets blown to bits, and now this! I cannot believe it. They're normally well-prepared and skilled in the dark arts. My guess is that they've tried to do everything 'below the radar' and thus be deniable if it goes wrong, but you do need to scope out your target and find its weak spots before you can hope to attack it successfully. I guess that they've prioritised secrecy over effective execution.

I think I'll come up for a few days this coming week, have a look at the damage and see if there is somewhere nearby we could set up a genuinely secure laboratory. Piet and I have been talking about the point you made, about how the purification technology could be an industry game-changer. We agree and we want to pour more resources into speeding up the development. Selling the rights to the deposit will bring a nice cash pay-out, but licensing income from the technology could last for years, keeping us all in the style to which we would like to become accustomed."

"I agree, Luc, but I think we should hive it off into a separate business, say KLP Holdings, registered in somewhere like Labuan, Cyprus, or even Delaware in the US, which would be the holding company for a separate IP licensing company and a second one developing separation and purification technology."

"Labuan - where's that?"

"It's an offshore financial centre on an island just off Sabah and is legally a Malaysian Federal Territory."

"Isn't that a bit near China?"

"Not a problem; the only physical asset we would have there would be a brass plate in the lobby of one of the international accountancy firms. If you set up an offshore company there you can't employ anyone in the country, but it's got strong secrecy laws, an international banking and accountancy infrastructure, very low corporation tax and you can park your profits there without risk until you decide what you want to do with them."

"Interesting. I see you've been giving it a lot of thought."

"Actually, Delaware would be my favourite but for one thing."

"And what might that be, Miss International Finance?"

"Although there are no taxes payable on non-US business, if you do any business in the US you get involved with their famous IRS and I'd rather not. Why don't you get Ton to look at the options and we can discuss it when you come up? And let me know your flight details and I'll meet you. I'm going back to London tomorrow, as I need a couple of days in the office first, so if you fly into Schiphol on

Wednesday, we can get down to looking for premises then."

"OK darling, I'll see you then."

*

CHAPTER 35

The phone on Minister Zhang's desk rang. When he answered it, his secretary said that an under-secretary from the Ministry of Foreign Affairs was on the line.

"Zhang here, Comrade Under-secretary, what can I do for you?"

"Comrade Minister, there has been a diplomatic incident in The Netherlands. It appears that two men from the Embassy's security detail were caught trying to break into a secure laboratory in Delft University. They were caught by the local police and, on interrogation, have claimed diplomatic immunity, immediately elevating their predicament to my minister's office. This reflects badly on our diplomatic mission in the Netherlands and has the potential to derail negotiations with the Dutch Government on accessing some of their water management technology and expertise.

"The Dutch police have returned the men to our embassy, declared them 'persona non-grata' and have given them three days to pack up and leave the country. Our understanding is that they were acting on instructions originating from your office. My minister would like to know what the hell is going on."

"Perhaps I can meet with your minister and explain."

"My minister is very busy at the moment. Would it not be possible to explain matters in a memorandum?"

"I think not, Comrade. I would rather explain matters face-to-face so that I may answer any further questions he may have without delay."

"Comrade Minister, I will check my minister's availability and let you know."

Putting the phone down, Zhang thought for a minute, then called his secretary, asking her, "Track down the Commercial Attaché at our embassy in the Netherlands and put him through to me immediately."

*

"Comrade Minister, this is Li-Fen, Commercial Attaché at our embassy in the Netherlands. How can I be of service?"

"You can start by explaining to me why two idiots from the embassy not only failed to get into the South Africans' Laboratory in Delft but got caught and have precipitated a diplomatic crisis following explicit instructions to mount a totally deniable operation."

"Comrade Minister, it didn't seem to be a particularly difficult assignment. Break into a laboratory, photograph everything, collect all the paperwork lying about, together with samples of any unusual reagents on view. Destroy any experimental rigs and leave.

"Except it wasn't what they expected, sir. They spent nearly an hour trying to get through the lab door without success - who knows what that is made of, and then the police arrived. They knew they couldn't tell the police the truth about their mission and thought the easiest way out was to claim diplomatic immunity, failing to realise that it would provoke a diplomatic incident and cause them to be expelled from the country."

"Do you only employ incompetents, or were these idiots specially selected for the job?"

"Comrade Minister, I am a most unworthy Commercial Attaché; you have my most abject apology. I have failed you and I have failed the Chinese People's Republic."

"You have indeed, *former* Commercial Attaché Li-Fen. You have caused me and the Ministry and The People's Republic of China to lose face, a lot of face. You will hand over your responsibilities to your deputy and return to Beijing immediately. You are an utter disgrace. Let my secretary know when your plane will arrive in Beijing and I will have you met and brought to my office to explain yourself as soon as possible."

Zhang slammed down the phone, waiting for his summons to the Ministry of Foreign Affairs and wondering how he could defend himself from the inevitable roasting he'd get and how he could live down the loss of face that that idiot had precipitated.

*

"What on earth are you mixed up in, Katya?"

"I'm not mixed up, as you put it, in anything Dad. You know how my rare earth trading business works - well, most of my products now come from China and in the last few months they've put the squeeze on exports, making my business difficult. Their game plan seems to be to sell what they decide to export at very low prices, driving non-Chinese producers to mothball their plants. At the same time, they are offering end users unlimited supplies if they are prepared to set up manufacture in China. Some are willing, mainly those whose products are reasonably simple to make, like magnets. Many are not because of the cavalier attitude that the Chinese have toward patent protection and intellectual property rights, so they are unwilling to set up technically complex manufacturing where all their trade secrets and know-how can be pilfered.

"Coincidentally, Piet de Bruin had financed Luc into prospecting for other rare earth deposits and he has been successful in finding a big one in Mozambique. This is the basis of our project. Unfortunately, the Chinese got to hear about our activities and see us as potential disruptors of their master plan. In turn, they are trying to disrupt our activities, and that is where my difficulties have come from.

"The English, South African and now the Dutch governments have heard about our project and want it to succeed because of the risk to the Western electronics and defence industries posed by the Chinese and their attempts to dominate the global market. Thus, we now have high-level multi-government support and protection for our project. That is why when I went into Delft University yesterday evening, I found the attempted break-in to our labs being dealt with by the Marechaussee and not the local police."

"Hmmm, I'm not totally convinced, but tell me, how come Piet is involved in rare earths? I thought that South Africans were exclusively focused on gold and diamonds."

"They are, but there used to be a significant rare earth mining industry in South Africa which ran down across the 1960s, as the local producers either couldn't or wouldn't adapt to changing market requirements and competition. Piet looked at the possibility of re-opening a couple of these old operations but their legacy issues of ground contamination and the costs of soil remediation and of removing old, rusted and outdated equipment before you could start work convinced him that he'd be better off somewhere outside the country with a totally new deposit – and Luc found one."

"So now you've got well and truly up the noses of the Chinese Government and they are trying to shut you down."

"Yes Dad, but our operations are secure; the door into the Delft laboratories stopped the burglars, no probs. Luc says the only way through it in a reasonable time would be by using something called a thermal lance and you can't carry one of those in your back pocket. Even if you could, the noise, heat, smoke and fumes it gives off would trigger any fire or smoke alarm system."

"I'm not worried about your laboratory; it's you I'm concerned about. I know we lived in some fairly rough places while I was still working in the field, but we always lived in secure compounds and had bodyguards to look after us. You're wandering around on your own and I don't like it. Can't that man of yours provide you with protection?"

"Yes, he can but I don't want to wander around here or in London with bodyguards making me look like some Russian oligarch's poule deluxe. I can look after myself, as I proved in London."

"I'm still not happy. If you don't set it up, I will."

"Look Mum, Dad, I'm going back to London tomorrow to square things off ahead of the holidays, but I'll be back next Tuesday night for Luc, we can discuss it then. OK?"

"OK, but we will discuss it properly – with Luc!"

*

Luc rang Piet to tell him about the attempted break-in to the Delft lab and that he was going to fly up to Holland on Tuesday evening to assess the situation.

"Will you be meeting Katya?"

"Of course."

"Well we need to talk before you go, let's have dinner together this evening, I'll get Mary to book us a table at The Codfather and see you there at seven."

*

With their orders taken and their glasses filled, Piet looked hard at Luc and said: "I have the impression that you're serious about Katya and you will probably meet David and Saskia, mummy and daddy this time around."

Luc looked sheepish for a moment before he said. "Yes Piet, she is very special. I've never met anyone like her. She's gorgeous, bright and brave, and I think I'd like to spend the rest of my life with her."

"You've got a bit of a problem to solve first. Katya's life and her business are centred in London, yours are here in Cape Town. Finding a compromise won't be easy."

"No, it won't. Assuming our Mozambican venture is successful, money won't be an issue. Maybe we can both sell up and go and do something else together."

"That would be a huge step – both of you stepping away from the separate businesses you have each built up over the last few years. You'll have decide on a plan that suits you both, otherwise either you or she will become bitter and twisted about the new path you've chosen. I've really got skin in this game. I have known her since she left school, I've followed her academic career and I helped her get started in her trading business. In many ways she's been the daughter that Molly and I never had. And you know our relationship - I feel that I am a second father to you also. I don't want to see either of you making a decision you'll come to regret, but never forget that you can come to me any time, even just to talk to yourself at me."

"Thanks Dad!"

"I mean it, Luc. You seem to have complementary qualities, and I do think you would make an unstoppable combination, united in a common aim. I just want to do what I can to make sure that it'll work out for both of you.

*

CHAPTER 36

Katya returned to Wassenaar on Tuesday evening and was standing across from the door to the customs hall in Schiphol the following morning as Luc walked through it, pulling a roll-along case. She waited until he cleared the barrier then rushed over and embraced and kissed him.

"Oh Luc, I've missed you so much, darling."

"Me too, lover. But I'm here now and I have news for you. Ton and Piet loved your technology licensing idea and I have decided to open an office either here or in London to test the waters."

"Oh darling, I really like the sound of that; 12-hour flights in between kisses aren't exactly romance friendly."

"Hang on Kat! Nothing's fixed yet!"

"I know but this means that the wheels are turning. Let's get going. I'll give you the details en route." They turned and walked out to the car-park, found her rented Audi, got in and headed down the A4 to Delft.

*

Standing at the lab door, Luc got down on one knee and looked at the places where the intruders had tried to break in. "Yes, it really works," he said taking out his phone and asking her to hold his pocket tape-measure. "You said they had burned out three grinder disks and only got this far?"

"Yes, at least if they wrecked more grinding discs, they weren't lying on the floor."

Taking some photos on his phone, with Katya holding the tape-measure stretched across the damage, he said, "Excellent."

"What is it anyway?"

"The door? It's a high security tungsten/tungsten carbide composite which is very difficult to make or to damage, and bloody expensive with it. You've only got this door because we're evaluating it for the developers. You're looking at around $20,000 for just that door and frame."

After he'd finished checking it out, Katya looked into the retinal scanner, waited for the whirring sound and as soon as she heard the bolts being withdrawn, pushed the door open. André came to greet them and they went into the conference room.

"Coffee, please, André for two thirsty travellers, and can you ask the rest of the team to come in?"

A few minutes later, with everyone sitting around the table looking expectantly at Katya and

Luc, he stood up and said that he understood there had been an attempted break-in on the previous Saturday night. "This has made us re-think this R&D setup. It is handy being situated inside a chemistry department. If you need something in a hurry, it is entirely possible that you can get it in minutes from the departmental stores. But, and this is a very big 'but', site security is poor and we don't control it. Katya and I are going to look at other premises this afternoon somewhere in this area where we can set up a free-standing and secure R&D facility.

"The work you've done looks like providing the platform for a separate technology licensing company selling to REE companies around the world. Of course, this requires an associated technology R&D company to push the technology forward, build our patent portfolio and offer technical support to the licensees. We see your future as the core team of this expanded technology group. Our new premises will be larger than these, with room for the additional staff you will need and with all necessary facilities, yet hopefully within easy commuting distance for you all. Your work has been excellent, so we are willing to inject the necessary funds to let you extend, enlarge and accelerate the programme. We're aiming to build a world-class technology licensing business reaching across the rare-earth industry and into the critical and strategic metals space."

With that he sat down and looked expectantly around the table. A stunned silence filled the room.

André looked around the table, cleared his throat and asked, "Does this mean that our jobs won't just continue but will actually be expanded?"

"Yes, you've done a great job here and we want you to continue, but with a more ambitious programme and more resources to build a more comprehensive technology and patent portfolio. Wherever we choose as our new base, we hope you'll stay with us and build on your achievements to date.

"Now I'm sure you will all have lots of questions. Can you send out for some sandwiches and we can continue this discussion over lunch?"

*

"They seem quite happy," remarked Luc as they drove out of the university campus.

"Yes, so far so good. Have you lined up a commercial estate agent?"

"Yes, I set up an appointment for this afternoon with an outfit called Van Doorn and Hegt. The brief I'm going to give them is to find us a nondescript looking, fully serviced building somewhere in the Rotterdam/Hague area of around 10,000 m^2, complete with permits to operate as a research laboratory."

"That sounds quite big."

"Not really. We're going to construct another building inside it, along the lines of my Internet unit in Cape Town. In other words, an apparently boring bog-standard industrial unit with a high-security inner shell – roof, floor and walls - which will keep out both the curious and those of evil intent."

"How much is that going to cost?"

"Not sure, but we'll have to live within the budget Piet has set."

"How much is that?"

"He hasn't said, but he seems to think that we can take all the kit from the Delft lab to keep costs down."

"It doesn't sound too bad, especially if you can take some of your stuff from Cape Town as well."

"You've seen through my plan."

"What do you mean?"

"To use part of the unit for Internet security."

"Yes, I had got there, and it makes a great deal of sense to put your Internet security and our laboratory operations under one secure roof. Easier to keep secure. But you won't be able to protect half of it in a cellar."

"Why not?"

"As soon as you dig down you'll hit the water table and that'll be that. Most of The Netherlands, especially around here, is at or below sea-level. Unkind foreigners say The Netherlands isn't really a country, so much as a bit of dried-up sea. It does mean we've got the world's best hydraulic engineers."

*

As they drove away from the estate agent's offices, Luc was in pensive mood. "I just hope that guy understood that we're serious. He didn't seem too convinced."

"Oh, I think he understood all right, especially when you detailed what we're looking for. I just don't think he's got anything suitable on his books right now, which means he'll actually have to get off his fat arse and do some work for his fees."

"Maybe. I hope you're right. What's next?"

"Let's head back up to Wassenaar and my folk's place. We can stay there tonight and have dinner. I also know they want to have a serious chat with you."

"Oh, what about?"

"My personal security in light of what's happened over the last few months. No matter what I say, they seem to think their little girl is in ongoing danger and can't look after herself."

"I agree about the danger, and I'm not sure about your ability to defend yourself against all comers either, OK in close combat, as you've demonstrated, and I guess you can handle firearms too, but I'm not sure how you'd cope with a kidnap attempt. Outnumbered, overwhelmed, locked up and then subjected to God knows what. We need to make sure that doesn't happen."

"What would be the point of kidnapping me? I couldn't run a lab for them. I've been away from the bench for too long."

"Yes, but our initial patent applications are due to be published in about fifteen months, unless the Dutch government puts a secrecy order on them. I don't think it's likely, but if they wanted to, they could make a case that the technology had a strategic value in the procurement of advanced electronic warfare systems. This would mean we couldn't file outside The Netherlands and the local filing itself would be secret. Assuming they don't put the block on it, and they are published, you could be kidnapped and made to supervise work in China under duress when that happens. And you only have to look at your attempted entrapment in the DRC by 'yellow fever' operatives to realise that the threat is real. We may hear from Hennie tomorrow or Friday as to who was pushing Mampata's buttons and see who is orchestrating the difficulties we've had to deal with"

*

Minister Zhang tossed and turned in his bed, unable to sleep despite having spent some hours in the soothing company of his favourite mistress and then drinking a whole bottle of Maotai before retiring. The Minister of Foreign Affairs had given him a 'slot' just after four that afternoon and by the time he had finished shouting in Zhang's face, he wondered how long it would be before he was called before the Party's Discipline Inspection Commission for trial and re-education, otherwise known as punishment. There was no doubt that he would be referred to them. The Dutch debacle had made waves outside the cosy coterie of the Politburo and had apparently made the Dutch government extremely angry. Bad for China, bad for trade, bad for Zhang.

The question was: what form would his re-education take? He would lose this apartment, his mistress, his chauffeur-driven car and all the perks that went with high office in the party. The rewards for apparent conformity, for the long years of only saying and doing things in public or private that fitted in with party policy, irrespective of what he actually thought and felt – and all because he tried to stop the South African's project and acquire their assets in support of the Party's plans. But he had failed.

No chance of sleep. Zhang got up from his bed, pushing his sleeping mat onto the floor. He pulled on a robe against the cold and went through to the kitchen. Turning on the light, he took a jug of water from the fridge and drank it all. He thought that if he was lucky, he'd be sent for re-education in the principles and values of the Party. If unlucky, he would end up in a labour camp where even basic survival was not a given.

He decided to get dressed and go in to his office. He would save as much face as possible by working normally until they came for him. They came at mid-day . . .

CHAPTER 37

As they were finishing dinner with Katya's parents, David turned to Luc, saying, "I'm very worried about Katya. Ever since she started working with you and Piet she's been under attack, directly in London and indirectly here and in Africa. She says it's all a Chinese attempt to disrupt your project, but that it is all under control. I don't buy it Luc. Tell me, honestly, how much danger are you in?"

"David, its much less now than it was a couple of months ago. The English, Dutch and South African Security Services know what we are doing and they seem to want our project to succeed because of its strategic implications, so no, I can't say there is no danger, but it is containable and we expect to sell our project on to a big mining company within the next few months. At that point, there will be no risk.

However, your daughter's skills have created a new refining, separation and purification technology which we will be commercialising via a separate licensing company and there will be further risks when that is up and running. Our Chinese friends will want to steal the technology for themselves, and that could be problematic."

"Why don't you just sell them a license too, cut the risk and simplify your lives?"

Katya chipped in, "That's not an altogether bad idea, Dad. Rather than spending money protecting ourselves, we can draw income from the prospective attackers instead. At this point it looks as if the technology will reduce the cost of extracting and refining rare earths to a few dollars per kilo. At that level, Western companies like Molycorp in the States would start coining it, even at the current prices being charged on the limited amount the Chinese are willing to export."

"What do you think, Luc?"

"I'm not sure. We need to sit down with Piet and Ton and work through the whole picture, and we certainly don't want to put the Chinese in a position where we wouldn't be able to sell a license to anyone else."

*

At breakfast Katya asked Luc what he was hoping to do that day.

"I've an appointment with your National Cyber Security Centre later this morning - some guy in the Market Development and Partnerships Division - in the hope that I can get some Government support to transfer my South African business to The Netherlands. We've been in contact over the last week or so and he's invited me to come and talk. I also know he's spoken to some of my government contacts in South Africa, so it shouldn't be a wasted trip."

"Sounds interesting."

"I hope so. Weather, food and wine apart, Cape Town is becoming an unpleasant city to live and work in. Another couple of my parents' friends were attacked last week."

"Serious?"

"It could have been, but their alarm system gave them time to break out their guns and a scare the bastards off with a few 12-bore rounds. It turned out that they'd been given the gate codes by their gardener, or should I say ex-gardener. One of the intruders is in hospital with a load of shot in his hopefully, very sore arse, and the gardener is in jail."

"Where do they live?"

"Just a couple of streets away from my folks. It has certainly shaken them, and I think they could be persuaded to leave now. I just don't know. Anyway, I'd better get ready."

"Where's the meeting?"

"Just down the road in The Hague."

"I'll run you there."

*

Luc came away from the meeting with a smile on his face and walked over to the coffee bar where Katya said she'd wait for him. As she saw him through the window, she came to the door to greet him.

"How did it go, darling?"

"Very well, I think."

"You think?"

"Yes, we seem to have the basis for accreditation to the National Cyber Security Centre, or the NCSC as he kept calling it, but I need to see official confirmation of what was on offer. In my experience, there is frequently a disconnect between meeting-room chat and the eventual official offer."

"I've found that occasionally too. Did they offer you any funding?"

"There is apparently a low-interest, government-backed loan scheme for which we'd be eligible provided I agreed to commit €500,000 for a minimum period of five years."

"Would you?"

"Not sure, let's see what the Brits can offer. Meanwhile, let's have lunch and head to London."

"No point."

"What do you mean?"

"Tomorrow is Christmas Eve and I know you hard working types regard holidays as an irritating diversion, but the UK and most of Europe will be closing down about now until the New Year. There is absolutely no chance, none, rien, nada, keine, zilch, of getting anything meaningful done until the third or fourth of January, which means we've got ten days to relax and have a bit of fun. I don't know about you, but I'm ready for a bit of R&R. Since the beginning of September, my life has been turned upside down. First the Chinese screw up my business by limiting REE exports; then I meet up with you and Piet, leading to the 'Shoot out at the OK Corral' in Mozambique, your hospitalisation, a direct physical attack on me in London, the Delft lab is attacked, there's more trouble in Mozambique and then a plan to kidnap me in the DRC. At least I've not been bored, and a bit of fun is definitely on the cards.

Let's stay here until Boxing Day and celebrate Christmas with Mum and Dad, then head off to Switzerland to ski and bring in the New Year. Bart and Marietta - remember them? - have been going to Davos for the week after Christmas for years and this time Marietta has dug her heels in. After the hellish weather we've been having in London, she's given him an ultimatum: the Caribbean or the divorce courts. Wisely, he's elected for the Caribbean and Marietta has asked me if I'd be interested in taking up their hotel reservation in Davos for a week from the twenty-seventh of the month. Typically, it's a suite facing out to the mountains."

"Sounds OK; what's it like?"

"If Marietta liked it, you and I will. Besides, trying to book a room in a decent pub in Switzerland at a week's notice at Christmas is impossible. Let's do it."

"OK, you win. I could enjoy a break and a Dutch Christmas, followed by a Swiss New Year. Sounds good."

*

CHAPTER 38

David and Saskia were delighted to have Luc and Katya as Christmas guests. After all, they seldom saw Katya at this time of year and Luc's presence was a very welcome bonus. Starting at lunchtime with champagne and festive nibbles, the four of them were soon chattering away when the doorbell rang.

Katya answered it to find Aunt Miep and Uncle Anton on the doorstep.

"Merry Christmas Katya, we thought your mum and dad wouldn't mind if we dropped by and had the chance to meet your Luc, so here we are."

"Great, we're delighted to see you. Come on in."

"Mum, Dad – it's Miep and Anton come to meet Luc!"

Saskia came to the door, kissed them both, led them into the sitting room and introduced Luc.

"Champagne?"

"Please."

KATYA'S CHALLENGE

Luc did the honours and soon they were interrogating him as to who he was, what he did, where he came from and how he had got together with Katya. He took it all in good part and felt very comfortable. They were lovely people, he thought, and obviously loved David, Saskia and Katya.

Miep and Anton left shortly after six, floating on a lake of champagne and wrapped in a cloud of warmth and happiness. Katya went through to the kitchen, where Saskia had prepared some Indonesian dishes that just had to be heated up.

They sat around the kitchen table eating, drinking and putting the world to rights until bedtime.

Curled up next to Luc she asked, "Happy?"

"Yes, it's been a lovely day and I feel that your folks and I have got to know each other a lot better. Saskia's very warm and has quite a sense of humour, which I like."

"When I was helping to put things away after the meal, she told me she thought that you were good for me and that if we ever decided to marry, she'd be very happy."

"Wow! A prospective mother-in-law's blessing – it doesn't get any better than that."

"Idiot! Go to sleep."

*

They spent Boxing Day quietly, with a long walk along the beach, wrapped up against the wind, then back home for mulled wine and a prawn curry, followed by another evening discussing coffee, brandy and the year to come

*

They arrived in Davos early on Monday evening, having had to take a train up from Zurich. The change of name on the booking caused no problems, and as the porter shut their suite door behind him she threw her arms around Luc and kissed him hard. Pulling back, she said, "One whole week and nobody to mess it up for us. Wonderful! I'm going to have a shower and get ready for dinner. The restaurant here has quite a reputation and I'm famished."

*

Back in London, breakfast was early on Tuesday morning, with Luc heading off for a meeting with someone from the National Security and Intelligence Office's cybercrime unit in Whitehall. "I have no idea who this guy is," said Luc, "but it's been arranged through the London office of Piet's accountants and will at least start me on the trail. They claim the Brits can offer some serious grant funding to companies like mine and, interestingly, they have a juvenile programme that sounds kind of like the one in Cape Town 'though I expect your jails are less unpleasant than ours. We'll see."

"Promising," said Katya. "Have you an agent lined up to find premises?"

"Yes, after lunch in a suburb called Ealing."

"I'm afraid I can't come with you, as I need to go into my office, now in fact. I'll see you there around six this evening and then we can go and have a drink and a bite to eat."

Standing up, she went and grabbed her briefcase, kissed him on the lips and headed off saying, "Please lock the door when you leave."

*

When Katya arrived at her office, Mark was waiting for her in reception. "Hi Katya, I think that the clouds are starting to possibly think of trying to consider lifting."

"How?"

"The magnet business may not be dead after all; I've had three of our customers call asking if we can source high-strength magnets for them from China. They don't want to deal with the Chinese directly and the proposal is that they give us specifications and we have them made in China without disclosing the identities of our customers. This could be exactly what we need. I'm still confident that we will keep our 'mission critical' customers, and this could allow us to get back some of the others by acting as procurement agents."

"Have you spoken to Tommy Chung?"

"Yes, I was on to him yesterday morning and he seemed quite enthusiastic."

"Quelle surprise! I imagine that he saw the restrictions on REE trading hitting his commission income and this would be a way to increase it instead. His commission is paid on the FOB[17] value of the shipment, and fabricated goods always cost more than raw materials. It'll help us a lot too. Well done."

*

Jean rang through to Katya's office just before five to tell her that Luc had arrived. "Send him through in about ten minutes, please. I have to finish dealing with this contract before we shut up shop."

Ten minutes later, Luc knocked on the inside of Katya's office door as he entered. "I do enjoy looking at work," he said. Katya smiled, picked up an eraser and threw it at him.

"Hi, I'm just finishing up. I've got a draft supply contract here that reads as if it was translated into English from the original Japanese by a dyslexic German junior schoolboy. If I hadn't seen dozens of these before, I wouldn't have a clue as to what they want. Anyway, that's it; if they accept my amendments, then we've got a deal. If not, then they can go and take a flying leap at themselves. Just let me lock up and we'll go. I'm dying for a nice, long and cold G&T."

---

[17] FOB = Free on Board – including the costs of transport to the dock, loading and securing the goods on board the ship

"Seconded! Guess what - I've been offered both accreditation and grant funding by the English Government if I open up shop here. They've been asking around in South Africa and it seems I've had glowing references. Their man is going to confirm everything in writing and is basically asking 'when can you start?' A bit of a difference from the Dutch approach."

"I'm not surprised."

"Also, I spoke to a commercial estate agent after lunch and he said he's got a couple of properties on his books that may be suitable."

"Where are they?"

"Down the motorway towards Heathrow in a suburb called Ealing in the west of London. He had photos and interior plans for them both. They both look potentially suitable so he's going to open them up for me tomorrow morning."

"All together a positive day, then."

"No doubt about it."

"Maybe it's because we have so many foreign businesses setting up shop here. Oh, and by the way, Piet called just after lunch to say that Eusebio's people had just faxed through a draft of our mining and refining license. He said you've not to get too excited, as it's all written in Portuguese and he's sent it out for translation. He'll get it back on Thursday and will look at it then.

Oh! I nearly forgot; Hennie's men got some information out of our friend Mampata. He claimed that he was set up in Kinshasa on direct orders from a Minister Zhang. He apparently heads up Beijing's Ministry of Mineral Resources. It seems that he is absolutely fixated on mopping up the international rare earths business for the Party. Mampata also indicated that he thought Zhang had more than the Party's interests at heart as he'd been told to set up his operation in total secrecy and only to communicate with Zhang directly, and especially not to have any contact with the Chinese Embassy in Kinshasa."

"It sounds as though this Zhang has gone rogue and has been trying to close us down for his personal glory."

"It does rather, but this at least lets us know for certain who and what has been attacking us. It doesn't remove the threat, we just know now that we are facing a private, but very well connected, operation."

"Is there anything we can do to derail it?"

"I'm not sure. I'll have to give it some thought. Anyway, let's go. I can feel the ice melting in our G&Ts."

*

Katya, Piet, Luc and Ton sat around Piet's boardroom table, each with a copy of the translated Mozambican license and their draft prospectus in front of them. They'd all received their copies of the prospectus on the previous Friday and had time to study them in detail but had only seen the license the previous evening when it came back from the translation bureau.

Piet started off the discussion, saying that as far as he could see, the license was reasonably OK. "We have sole and exclusive rights to mine and refine the ores from the deposit. He's still asking a 3% royalty on all products refined on site, which is reasonable, and there are no restrictions preventing us selling on our rights in the project. There is, however, a time clause that I'm not so happy about. If we fail to get things up and running within two years, all rights revert to the government with absolutely no compensation for us."

"That's a bit steep. Do you think we can get the kit together and get the mining and refining up and running in that time frame?" asked Luc.

"It depends to an extent on their definition of 'up and running,' which isn't specified. I think we can insert our own definition along the lines of 'all equipment installed and operational.' Provided they accept that, then I think it's possible to meet the deadline, but we may have to settle for second-best kit or second-hand kit if we're to meet it. I mean, it's open-cast mining and there's no tunnelling involved; we just need a dragline excavator and a ball-mill to extract and grind the ore for smelting; the fluid-bed kit is available on a nine-month lead and the refining kit is simply a set of glass-lined columns, pipes, valves and pumps, so it seems doable. Commissioning will be the big issue.

Katya, assuming we get everything delivered to site within twelve months, do you think that working with contract plant engineers and the teams from the Wit and the Delft labs, you could be up and running twelve months after that?"

"Very tight, 24/7 work schedules and pray to God that nothing critical breaks. I assume you're going back up to Maputo to seal the deal?"

"Yes."

"Why don't you get him to give us another twelve months? I'm sure he wants this to succeed every bit as much as we do, and if we present him with a procurement bar chart with somewhat generous time allowances for the delivery of the major bits of kit, he will agree. He's not a stupid man and while he doesn't want us to sit around on our arses, he's got to be reasonable if he wants results. Three years seems like a more realistic timeline."

"OK, I'll go back to Eusebio with our operational definition and the extended timeline. Now, moving on to the prospectus, does anyone have any issues with the data as presented?"

"Not as stated," said Katya "but I am unhappy about the valuation numbers we've put in there. I am in complete agreement with Luc's estimation of the amount of recoverable ore and Alex

Stewart's assays of the REEs and their concentrations. No, my problem is with our valuation. When I first went up to Camp 25 Luc had arrived at an estimate of the amount of recoverable ore and its REE content. Using average REE prices from early 2010 I came up with a 'back of a cigarette packet' valuation of $20 billion. I only got copies of all of Alex Stewart's assays a week ago and now believe that $20 billion is a serious underestimate. Market prices, metal by individual metal, have risen between four-fold and twenty-fold over the last few months and while I don't think these higher prices are sustainable over the life of the project, $20 billion is far too low."

"Well, you're the saleswoman," said Piet. "What should it be?"

"At least $80 billion on my long-term price projections and as much as $300 billion at today's market prices."

"Which would imply an asking price of around $30 billion."

A stunned silence followed his words.

"$30 billion," echoed the others.

"Let's be realistic" said Kaya "Today's prices are unsustainable. At these levels, customers will find ways to reduce their usage, even substitute rare earths with lower cost alternatives, so I see prices returning to more historic levels, bringing me back to my $80 billion valuation with an $8 billion asking price

"We'll never get that," said Piet. "Don't forget that all we actually have is just a scoped-out claim. The eventual buyer must do his own due diligence to confirm our estimates of the size of the ore body and its REE content. He'll then have to make his own calculations on the costs of extraction, smelting, refining and purification. Our unique selling point is that we have Katya's technology, together with a source of natural gas on-site at Camp 25."

"Do any of our target buyers have that kind of cash?" asked Luc.

"I think one of them does, but it's not about cash in the bank," said Ton. "These companies give the banks a charge on the deposit and they can then draw down cash to a pre-agreed limit as necessary. It's a bit like getting a mortgage on the ore deposit. I'm sure that while our eventual deal may approach $8 billion, it will involve staged payments and possibly royalties over a number of years. Typically, all or most of the income from the project goes first to the bank to reduce the outstanding loan, with the balance going to the operating company."

"I've come across this a few times. It just adds an extra layer of bureaucracy to each sale of finished product which, by then, will be owned by the bank," said Katya. "The bank needs to authorise every sale; these have to be made against banker's drafts to ensure that the proceeds come to them first. We just need to decide on a payment schedule that meets our needs and can be financed within the lifetime of the project."

"Not the lifetime of the project," said Ton. "We should aim to have all of our cash within a couple of years of their cash-flow turning positive, say five or six years from signing off on the deal, with at least 10% up front."

Piet chipped in to say, "This looks like it's going to be one of the most complex negotiations I've ever been involved with. I'm going to need a lot of support from our lawyers and accountants.

"I'll amend the prospectus and send it over to the lawyers. I need them to go through the final draft. We can't afford to get it wrong. I'll also go back to Eusebio with our proposed alterations to the license. I'll call him and try to fix a meeting in Maputo next week to sign off on the license and pay him his initial 'fee.'

I briefed the accountants last week, as well, and they were salivating at the prospect of the fees they'll get from selling the business on."

"Why don't you put the process out to competitive tender?"

"I would, Katya, but I know these guys, I trust them, and we will negotiate an acceptable fee. They're not stupid and will accept the logic that 10% of something is always better than 100% of nothing."

CHAPTER 39

Both former General Tang and ex-Minister Zhang were transported to Qingcheng prison in early January 2011, within weeks of their respective arrests. As high-ranking prisoners, they were spared manual labour, but that was pretty much the limit of their privileges. However, both still had good connections outside the prison, Tang via officers formerly under his command but still loyal to him personally and Zhang able to call in favours from his time at the ministry. Neither were openly acknowledged but their influence could be seen in little ways.

These connections began to bear fruit almost immediately. The guards were almost, but not quite, respectful towards their charges; both men received better rations than the other prisoners and they were assigned to work in the administration of local state-owned businesses, where their former rank, status and abilities were respected.

As the result of an administrative mistake in February, they found themselves both working in the planning office of the Beijing Plastic Shoe Manufacturing Industry. Recognising each other, but not allowed to speak, they resorted to passing messages written on paper pilfered from the supervisor's desk at meal times.

*

Piet was shown into Eusebio's conference room by the same secretary he'd met last time. Eusebio entered about three minutes later, shook hands with a smile, and sat down. "So, do we have agreement?" asked Piet.

"Yes, we're happy to accept your definition of up and running and to extend the period from two to three years. We didn't realise the length of the lead times for some of the critical bits of equipment and we would not want the project to fail because of a delay in getting a key piece of equipment delivered to the site."

"We can sign?"

"Provided your initial payment is made."

"The money is in place; it just requires a phone call from me for it to be transferred to your account. After that it will take less than fifteen minutes for it to show up in your balance. Why don't we sign, and I'll stay here until you have received the money?"

"Agreed."

With that, Eusebio called his secretary and told her to come in with the papers and another clerk to witness the signing of the documents. The documents were signed off and Piet asked to use a phone to release the funds.

*

Half an hour later Piet was $100,000 poorer and in a taxi on the way back to the airport. He'd asked Eusebio if he could buy him dinner to celebrate but had been good-humouredly turned down. "It doesn't do me a lot of good to be seen in public here with South African businessmen. However, I do expect to be entertained royally next time I'm in Cape Town or wherever the Advisory Board Meetings are to be held."

"Naturally."

Eusebio escorted him down to the lobby, where his taxi was waiting, and said farewell.

Once at the airport, Piet called his secretary to tell her the deal was done and that he was on his way back to Cape Town with the license. He asked her to call Katya, Luc and Ton with the good news and said he'd see her in the morning. He sat in the business lounge and went back through the license papers, smiling in satisfaction as he saw the amended clauses and the official Mozambique Government Seal by Eusebio's signatures. *Job done – but now the real work begins,* he said to himself.

*

Of the four pre-selected candidates to purchase their project and take it through to commercial operation, Ramontain had responded first and fastest so a preliminary meeting was set up for the middle of the following week in Cape Town.

An excited Katya flew into Cape Town on Tuesday morning, ready for the negotiations with Ramontain the following day. Going straight to Piet's office, she found Luc and Ton sitting with him at the conference table.

"Hi guys, are we all ready to have our wicked way with Ramontain?"

"Nearly," said Piet, "we just need to be prepared for their hot buttons and rehearse our responses."

"Surely the best way forward is for us to ask ourselves what we would want to know if we were in their shoes."

"Agreed."

"What bits of our data do they have?"

"Just what you saw in the prospectus."

"They haven't seen our element-by-element percentage breakdown?"

"No, and from what you said last time, Katya, this has to be the icing on the cake. Our deposit contains more than 30% dysprosium, europium and terbium, which puts the average value of the combined extracted metals 'package' at around $350/kilo or more."

"My point exactly - $80 billion is a conservative estimate."

"But estimate is all it is at this point, Katya. It's not hard actuarially proven fact, but I do agree that it is a good negotiating point."

"I imagine their due diligence will include visits to Camp 25, The Wit and finally Delft to see the clever end of the process. Given where we are now, I'm confident that we can give them a mouth-watering show. Do you think they'll swallow an overall $80 billion valuation for the deposit, especially when they see the average elemental analyses?"

"My guess is a conditional yes, subject to due diligence, and their acceptance is bound to be hedged around with all kinds of conditions, all aimed at reducing the value of the ore body in our eyes and hence their eventual pay-out. I think today will only be a preliminary meeting and the serious discussions will come in a week or two, once they've seen Camp 25 and the two labs.

Presumably you'll lead on the visit to Camp 25, Luc? And you'll do the same on the lab visits, Katya? I also think you should show them the same demonstration that you gave Eusebio."

At the end of the meeting, Luc left to take Katya to her hotel, where they agreed to meet up later for dinner.

*

Luc stayed with Katya that night and they discussed the relocation of his security business to Europe.

"I'd prefer it if you set up shop in or near London," said Katya. "That way we can sit on top of the technology, keep my trading business running and enjoy London's social scene. I know it doesn't offer you much in the way of an open-air life, but we could buy a chalet in the foothills of the Alps Maritimes, within easy reach of London, for climbing, swimming and sunshine in the summer and skiing in the winter. There's also good climbing in north-west England and Scotland, plus skiing in northern Scotland. On the other hand, The Netherlands are not noted for their mountain ranges; skating and ice-hockey are really the only winter sports."

"That sounds very tempting. I'll think about it, but it eventually comes down to good old-fashioned cash: which location will have the lowest start-up costs and where can I hang on to more of the profit?"

*

Immediately after breakfast, Katya and Luc headed for Piet's offices for a last-minute briefing before their first meeting with the Ramontain team, who turned out to be their CEO, Chief Chemist and Chief Geologist.

Their CEO Jack Schulz, took the lead, saying that the Future Metals proposition looked interesting, but they'd need a lot more data before they could evaluate it properly. "For instance, how sure are you of your mineralization figures and what is this low cost, high quality separation technology?"

Luc answered first. "The mineralisation figures are the results from 4 drill-holes at each of 25 sites across the deposit, 100 cores in total. These were assayed by the Alex Stewart International Laboratories in Zambia and we have every confidence in the accuracy of their results and that we're looking at a rich and major REE deposit."

"OK, I'll concede that; we use Alex Stewart ourselves."

"What do you think of the metals percentage analysis?"

"You hadn't sent that to us in advance, but they look very interesting: high dysprosium, europium, terbium and neodymium contents, no thorium. How did the deposit originate?"

"We reckon it is a mixed alluvial ore body, washed down from the eastern Zimbabwean Bvumba mountains at the end of the last ice age, which might explain its slightly unusual composition. It is mainly clay with a high loading of monazite crystals, and very friable when dry, excellent from a mining and processing point of view."

"OK, but what's this separation and purification process you claim so much for?"

Katya said. "Jack, it is proprietary technology that we've developed in-house, and I can only tell you at this point that it is a high-efficiency molecular sieve system. Why don't I show you a short presentation?"

"Please."

Switching on the projector, she began by saying, "You will be aware of the messy and environmentally disastrous processes used by the Chinese? Well, these pictures were taken earlier this year at two of the largest Chinese REE mining and processing sites. Kind of a toxic moonscape, isn't it?

"Well, our process is nothing like that. This jar contains samples of the ore from the deposit, a friable clay. Now we grind it to a powder and smelt it in a fluidized-bed calciner to recover this mixed metal. This is a sample of the recovered metal and this jar contains the calcined ore powder, excellent as a concrete additive and with no adverse environmental impact.

"We then dissolve the mixed metal in nitric acid and separate the individual metals via these columns. The pure nitrates can then be treated to deliver oxides or processed through to the metal itself.

"I have prepared these samples for you to take away and confirm what I've just told you."

"Impressive, but what about the process effluent?"

"This jar contains a sample of it. Colourless, odourless, pH 6.8, almost neutral and with only low ppm traces of the rare earth metals, it can be discharged direct to sewer or even a river course."

"How much do you generate?"

"I've always been an advocate of processes that 'eat their own tails,' and this is no different. Each kilo of rare earth oxide only generates a net one litre of waste-water like that in the jar there, over the whole process cycle."

Katya was then bombarded with questions from the Chief Chemist, Kurt Weber. These she either answered in full or said she could only divulge the answers once they had a deal. "Our molecular sieve technology has much wider applications than this and we are waiting for confirmation of our patents before we talk about it in any detail."

This was accepted and they moved on to discuss the logistics of site access, and the fact that there was a natural gas well on-site that could supply all the energy requirements of a REE refinery.

Piet brought the meeting back together and asked, "Do you want to take this further?"

Jack said, "Very much so. However, prudence demands that we do detailed due diligence, both on the site and on the processing."

"Not a problem," said Piet. "Luc and Katya can take you to the Johannesburg laboratory, then around the ore body and finally on to the Dutch laboratory doing the clever stuff. I estimate that visiting all three sites will take you a maximum of ten days between travelling time and site evaluation, so let me know your availability and I'll make the necessary arrangements. For simplicity, I suggest that you start the trip at the Johannesburg lab, then on to the site and finish your visit in Delft. That'll cut travelling time to a minimum."

Jack Schulz consulted his diary and then said: "I had hoped we could get to this point fairly quickly so I could rearrange my schedule to make the due diligence visits in ten days' time. Would that fit with your plans Piet?"

"No problem here provided both Luc and Katya are available, we can arrange your visit starting a week this coming Tuesday. This gives Katya time to get back down to Cape Town from London."

Luc and Katya nodded their assent to the proposed timing. With that, Piet brought the meeting to a close and said he'd arrange transport for them back to the airport.

*

CHAPTER 40

Luc and Katya flew into the O. Tambo International Airport on Monday evening and took a cab to the Fairway Hotel. "This is where I stayed last time I was here, so I got Mary to book us all in here for tonight. I expect that we'll fly on up to Camp 25 for tomorrow night. I'm not sure when the Ramontain guys will show up but we can leave a message for them at reception."

On checking in they found that the Ramontain party had just checked in ahead of them, the same team who had met them in Piet's offices in Cape Town. Katya phoned Jack Schulz in his room and arranged for them all to meet up in the bar at seven, prior to eating dinner together.

Over a couple of drinks everyone relaxed and during dinner Luc asked Ramontain why they were so interested in the project. "Simple," said Schulz. "With the Chinese squeeze on the REE market, we scented an opportunity and on paper at least, your project ticks all the boxes. We have been looking at other options, including re-starting the South African REE business, but it was really messy, with a lot of site legacy problems and rusted-out kit, so we walked away from it. I know Piet of old and when he contacted me, or rather when your accountants did, we absolutely had to come and have a look-see."

"I think you'll like it. I was prospecting on a purely speculative basis up in Mozambique and could hardly believe what I'd discovered. Piet has acted as the angel in financing the project so far, and Katya's chemical insights have allowed us to come up with a nice, clean process. However, none of us are miners, hence the decision to put the project up for sale."

At the end of the meal, Katya detailed what they'd see during the following day's visit to The Wit and with that they parted company. Luc and Katya went for a wander around the hotel grounds before retiring for the night.

"Guess what?" asked Luc

"No idea - you've won the Lotto?"

"No, better than that, when I checked my emails before dinner, there was a message from the lawyers in London; I now own a factory in Brentford, the new headquarters of LKF International Ltd. They sent me some photos a couple of days ago and couriered a set of plans over, which were delivered last night before you arrived. I made an offer first thing this morning and his email was an acceptance of my offer."

"You mean to tell me you've been keeping this to yourself since I arrived last night and all day today?"

"I didn't want to say anything in case it all fell apart. But it didn't, and you know what this means?"

"That you're moving to London."

"Yes!"

"When?"

"As soon as I can make all the necessary arrangements in South Africa and the UK. I'll probably have to travel to-and-fro for a bit, but I expect to have everything sewn up inside six to eight weeks."

"Fantastic, darling! Will you move in with me?"

"If you'll have me."

"Yes – and with all my love."

Arm in arm they walked around the hotel before Katya turned to him, threw her arms around his neck and kissed him hard. "What wonderful news and what a wonderful evening! Let's go to bed and celebrate!" she said, smothering his face with kisses.

*

Luc had arranged a minibus for nine o'clock to take them all to Witwatersrand University, and it deposited them in front of the Geosciences Building just before ten. Adam Smith was waiting for them at the entrance and after the introductions had been completed, he took them up to the lab.

Smith looked into a retinal scanner and a clicking, whirring sound signalled the unlocking of the door. "I see Luc has beefed up your security," remarked Katya.

"Yes, this high-security door is really something," said Adam, leading them into the conference room, where Jim and Leonie were standing by expectantly and coffee was set out ready.

"Gentlemen, there are a couple of things I need to say. Firstly, what goes on here is highly confidential, so we cannot allow you to take pictures. Please put your cameras, mobile phones, etc., on that table over there. Leonie here will make sure they come to no harm and you can pick them up again when you leave.

"Secondly, when you go through to the laboratory itself, we need you to put on protective gear. It is very hot and I strongly suggest you don't touch anything, as many of the exposed parts of the kit are running at over 700 Deg.C. Jim will explain what is happening."

Suited, helmeted and visored-up, they followed Jim into the Furnace Room. It was hot and quite noisy, as the fans driving the calciner were running flat out. Katya noticed that hoods had been placed over all the dials so that no-one could play the old trick of using a pencil stub and little pieces of card

KATYA'S CHALLENGE

in their pockets to surreptitiously record the key operating readings displayed.

Jim showed them the raw ore, the crushed ore being fed into the unit, and reduced ore coming out the other end. He showed them the mixed metals being collected in small ceramic troughs under the bed.

"You can see that it works well, and this little baby is processing 20 kilos of ore per hour. We're currently getting 95% recovery of the metal contained and we're in the process of having the next size up calciner delivered to Camp 25. We really can't run anything larger in here and have had to move up to Mozambique. It's all good, though; we'll be sitting on top of the ore and can forget about all the hassle of shipping it down here and processing it in a confined space.

"Now let's go and look at the analytical side of things. Jasmin and Ravi will talk you through it."

Happy to be out of the furnace room, they stripped off their helmets and visors and went over to the analytical equipment on the lab benches. Jim introduced the visitors and Jasmin talked them through the ore sampling process, followed by acid extraction and analysis of the REEs. Comparing the Alex Stewart assay results with those on the metals collected from the furnace had allowed them to come up with an accurate process yield.

"Very impressive," said Kurt. "Do you have historical results we can see?"

Ravi nodded and led them back to the conference room, where he produced a binder of analytical reports. "You'll see we didn't get it right to begin with, but Jim has steadily pushed the efficiency up to 94-95% and our results match Stewart's very closely now."

"Can we have copies?" asked Kurt.

"No problem, I actually made up this set for you," said Ravi, handing them the folder.

"How about a spot of lunch?" asked Luc as they returned to the conference room.

Adam had arranged a finger-buffet lunch for them and as they were enjoying it, Jack said, "That's a nice little team you've got here, Adam. They radiate enthusiasm and commitment and their work seems to be of a very high standard. Do they come with the deal?"

Katya said, "That's a matter between you and them. We've got plenty of development work in the pipeline for the team, but we'll leave the decision to them. We employ them, but we don't own them, so it's their choice.

"But gentlemen, I think we've shown you everything here that you can see in advance of a contract. We should be heading for the airport and if we leave now, we can be up at Camp 25 for dinner."

They said their thanks and goodbyes. Adam saw them to their minibus, and they drove to the airport. The scheduled flight times were unhelpful, so

Luc had arranged a charter jet for their party, and they were airborne within an hour and a half of leaving the university.

*

Landing at Beira, Katya had a sense of déjà vu as they taxied over to the private aircraft stands. The immigration jeep drove out to the plane, checked and stamped their passports before retiring to the terminal building.

Luc led them over to the Chinook, whose rotors were already turning. "I'm afraid you've all been downgraded to 'goat class' for the next leg of the trip. It's the only feasible route to and from the camp at the moment."

They climbed aboard, strapped themselves onto the cargo netting lining the interior and settled down on some tarpaulins for the flight.

*

On arrival, Luc led the Ramontain team to a four-man dormitory hut, showed them the facilities and told them of the water restrictions, saying that they should all meet up at the lounge hut over there before dinner, so they could agree the schedule for their site visit the following day.

Feeling relaxed, they enjoyed a couple of beers, and Luc suggested they should begin tomorrow with a look around Camp 25, followed by a Chinook flight around the ore body. They could land at any of the other drill sites that interested them, then return to camp for a Q&A.

Dinner was a choice between chicken piri-piri and prawn bhuna, made with fresh prawns that had come up in the Chinook with them. The canteen hut was almost empty compared with Katya's last visit, as there were only a couple of technicians and a squad of soldiers left on-site.

Jack asked Luc lots of questions about the extent of the Camp, and he gave them the story behind the decision to make this the proposed centre of the mining and refining operations, minimising ore transport and taking advantage of the 'free' on-site natural gas field.

They retired to the lounge hut after dinner for coffee and cognac. Soon after, Jack said they'd retire to their hut for a good night's rest and would meet up again for breakfast at eight o'clock.

*

As the Chinook flew over their concession, Luc pointed out the perimeter markers and identified their drilling sites. They touched down at four of them and saw evidence of the drilling operation and the tracks through the bush that had been made to get the drilling rig from site to site.

"The whole site has just a thin covering of scrub across it, which poses no problem for clearance. The overburden of topsoil varies in thickness between three and four metres, making exposure of the ore bed easy for excavation. We've agreed with the Government that we'd work across the deposit, putting the overburden on one side, mining and processing the ore, back-filling the site with the reduced material, unless it is wanted elsewhere, and topping it off with the overburden."

"Very ecologically responsible," said Jack. "How thick is the ore bed?"

"Variable - it's lenticular, eleven hundred metres thick in the centre, thinning to around four hundred metres at the edges, where it comes up against a basalt rock wall which effectively contains it. The whole area was probably under water at one time and the REE deposit concentrated in the centre as the ground shifted. That might also account for the natural gas under Camp 25," said Luc.

*

After four hours of flying, landing to examine drilling sites and taking off again, they landed back at the camp for some lunch before flying back down to Beira.

Glad to leave the noisy Chinook, Katya had been observing them closely across the morning and had seen their interest growing by the minute. It was, after all, an excellent operation. Luc had done a first-class job of managing the definition of the ore body with hard data to back up every assertion. Adam Smith's team had performed brilliantly, and all that now remained was for them to be impressed with the work going on in Delft. She smiled to herself. *Almost 'in the bag!'*

"I've organised things so that your visit can be completed in a week and have booked a Citation jet to fly us up overnight tonight to Rotterdam, meaning that with any luck you'll be able to fly home on Friday," said Luc.

"Sounds good," said Jack. "You've managed to organise our time very economically. Depending on what we see tomorrow, we should be able to come back to Piet next week with a conditional offer. If that is the case, we'll need another meeting very soon to thrash out the detail."

Katya said she expected they would like what they saw in Delft and suggested that they had an early dinner prior to taking off for Rotterdam.

*

The Citation came in through a clear, cold winter sky to land at Rotterdam. The flight attendant had woken them an hour earlier and they'd all had time to wash, dress and have a light breakfast. They had cleared customs and immigration and were walking onto the arrivals concourse when André spotted them and came over.

"Welcome Katya, Luc and gentlemen, I have a minibus waiting outside to take us to the labs. Do you need food or to do anything before we go?"

Everyone said no and they walked out to the minibus, climbed aboard and were driven to the

Chemical Technology Building. As they stepped inside, Katya said, "This is where it all started for me; I did my doctorate here, focusing on the synthesis of molecular sieves with very precisely controlled pore sizes. Upstairs you will see about the twentieth iteration of my research work, which now allows us to separate individual rare earth metals from a mixed solution. This is the basis of our mining and refining license."

Kurt asked, "Is this all your own work?"

"The concept and initial work is all mine, but what you will see in the lab is the product of a dedicated research team building on my initial concept."

André opened the lab door using the retinal scanner as Jack remarked on their security. "Essential," said Luc. "The technology is extremely valuable, as it allows us to separate metals which cannot easily be separated by conventional processes, like cobalt and manganese, for instance, and all of the rare earth metals. We are aware of interested parties who are prepared to go to extreme lengths to steal it."

Leading them into the conference room, André asked them to leave phones and cameras on the table. "They'll be quite safe here and you can pick them up when you leave." He then called Thijs and Johan into the room, introduced them and asked them to show the visitors the separation process.

Walking into the lab, they saw a long, wide bench covered with turntables, each carrying three glass columns, through which liquids were being pumped.

"Each set of three cylinders is filled with a metal-specific molecular sieve, the first set stripping out europium and so on down the atomic radii."

"Why groups of three cylinders?"

"One in use, one being stripped and one on standby. If you look at the top and bottom of each cylinder in use, you'll see spectrophotometers linked to that computer monitor over there. If you look at the screen, you'll see that the concentration peak for each metal in turn is high at the top of the cylinder and almost invisible at the bottom. The spectrophotometers trigger the switch of cylinders when the one in use is saturated.

"Look, there are the dysprosium columns switching now! The column in use is almost saturated and is being rotated to the stripping station while the standby is being brought on line. The separation we achieve is better than any available using any other technology. You don't need to take my word for it; Katya has agreed that you can take samples from any point in the process train and subject them to your own analysis back home."

*

By mid-afternoon, all their questions had been answered and they were ready to leave, along with a box of samples.

"That's an impressive piece of work, Katya," said Jack, "and thank you for your hospitality and openness. It gives us confidence in your proposal. We'll get these samples analysed next week and if they confirm what you say, I'll be back to Piet within the next couple of weeks to move things on to the next stage."

"I've arranged transport for us all up to Schiphol. I believe you're heading for Switzerland, while we're headed for London," said Luc.

CHAPTER 41

A month passed before Tang and Zhang were able to agree that their current ignominious situation was the direct result of the activities of the South Africans in Mozambique, compounded by the failings of their own subordinates, and absolutely nothing to do with their own shortcomings. From there it was but a short step to agreeing that some form of retribution had to be arranged, ideally 'termination with extreme prejudice,' as the American CIA put it. Their elimination would restore face to both men and perhaps give them grounds to appeal for early release from prison, depending on whether the Chinese state could acquire the rights to the Mozambican REE deposit.

Agreement was one thing; deciding on the means and instruments of their retribution was more difficult, as there is a limit to the dialogue and planning that can be achieved via cryptic paper messages. Zhang, as the more diplomatic personality, started working on the administration supervisor with the objective of getting permission for him and Tang to work in the same sector of the administration office, which would make direct spoken communication between them essential and would not be in contravention of the terms of their imprisonment.

By early March, the two men were working at adjacent desks and being treated almost like regular employees. By mid-April they were allowed to eat lunch together and they could get down to detailed planning.

Both men, driven by resentment over their status, had quickly agreed on what, where, how and when their retribution should take place. Friendly employees at the factory were persuaded, with the help of some cash, to carry sealed envelopes to addresses in Beijing and return two weeks later to collect similar sealed envelopes and deliver them to the men.

*

Luc rang Katya just as she was packing up to go home for the night. "Guess what Kat?"

"No idea – the British government is going to offer you honorary citizenship?"

"Better than that: the first tranche of Ramontain's cash is in the bank. You, Piet, Ton and I are all multi-millionaires!"

Katya sat down behind her desk again. "Darling! Has it really all gone through?"

"Without a hitch, and with the simple four-way split we agreed, we are each $98 million richer."

"Not $100 million?"

"No, remember we agreed that Piet should recover his expenses from running the project in the first place - everything from funding my exploration through paying for all the kit and labour involved in the drilling programme, the security, assays, lawyers and accountants' fees, etc. That basically came to eight million dollars, hence the deduction."

"That's OK by me – he took a hell of a risk with his own money and this is a pretty fair pay-off. Mind you, it's just a pity that Piet had to agree to staged payments against milestones."

"Don't be greedy Kat. It's more money than either of us could have expected to get, and it brings with it a contract for your continuing involvement in the project. Can you call Ton tomorrow and tell him where you want your share deposited?"

"Will do. I certainly don't want HMRC to get its sticky hands on it before I've had time to decide what I'm going to do with it. I think I'll park it in Labuan as a first step."

"You've set up facilities there?"

"Yes, when I was working in Belgium, my old friend Jan van Vliet used to witter on about keeping the profits from his trading successes safe from the taxman, informing me of the relative attractions of various offshore jurisdictions. When I started making some real money, I took his advice and established my own little nest egg to tide me over the inevitable bad times that come to any trader."

"So now your nest egg is about to become a clutch of eggs – lovely. What are the advantages, darling?"

"They charge you a maximum of six thousand US dollars each year to maintain a local registered company, irrespective of the profit it makes. You can't employ any of the locals and your business activities can be anywhere in the world except there. You can leave your cash sleeping peacefully in any currency in the bank, until you want to use it elsewhere. From an English tax perspective, it's fine, as you don't pay tax on it until you bring it onshore, and as you may be investing in another overseas activity it's not too difficult to keep your tax payments to a minimum."

"Sounds good. Could you fix the same deal for me?"

"No problem, but we'll need to take a week out to do it. Around two days travelling each way, a day to do the business, and a couple of days to enjoy doing it. You'll also need to bring notarized copies of all your key documents - birth certificate, driving license, proof of residence, etc. - with you."

"By the way Kat, your contract deal runs for two years to scale up the REE separation process to production levels: $20,000/month for you with a further $1 million success fee if you do it in under two years. All materials, equipment and labour expenses chargeable to Ramontain."

"Sounds good, I'm pretty sure that we can do it and the million-dollar success fee means I can really incentivise the team. I never mind paying out of profit but I sure as hell resent paying out up front.

"We get a further stage payment when all the necessary kit is on site and commissioned, a further $400 million. We then start receiving royalties of 3% on the ex-works value of all material shipped for five years, subject to a minimum of one hundred million dollars per annum. Piet's done a pretty fair job."

"Absolutely, I'm quite used to seeing sums like this running through our accounts as large contracts are agreed, financed and paid out, but this is different, it's all ours to do with what we will."

*

Four weeks later, Luc and Katya flew to Malaysia. Their flight from Kuala Lumpur landed in Labuan just before mid-day. They were met at Passport Control by a slim, smartly dressed man of obvious Chinese ancestry, whom Katya introduced as Fabian Chen of Waterhouse International Trust (Labuan) Ltd, the legal and accountancy firm that functioned as the registered office for Katya's offshore trading company. He spirited them through Immigration and Customs to an unmarked, chauffeur-driven black BMW X5 parked at the front of the terminal. Katya and Luc stood beside the car, perspiring in Labuan's mid-day heat and humidity, until their baggage arrived, pushed by a smartly dressed porter. Fabian ushered Luc into the back of the car along with Katya, then got in the front beside the driver. At the hotel in Victoria, he organized their check-in, saying that he'd leave them to rest up until the evening and would come past about seven thirty and take them to dinner. After more than 30 hours in transit and coping with an eight-hour time-shift, both Luc and Katya were dog-tired and went straight to their room.

In private for the first time in nearly day and a half, Katya stripped and stepped into a hot, relaxing shower, feeling the dirt and weariness of the journey washing off her body and down the drain. Coming back into the bedroom, with her hair and body wrapped in towels, she set her travel alarm for six thirty local time, snuggled up to Luc and was asleep almost as soon as she lay down.

The buzzing of the alarm woke her from a deep sleep, climbing back to consciousness as from a deep and comfortable burrow. She showered for a second time, dried her hair, and dressed in a loose-fitting embroidered muslin top and white jeans. Luc followed her into the bathroom. Then, dressed in tan chinos and a white, open-necked shirt, he pulled on his jacket, leading the way to the lifts and down to their rendezvous. As the lift doors opened they saw Fabian walk into the lobby.

They met up, shook hands and stood awkwardly until Fabian asked what kind of food they would like to eat. Katya thought for all of about two seconds before saying, "Local, please." Turning to Luc she asked, "OK by you, darling? I love the food."

"Lead on. Malaysian food sounds interesting."

It took all of ten minutes to drive to the chosen restaurant, where they were greeted in the formal Malay manner before being conducted to their table in a slightly raised bay window, looking out over the harbour. Night had fallen while they had been getting ready and the lights of the yachts riding at anchor gave the view a festive air. A waitress came over and handed them hot towels and menus, followed by the wine-waiter, who handed Fabian the wine-list and asked if they would like an aperitif. Luc said he would just have a beer and Katya, remembering previous visits, said that she would have the same. Fabian made it three, smiling at them as the waiter left.

Dinner began with satay ayam (chicken satay), accompanied with gado gado (a Malaysian salad), followed by sambal udang (spicy prawns), sotong goring berempah (crispy fried squid), with nasi (rice) and roti (flat bread) on the side. All through the meal Fabian played the attentive host, being especially attentive to Katya, explaining what the dishes were and asking how she liked them.

Katya couldn't help but notice that his interest in her went beyond the politeness expected of the host. Smiling a lot at him, she mused that it would probably do their mission no harm at all if Fabian joined her fan club, so she started flirting back. By the time their coffees had arrived, she was the absolute focus of his attention.

Fabian excused himself for a moment and as soon as he was out of earshot, Luc asked, "What the hell are you playing at?"

"Nothing," she replied. "I'm working. If he fancies me, however little, we will get a lot more information from him, including the answers to the questions we forget to ask, than if he writes us off as a pair of arrogant, demanding foreigners. Softly, softly, catchee monkey. I'm sure that just asking for the information we want will take us into an area where he can either block us with the full panoply of Malaysian bureaucracy or interpret the rules favourably for us. I suspect he has some discretion and I want him to use it. Besides, I've heard Malaysian men are good in bed." She smiled.

Luc frowned, then relaxed as he saw she was teasing. "I hope you're right, but don't overdo it."

"Moi?"

He looked hard at her without saying a word and then grinned. The table had been cleared by the time Fabian returned. Sitting down, he leaned forward in his seat and looked at Katya. "Why exactly are you here?"

"You let me know a couple of months ago that LOFSA[18] are making some far-reaching changes

---

[18] LOFSA - Labuan Offshore Financial Services Authority,

to the rules for offshore companies. So, I want to take the time to understand what is going on and I wanted Luc to hear what is said and to meet you and Chee Tan in the office. I also want Waterhouse to set Luc up with his own Labuan offshore company and local bank accounts."

The rest of the evening passed quickly, and they were dropped off back at the hotel by nine thirty. Fabian's parting shot was that he would pick them up at eight thirty in the morning and take them to a meeting with Chee Tan, Katya's local director.

Katya woke early the following morning, still adjusting to the eight-hour time-shift. Tossing and turning for half an hour, she concluded that she was not going back to sleep and rolled out of bed. Leaving Luc sleeping soundly, she wandered through to the bathroom, brushed her teeth and had a reviving shower. Once she had towelled herself dry she looked at the bedside clock and saw it was still only six am.

She picked up the hotel guide and flipped idly through the pages until she came to the "Fitness Centre" which, she saw, opened its doors at six am. Thinking that it was time to do something physical for a change, she slipped on her athletics kit, put on her running shoes and topped it off with the room's towelling bathrobe, picked up her swimming costume, shower gel and room key, and headed down to the

---

the body that regulates offshore companies registered in Labuan.

sixth floor. She thought that she would be the only one there but to her surprise, found that there were already about ten European men and five or six Chinese-looking women pounding away on the equipment.

The receptionist gave her a towel and a locker key for the female changing room. Putting her bathrobe and swimming gear in the locker, she walked through to the gym. Choosing an unoccupied treadmill, she set it in motion and started running gently. As she warmed up, she turned up the speed until the dial on the grip bar said she was running at a steady 20 kph, or 12.5 mph. As she pounded along, she reflected on yesterday's events and the contrast between this and the office back in London. This was much, much nicer; in fact, she felt that she could get used to this. However, after fifteen minutes of pounding along like this, she turned the speed up another notch, and then another for a final sprint. As the belt slowed down and stopped, she stepped off and did some yoga stretching until her breathing returned to normal.

Looking at the clock, she saw that it was still only seven am - time for a swim. Back in the changing room she stepped out of her athletic kit, put on her costume, showered and walked out the other side to the pool. It was a large one for a hotel and Katya dived in and ploughed up and down for nearly half an hour. Emerging from the water, she picked up her towel and shampoo and headed straight into the showers. There were two young Chinese women showering there who made Katya feel a little uncomfortable. They were barely five-foot-tall, making her feel like a giantess, being a full head taller. They kept looking at each other, then at her and started giggling in what she had come to recognise as a typically Chinese way.

Back in their room she got ready for the day - and for breakfast. Over a buffet breakfast of fresh fruit, yoghurt, croissants and coffee she outlined the agenda that they should follow at the meeting. "We need to be quite clear about what we want to have and how it should be administered, otherwise we can end up in a bureaucratic swamp. Agreed?"

"Absolutely, you've done all this before and I'm happy to follow your lead. It's all new terrain for me."

*

Arriving at the Waterhouse Trust's office building in the Financial Centre, Fabian took them straight up to Chee Tan's office, where Luc was introduced, and they were served coffee. Getting down to business, Katya asked Chee Tan to explain the changes to LOFSA's rules and regulations. There didn't appear to be any change that impacted on her operations, so they moved to set up Luc's new company, LKF (L) Ltd, and open two bank accounts, one with a local Labuan bank for day-to-day local expenses and one with the local branch of Barclays Bank for international transactions.

"Who do you wish to nominate as signatories to operate these accounts?" asked Chee Tan.

"I'm sure that Mr Kruger will want you or Waterhouse Trust to be the additional signatories on the local account, and I think that Mr Kruger will agree to us both being signatories on his Barclays Bank account. I also want him added as a signatory on my Barclays Bank account."

"May I ask why?"

"Simple - if anything happened to either of us at the moment, the money in these accounts would only be recoverable with a shed-load of administrative complications. This way an eventual survivor can draw on the funds without problem."

"You are right and certainly looking ahead, Ms Francis."

"Yes, I find that it pays to do so."

"If you can leave your documentation with me and come back this afternoon around four, I will have all the necessary paperwork drawn up for your signatures."

"Thank you, Mr Chee, we'll see you then."

*

The chauffeur-driven BMW dropped them back at the hotel. "That was pretty painless," said Luc.

"Yes, because I knew what to expect and we had all of the necessary identification paperwork with us. I hope you don't mind being regarded as a South African resident in the UK."

"So long as it is advantageous for tax."

"It is – anyway, let's have a light lunch here in the hotel before retiring upstairs for a siesta."

"Good thinking."

*

Katya awoke to the feather-light touch of Luc gently caressing her breasts, before he explored her body further, trailing his fingers across her stomach and ending up between her thighs. She responded sleepily, before coming fully awake and reciprocating. They made sensual, leisurely love, with increasing urgency as they neared, then reached, their climaxes.

Showered and dressed, it was time to return to Waterhouse Trust and complete the paperwork. Down in the lobby Katya asked the concierge to get them a taxi, only to be informed that a car was waiting to take them back to their appointment.

Back in Chee Tan's office, they were offered tea before Luc and Katya were presented with a pile of papers to sign off. Job done, Luc turned to Chee Tan and asked when the account would be operational, so he could deposit funds and also how much he had to transfer to Waterhouse Trust to settle his account.

*

Back in the hotel, they headed for the bar and a couple of beers. "That was all pretty damned reasonable," said Luc. "Change out of $8,000 to establish my offshore company, open my bank accounts and pay Chee Tan's first year director's fees."

"I did say it was pretty good and pretty good value. Now what do you want to do for dinner?"

*

As they were enjoying their coffees and liqueurs, Katya said, "We're not flying out until Friday afternoon, so how do you fancy a tour of the island?"

"Is there much to see?"

"Not really. Labuan is all about oil, gas and money. The south of the island is basically just an industrial zone and there's not much else to see unless you're into temples and mosques."

"Then why don't we fly back to Kuala Lumpur in the morning and have a couple of days there before we fly out?"

"I could enjoy that. A bit of Malaysian retail therapy would be good and quite different from anything we'll see in London, Amsterdam or Cape Town. I'll book us into the Mandarin Oriental."

*

The following morning, they checked out of their hotel and flew back to Kuala Lumpur. They spent the next couple of days exploring the city, shopping and sight-seeing, including a trip up the Petronas Twin Towers, from which they had a fabulous view over the city.

KATYA'S CHALLENGE

Katya had a ball. "It's ages since I've just spent a day in a city with nothing to do but enjoy myself, shop, eat, drink, wander about and gawp at my surroundings."

Luc agreed. "Me neither and I think it's time we had a proper break. In a couple of months, our research laboratory cum computer security facility will be up and running. You say that your business is getting better since you added the sourcing of REE-based components to your core REE business. Give it another month or so and we could have a proper holiday.

Have you ever been on a safari?"

"No. Aren't they all a bit rough and ready? In return for being able to see big beasts in the wild, you are allowed to get eaten alive by mosquitoes, bitten by snakes, have the opportunity to sleep under canvas on a lumpy camp-bed, wash in cold water and eat really bad barbecue? I don't fancy that at all."

"That's what it used to be like, but the safari park owners cottoned onto the fact that the people with the money would only come if they upped their game and made the whole experience much like a luxury hotel, with chauffeur-driven transport around the animals and really good food. They made the changes and I'm sure you'd love it."

"OK, I'm prepared to give it a go, provided it is luxury all the way."

"Right, you're busy reshaping your business and I'm a couple of months from getting my European base up and running, so let's arrange to go in August, let's say the middle fortnight. I suggest the Kruger National Park. It's got everything and good facilities."

"No relation?" Katya asked with a smile.

"Not directly, but it is named in honour of a Kruger ancestor."

"Looking forward to it."

*

Over lunch Zhang and Tang went over the replies they'd received from the Cape Town Consulate. "We've got both political and army agreement from the Cape Town Consulate," said Zhang. "Removing the soldier and the woman from the project will bring it to a halt, giving our people the chance to move in and take it over."

Tang said, "While I agree, I still think we should attempt to take the woman prisoner. We know she's the brains behind their extraction and purification process, and I'm sure we can persuade her to show us how it's done."

"I'm not sure we need to; their patents will be published in the next few months and I am sure our chemists can work their way past any misdirection in them to arrive at the real process. Persuading the kind of woman we now know her to be could be difficult, and if we succeed in breaking her spirit, she might be useless. I have asked my successor at the ministry to keep a lookout for their publications, get copies as soon as they appear and set our chemists to work. Much better just to eliminate her."

"I half-agree with you, comrade. It will be tidier that way but we might be able to get to the details of the process quicker with her help. Ultimately, it's not about that, is it? Our loss of face is compounded every day they remain alive, and I think I've been able to fix it for them to be put under surveillance until we find an opportunity to deal with them in line with the plan we agreed upon."

"Our plan, comrade, must prevail. I really would like to be released from here and enjoy the freedom to walk outside without being under the eyes of the guards. We've managed to get some privileges, but they're a long way short of walking free, eating what we want to eat, wearing our own clothes, sleeping with our women, making our own decisions – think of it. We just need to wait and watch . . ."

CHAPTER 42

Luc came bounding up the stairs to Katya's offices on Friday evening. Jean let him in asking: "Where's the fire?"

"Nowhere, it's just that I've finally got the keys to our finished and fitted-out business unit in Ealing and I have to tell Katya."

"Congrats – I'll buzz her and tell you you're here. Katya, Luc's just arrived and has some hot news for you."

"Oh? Send him in."

"Kat, darling, it's done, finished and complete. We can move into our new premises tomorrow. I can get back to my business and you to your labs. My guys have sorted out the security and we can go along tomorrow and set the system up to give you retinal scan access to all areas."

"Wonderful!" She came around her desk and hugged and kissed him with enthusiasm.

"Let's pop down to Scott's for a celebratory glass of champagne and dinner. You clever darling, you must be one hell of a project manager. I didn't expect we'd have been able to take possession before the end of next month. Very well done and congrats again. Have you told the team from Delft?"

"Not yet. I thought I'd wait until Monday to break the glad news, until you've seen it and declare the laboratory suite fit for purpose."

"Fair comment. I can be quite picky when it comes to approving laboratory facilities and I don't like things to go off at half-cock. I can check it over tomorrow and hopefully give it my seal of approval. When do you think we should move the team in?"

"As soon as we sort out their accommodation. Our estate agent has been sussing out a small apartment block that is for sale near the labs and if you give your approval, we can hopefully move them in during September. I had thought of incentivising them by giving them ownership of 10% of their apartments for each complete year they stay with us."

"Not a bad idea, but how do we square that if we have to get rid of someone?"

"They'd lose their share and given the price of flats in this area they will have a very strong incentive to be good boys and girls."

"OK, but I need to think it through. Meanwhile, I feel a there's a glass of champagne sitting in the bar down the street that's dying to kiss my lips. Why don't we ask my team to join us for a drink? They've known something big was going on;

now we can tell them and have a party."

"I'm up for that, let's go!"

*

Four bottles of champagne later, Marijke, David and Mark wove their way to waiting taxis while Katya and Luc sat down to a lobster dinner.

*

Back at the flat, they fell into a dreamless sleep, wrapped in each other's arms.

*

The taxi dropped them off at their new unit and Luc used the scanner to gain entry. Moving to the console behind the reception desk, he pressed some keys, picked up a scanner and asked Katya to look into it.

"Move your eye around a bit so that it'll recognise you from any angle."

A few seconds later there was a loud 'beep' and Luc put the scanner back in its slot.

"That's you authenticated. You'll need to look into the scanner to enter the building, again to enter your lab suite and also if you want to get into hacker central."

"All very hi-tech and was I seeing things, or have you fitted a nitrogen lock here, the same as in Cape Town?"

"Exactly the same."

"Trusting, aren't you?"

"Absolutely – not! Anyway, have a good nose around and check that everything in the lab suite is as specified."

An hour later she'd checked the lab suite and joined Luc in 'Hacker Central' as he ensured that all the equipment was working as specified.

"Well, that's the launch pad for the next phase of our lives in place, in working order and ready to roll."

"Well done us!" said Katya, looking forward to getting things up and running.

"We had better get away on our safari holiday ASAP. Once this is operational, I don't expect we'll have much time for holidays before Christmas."

*

Katya and Luc flew overnight from London to Johannesburg. Clearing customs and immigration, they took a taxi to the Fairway Hotel and checked in for a couple of days prior to travelling on to the Kruger.

"Might as well pop over to Witwatersrand University and make sure that all traces of our activities have been removed, but first, a shower and a proper breakfast," said Luc.

"Agreed. I wouldn't like to think that anyone had left an important notebook down the back of a drawer."

"My guys will have done a pretty thorough job, but it never does any harm to check."

"Bags the shower first."

"OK." And with that Luc started to unpack his stuff before undressing and following her into the shower. Rubbing her shoulders, he said, "Just making sure you're properly relaxed after that long flight."

She giggled and felt his hands explore the rest of her body before she turned and threw her arms around his neck, kissed him and said, "This is nice" as he picked her up and carried her through to their bedroom.

*

Downstairs in the dining room, they had a leisurely late breakfast, then got the concierge to find them a taxi to take them to the university. Half an hour later they were dropped off at the geosciences building and walked in the main door. There was no-one about because of the holidays, and they took the lift to the third-floor laboratory without being challenged.

The door of their former laboratory suite was unlocked, and they walked in to a deserted set of labs. Clear benches, empty cupboards and empty drawers. The only indication that these rooms were laboratories, were the benches, fume cupboards, sinks, water and gas taps. They went around the labs systematically, checking and double-checking for any item or indication signposting the work that had been carried out here and were happy to see that all evidence of their occupation had been removed.

"The new setup at Camp 25 seems to be coming along nicely; I've spoken to André a few times in recent weeks and he said that he was expecting the 100-500Kg per hour calciner to be delivered around about now. By the way, what happened to the security door setup?"

"It was crated up and sent to the UK. It's part of the security system on our new facility; didn't you notice it?"

"Not really. I was much more focused on our new labs. Well, not much to see here; let's head back to the hotel."

They managed to pick up a taxi on its way out of the campus and were back at the hotel in time for a late lunch. Over coffee they discussed their safari trip.

"Early morning or dusk tend to be the best times to see the most interesting animals, so I suggest we take it easy for the rest of today and head for the park after breakfast tomorrow. I've booked a local charter to fly us over there. Meanwhile, let's do a guided tour of the city, then dinner and bed."

"Sounds good to me but tell me more about why you decided to relocate to the UK. Back in

December, it sounded as though you were only committing to a European branch office. Then in February you come over to join me in London, and now you are opening up your headquarters in west London. You've never told me what actually drove your decision. You've kept glossing over it in the last few weeks and I'm really curious to know what drove you."

"In a word, you."

"But why?"

"I've never met a woman like you Kat, and I couldn't see you settling in Cape Town. So if we are to be able to build our lives together, the mountain had to come to Mohammed. You would find doing business out of Cape Town very difficult, while doing business out of London is not at all difficult for me. I sold my physical security business to Hennie last month. He insisted I retained a small stake in it and has promised me VIP status if ever I need things done. He's happy, I'm happy and I hope you're happy."

"Oh darling, yes, very happy."

*

After breakfast the following morning, they packed up and took a taxi back to the airport. Once there, Luc had their pilot paged and they sat in the check-in area until a wiry, middle-aged man wearing a gold-braided uniform shirt, trousers and cap approached. "Mr Kruger for the Kruger?"

"That's me," said Luc, standing up.

"I'm Noah, your pilot for this morning's trip to the Kruger. Now if you and your party will follow me, I'll lead you out to our plane, or should I say Ark."

They followed him across the concourse and out through a side door to what was obviously the private and charter planes' stands.

"That's our bird," said the pilot, pointing to an old but shiny twin-engine Piper Seminole done out in red and white livery with 'Capital Air Services' emblazoned along the fuselage. As they walked over to it, the fuselage door opened, and a set of steps were let down by a rangy blonde woman wearing a female version of the pilot's uniform.

Smiling broadly, she said, "Welcome aboard Capital Air Services' Safari Bus. I'm Trish, at your service for the trip. Please take your seats and put these headphone sets on so we can all communicate once the engines are running. Now what can I get you to drink?"

Katya asked for a nice, cold lemonade and Luc said he'd have the same. They settled into their seats, belted up and relaxed. Trish went forward, pulled up the steps and shut the cabin door.

Noah's voice came over the intercom, saying he was about to start the engines, and would they please fasten their seat belts ready for take-off. Trish came back from the little galley with their drinks, sat down behind the pilot and belted up ready for take-off.

With a roar and a shudder, the plane taxied off the stand and headed for one of the longer taxi-ways. They could hear Noah talking to the tower and then with a louder roar, the plane accelerated down the taxi-way and into the air. They heard the undercarriage retract and lock into place and the cabin quietened down as they reached cruising height.

Three-quarters of an hour later Noah came on and asked them if they wanted to go straight for the landing strip or if they would like to fly around for a bit and see if there was any big game roaming about.

"Let's have a look around first," said Katya.

Noah throttled the engines back and brought the plane down to five hundred feet and started quartering the airspace above the park. Both Luc and Katya were looking out of the starboard windows when Noah said, "Look out to the port side. There's a small herd of elephant walking away from us, probably heading for that watering hole up ahead. I think there may be some rhinos there as well. There were some there yesterday evening."

Katya said, "These are breath-taking. Just wandering towards their afternoon swim or whatever. It all looks a lot different from what you see on TV."

"Of course, nothing beats the thrill of seeing these big beasts walking free. Wait until your ranger takes you out tomorrow on safari proper. With any luck, you'll see lions, buffalo and even a leap of leopards. This park has the lot, along with loads of other beasties like troops of monkeys and herds of antelope. You've come at the best time of year. Winter isn't cold but the deciduous trees have shed their leaves, making it easier to see the animals moving across the veldt. You don't get mosquitoes at this time of year either, which is a real bonus."

"I can't wait."

"I'll take you in now. You're staying in the Sabi Sands Lodge, aren't you? I'll radio ahead to warn them we're coming in, and a ranger will come out and meet us."

*

Their lodge was light and airy, with an enormous bed in the bedroom, while the rest of the lodge was fitted out with every feature the most exacting guest could wish for.

"Not exactly a lumpy camp-bed under canvas, is it?"

Katya bounced on the bed and looking up at him, said, "Not exactly." Smiling, she grabbed him and pulled him down on top of her. "I think I'm going to enjoy it here."

"Me too. I've booked us in for an all-day safari tomorrow. We have to leave the lodge at seven in the morning, so we'd better get to bed early tonight. Meanwhile, how about going for a swim?"

Dinner at the lodge would not have disgraced a top Cape Town restaurant, with an emphasis on game dishes.

"This is so different from what I was expecting," said Katya.

"Do you like it?"

"Totally, darling, and I'm so glad I brought both my camera and field glasses."

*

The next two days passed quickly; the park ranger guiding them really knew his park and his wildlife. They saw a pride of lions close-up, several different species of antelopes, rhinos, more elephants, leopards and two herds of buffalo, along with vervet monkeys, some snakes and, at one watering hole, crocodiles.

They travelled each day in an air-conditioned Toyota 4 x 4 and the ranger stopped the vehicle frequently for them to take photographs and stretch their legs. They had picnic lunches prepared by the lodge and on the second day, they attracted the attention of a noisy troop of intrusive and inquisitive monkeys, forcing them to stop eating, pack up and drive on before finishing their meal.

*

Luc woke up suddenly. He wondered what had disturbed him when he heard it again. A creaking noise on the veranda outside their lodge. A sixth sense made him reach under his pillow for his pistol.

Reaching over to Katya, he woke her with his hand over her mouth and whispered in her ear, "Intruders. Get down flat on the floor on your side of the bed and wait till I call you."

With that, he slid silently out of the bed, tiptoed over to stand beside the door and turned on the light. A burst of machine-gun fire tore through the wall of their lodge and the door, throwing Luc back on to the floor. Katya didn't need to look further; she knew he could not have survived that fusillade. His hand flopped to one side, his pistol falling on the floor.

The door was kicked open and a couple of men of Asian appearance entered their lodge. Katya could see their legs from the calves down to their bare feet. One of them turned to the foot of the bed and emptied the magazine of his AK-47 into the mattress. The bullets went straight through it into the floor, filling the air around and under the bed with splinters, fluff and fibres.

A shocked Katya had seen Luc's pistol fall, but rather than panic, she was overcome by blazing fury as she saw the armed intruders. She thought she could just reach his pistol in the current confusion before she was spotted. Stretching out her arm, she could feel the pistol grip; curling her fingers around it, she pulled it silently towards her and checked that the safety catch was off, looked to see which way the men were facing, gathered herself together and stood up. One of the men was facing her; the other was looking out of the door. She concentrated on the one facing her; holding the pistol in both hands, she pointed it at him as he brought his AK-47 up to his shoulder, pointed it at her and pulled the trigger – click! Nothing happened; the magazine was empty.

As he reached to change the magazine, Katya took aim at his torso and fired. The bullet hit his shoulder, knocking him over as the other man turned around to see who was firing. As he brought his gun to bear, Katya fired at him twice, the first shot missed but the second split his skull like a watermelon as he fell over in a pool of his own brains and blood.

Turning back to the first intruder, she saw he'd managed to change the magazine on his gun and was pushing himself up against the wall while trying to aim his AK-47 at her. She fired at him again - and again - and again - until the magazine was empty.

Moments later a couple of park rangers appeared in the now-silent doorway.

"Hello, anyone in there? Are you OK? Hello?"

*

CHAPTER 43

Katya was slumped over the shattered bed, shivering uncontrollably and sobbing her heart out. The rangers walked carefully into the room, smelling gun-smoke and looking at the carnage and destruction that had been wrought. One of them went over to Katya and, putting his arm around her shoulders, picked her up and carried her from the room over to the camp's reception area, then called in the emergency medical service and the police.

After a quick phone discussion, the emergency service doctor in Skukuza[19] advised the rangers to take Katya to a quiet room and give her some diazepam, along with plenty of sweet tea to drink, and make sure she rested.

They'd given full details to the police, so they were not altogether surprised to hear a helicopter coming in to land in front of the lodge complex just before seven o'clock. The men who emerged from it

---

[19] The Skukuza Medical Centre offers a 24-hour emergency medical service across the Kruger National Park.

were a uniformed police Lieutenant Colonel and two plainclothes officers who did not identify themselves. They asked to be taken to where Luc had been killed and see who the attackers had been. The luxury suite was a blood-spattered charnel house. Inspecting the room, they checked the bodies of the suspected attackers for I.D. and finding none, produced a fingerprint kit to use on them.

"We may get I.D. this way but I'm not hopeful," said the older of the two plainclothes officers. Turning to the ranger, he asked, "And these two were shot dead by the lady?"

"Yes, Ms Katya Francis. She's recovering in one of the empty lodges."

"We need to talk to her."

"She's been sedated and I'm not sure she'll be very lucid."

"We know a lot about the lady, and I suspect that she'll be able to help us. All I'll say is that she's a very strong woman, mentally and physically."

*

The receptionist went into the lodge where Katya was resting to wake her up but found her sitting on the edge of the bed wrapped in a blanket. She was shivering in shock as she relived the attack and the fact that she'd just killed two men. "There's a senior policeman and a couple of other men here about last night's attack. They want to talk to you.

Are you OK for that, or will I tell them to sod off, as you're sleeping?"

"No, I don't want to talk to them, but I suppose I must. It's OK, I'll talk to them, but can you get me my clothes from the lodge and a jug of coffee first? I just can't face going back in there."

With a jug of coffee beside her on the table, and dressed in her own clothes, she asked them in and gestured to them to sit down.

"Ms Francis," began the older of the two plainclothes officers, "we are so very sorry for your loss. Mr Kruger was your partner in your Mozambique project, wasn't he?"

"You're from the SASS?"

The man simply ignored her question and then asked her to tell him all she could remember of the attack.

"It all happened so fast. Luc - Mr Kruger - woke me up, told me to get on the floor beside the bed on the side away from the door. Pistol in hand, he tiptoed over to the door and switched on the lights. There was an immediate fusillade of gunfire, through the door and the front wall of our lodge. He fell to the floor as the door was burst open and the attackers ran into the room.

"They didn't see me at first and one of them stood at the end of the bed and emptied his gun into it. The bullets ripped the mattress to shreds, filling the air with mattress stuffing and dust, but I could see Luc's pistol lying just within reach on the floor.

"I could see the attackers' feet from where I was lying and waited until they were facing each other, picked up the pistol, jumped up and shot the bastards dead. I went over to see to Luc, but he was dead. I counted five bullet wounds to his chest and head."

"And how are you?"

"Shaky, very sad and bloody angry. Luc and I were probably going to marry before the year was out, and these bastards have destroyed all that."

"You're a remarkable woman; have you been trained in countering terror attacks?"

"My father worked in the Niger delta for a while with Shell and his close-protection bodyguards taught me to use a variety of weapons in self-defence."

"They taught you well. Now you don't need to worry, there is no question of you being charged with murder or manslaughter. This is an open-and-shut case of self-defence and if we ever find out who your attackers were, you will almost certainly have done South African society a great favour by helping them leave it. We understand that your contact point here is a Mr Pieter de Bruin in Cape Town. Do you want us to contact him?"

"Please, I need to talk to him, to tell him what's happened, to decide what to do next."

"I'm sure you'll want to get away from here now. We can give you a lift to Jo'burg airport and we'll get a funeral director to come over and take care of Mr Kruger's body."

"Can someone pack up my stuff? I can't face going back into our lodge."

"No problem. While we're waiting, I'll call Mr de Bruin and explain what's happened, then let you speak to him."

He stood up and walked out of the lodge to make the call. Returning a few minutes later, he handed his phone to her and the three men left her alone.

"Katya, how are you, my darling?"

Katya burst into tears and went through the whole story again, punctuated by sobs, and ended up apologising to Piet for breaking down.

"You've nothing to apologise for. You've been through hell and acquitted yourself brilliantly. I understand the security squad are taking you back to the airport to get a flight back here. Call me when you know what flight you're on and I'll meet you. I'll also call the Krugers and bring them up to speed. They'll be devastated."

Finishing the call, Katya went into the bathroom and washed her face in cold water before going out to speak to the older security officer.

*

On board the South African Airways' 737 at O.R. Tambo airport, Katya was shown to her seat in Business Class. The plane's doors closed, and the flight attendants went through the safety briefing as the engines started. A few minutes later they started taxiing and were soon airborne. As soon as the seat-belt sign went out, the senior flight attendant came up to Katya with a tray holding a large cup of coffee and a large brandy.

Katya looked up, surprised, saying, "I didn't order these."

"No, but the gentleman who escorted you to the flight said you'd been through a great deal and that he thought this would help you get through the flight."

"Oh, thank you."

Reclining her seat and sipping the brandy, she tried to shut her eyes and sleep, but the events of the night kept replaying in her head. . .

*

On landing, she collected her bag from the carousel and walked slowly through to the concourse. She saw Piet standing in the Arrivals zone, looking suddenly older. He saw her and smiled sadly with his arms outstretched to her. He enfolded her in a comforting hug and she slumped against him and burst into tears, sobbing helplessly as he held her tight.

As her sobs subsided, he said "Come on home with me. Molly's made up a bed ready for you,"

They were both silent on the road to Piet's house and Molly came to the door when she heard the car. Together they helped her from the car into their living room and settled her on a settee. Molly disappeared to the kitchen, returning with a cafetière of coffee.

Pouring cups for the three of them, she sat down next to Katya and said. "Tell us what happened. We got a summary from the police, but I want to know what really happened"

"Oh Molly! It was horrible. Luc and I had just gone to sleep when he was wakened by a noise on the balcony outside our suite. He wakened me up silently and made me lie down on the floor beside the bed, away from the door. He collected his pistol and tiptoed over beside the door before switching on the main light. There was a burst of gunfire and he was lying on the floor when two men crashed into the room. I could see his pistol where it had fallen, grabbed it and stood up – and – and" before collapsing in heart-rending sobs

Molly said "Enough! The poor girl's still in shock. Let's take her through and I'll put her to bed."

*

By late afternoon, she'd slept and woke up feeling physically rested but incredibly sad. Molly said that the Krugers had asked if she would be up to seeing them.

Nadine and Marius came over in the late afternoon and after Katya had re-told her story yet again, the five of them sat around the coffee table in silence, each nursing a large cognac and lost in their own thoughts. Nadine was crying silently while Marius, his arm around her, held her tightly and was on the verge of tears himself.

Just then the de Bruijn's butler came through to say that Hennie had arrived, and could he see Miss Katya. There was an awkward silence for a few moments before Katya said: "Yes, show him in."

Hennie came quietly into the room, focusing on Katya with sadness in his face. "Is it true? Is Luc really dead Katya?"

"I'm afraid so, we were attacked in our lodge in the safari park. Luc didn't stand a chance." Sitting up straight and looking more animated than she'd been since she woke up, she said. "But I got the bastards, both of them, and they are both very dead."

"You're a very brave woman." Said Hennie, "We'll get whoever's behind this and I will personally destroy them – utterly.

Now before I go, I want you to know that if you need me to do anything, anything at all, you only have to ask."

Grim faced, he stood up and took his leave.

Later, after the Krugers had left, Katya asked Piet if she could phone her parents. He said "Of course, I spoke to them earlier and broke the news. You mum was very upset when I told her, and she cried even harder when I told her what a heroine you'd been. That was three hours ago and I'm sure that she's dying to hear from you directly."

*

CHAPTER 44

Ten days later, she stood in the front pew of the Kruger's local church together with Nadine and Marius Kruger, Piet and Molly de Bruin, Ton and Sophie Botha. Behind them were Mary Wynne and rest of the staff from Piet's office, watching as Luc's coffin was borne in by Hennie, Jan and four other sergeants in full dress uniform. To her surprise, she saw they'd been joined by 'Mr Smith' who'd obviously flown out from London. The service was simple, and Hennie gave a strong and moving eulogy that had tears coursing down Katya's face and those of his parents.

At the end of the service, as his coffin was lowered into the ground and the minister spoke his final blessing, Hennie and his men lined up beside the grave, put their rifles to their shoulders and fired three volleys, bringing the proceedings to an end.

Afterwards, the Kruger's had organised a wake at a nearby hotel, which was attended by their friends and several of Luc's former colleagues from his army days, all in full dress uniform.

KATYA'S CHALLENGE

Katya sat in a corner of the room, smiling sadly at those who came over to offer their condolences, wishing it was all over and that she could go home with Nadine and Marius, but before they left, Mr Smith came over to offer his condolences. He told her that they'd shut down Cathay (UK) Metals and deported their Chinese staff and he said that they would continue to keep a close eye on her security.

*

Two days later she was sitting in the Krugers' lawyer's office in downtown Cape Town for the reading of the will.

After bequests to his parents, Piet, and Hennie, the lawyer came to Katya. "Luc has left you his Internet security business, the funds in the LKF accounts in London and elsewhere, and the other fifty percent of his equity in Future Metals (Pty) Ltd. You are now a very wealthy woman."

*

In Qingcheng, former General Tang received a message in a folded paper handkerchief. He read it and on returning to his cell, removed one of the photographs from above his bunk and tore it into tiny pieces.

One down, two to go . . .

*

A week later, Katya was walking along the beach at Wassenaar arm in arm with her mother, tears running down her face and saying, "What the hell do I do now? Money will never be a problem, but I've lost the man I wanted to share my life with."

"Stay here for a few days and we can talk things through."

"Thanks Mum, I will."

"Do you think you are still in danger?"

"Well, Piet has checked with his pals in SASS and agrees with me that we don't think the attack in the Kruger National Park had the fingerprints of a state-sponsored operation. We think this was privately sponsored, possibly by this 'Minister Zhang' whose failures seem to have cost him his job, but not his influence. Piet has asked Benny Kim to see what he can find out and I've asked Tommy Chung to nose around Beijing for me to see if any high-ranking soldiers or politicians have unexpectedly lost their jobs in recent months. I'm going to find the bastard who organised Luc's murder and tried to have me killed. Then with Hennie's help it'll be an eye for an eye and a life for a life – no quarter given."

The End – for now

KATYA'S CHALLENGE

AFTERWORD

Anyone interested in finding out more about the rare metals business in the real world should read

David S. Abraham's excellent book:

THE ELEMENTS OF POWER

Gadgets, Guns, and the struggle for a sustainable future in the Rare Metal age

Yale University Press 2015

Printed in Poland
by Amazon Fulfillment
Poland Sp. z o.o., Wrocław